KILL MOST OF THE MISCREANTS

By Ivan Bering

I0641316

Copyright 2017 Ivan Bering

ISBN 978-0-9937100-5-6

SPECIAL THANKS

Thanks to my daughter Cathy for starting me

on this path and reading many versions of this novel.

Other Charlie Taylor novels:

Kill some of the Privileged: second in the series

Kill All of Them: third in the series

AUTHOR'S NOTE

My therapy demanded I start writing, the mantra: write what is important to you. For some time, this meant bugger all. But my analyst persisted, and I began with what I knew best: my work.

I tried to capture the turmoil and tension which existed when we reinstated the death penalty, and executions were an acceptable part of our ethos. Of course, with Prison Reform, everything escalated and the body count mounted.

It was not to be that easy; the writing had to be personal. Hence, this book includes personal logs of my struggles. These private records have been edited, and there are a few omissions; some events are too embarrassing to provide a full confession, vanity trumping accuracy. I'm sure you will be able to fill in the gaps; if you can't, by the last chapter you will know how much I care.

Charlie

Charles (Charlie) W. Taylor
Detective First Class Homicide Division

PROLOGUE

Neither of the two men classified their meeting as clandestine. Other Board members, had they known, would not have agreed.

They sat in the Judge's Chambers; one a lean man with the appearance of an academic, the other a large man who looked more like an ex-prize fighter. However, both presented the demeanor of authority.

Usually, he controlled his emotions, but the execution news was an unexpected body blow. "Steve you can't execute a Nobel Prize winner, a friend of the President! Jesus where is this coming from? And, why as Chief of Police, am I just hearing about this arrest? This is insane."

The taller man, standing by the window, also struggled with his emotions. "Hold on Dunc. At this point, I am the only one aware of the situation, and it is only my personal assessment of the incident which has me worried; his track record is not good, and this could lead to a guilty verdict and the death penalty. There was no arrest, and I only told you to give you time to think about the situation, in case an arrest has to be made."

"Shit what the hell happened? Dr. Max has been screwing everyone, particular the young ladies, for years...no drug or alcohol issues......no violence. We give celebrities all sorts of room, and with expensive lawyers, they rarely get convicted. So what the devil did he do this time?"

"Dunc, I'm going to keep this with me and not give anything out. If it develops, I'll probably get Legal to work on the case and gather all the evidence. Because I think it will turn to an Execution of an international superstar, there can be no mistakes; and right now I think you can't afford another high-profile case."

Dunc started to protest, but his heart wasn't in it; he knew what was coming.

Steve continued. "You have serial killers running rampant. A couple is killing ladies in high-end hotels. Then a rapist picking women off the street and brutally beating them. The hotel industry is screaming for an answer; the Mayor calls every hour and bars and clubs association screams business is in the tank because the rapist has women afraid to walk the streets.

And you have nothing. Am I right?'

Dunc knew he couldn't bluff or lie his way out. "You're right we have nothing. The hotel killers are unbelievable, and their crime scene yields nothing. The damn rapist is a sloppy bastard. We had DNA and fingerprints, but he has never been in our system or the military, because we get no matches."

"Do you still have your best homicide detective buried in the Record Section?"

"Yes and that is where that son of a bitch is going to stay. He can cause more shit in one week than most detectives get into in a lifetime."

"Dunc I understand he causes you grief, but he is your best. You need this kind of thinking to break these cases.

"Steve, be careful. Do you know many at the precinct call him 'Crazy Charlie'?

"I don't want to know the details, but you should know at the next Board meeting you will be under a lot of pressure and will be asked to show or provide a new approach to finding these killers. You have to give us something which shows there is a new strategy."

The Chief knew it was a lost cause. The Judge had appointed him and was the man who controlled the Sector. He resigned himself to the inevitable with one last protest. "Shit, that fucking Charlie will drive me crazy. He's in the same league as our Dr. Max, Nobel Prize winner, uncontrollable. Do you mind if I start crying?"

CHAPTER 1: WHITE ROCK PRISON

Most of the cells on death row stood empty, but the execution rate never faltered.

As another convicted rolled into the execution chamber, the head guard neared a panic state and screamed into his phone. "Peter, get the hell back up here. We need the gurneys and more body bags. I've got bodies stacked in the hall."

"I'm coming. I'm coming. The first two ambulances collided, then a tailgate door stuck, and we couldn't load the corpses. A goddamn mess."

"I don't care. Try running. If the Warden gets here before you do, we'll all be back in the shit."

"I hate this. It's all happening too fast. We've executed over half of death row in a couple of weeks."

Currently, White Rock prison functioned as two extreme zones. Inside the closed doors of the Interrogation and Execution rooms, the atmosphere was all business, logic, and control. Outside these rooms, in the hallways and corridors, chaos and confusion prevailed, as prison staff hustled to deal with the logistics of executed convicts, the influx of relatives, and demanding crematorium staff. In the yard, the temperature was over 100 degrees, and a traffic jam of ambulances competed for the next corpse. The mass executions at White Rock prison were the result of one man's brilliance: Dr. Max Armstrong.

Unfortunately, peer jealous frequently accompanies individual brilliance. His detractors complained he was too fast, skipped steps, jumped to conclusions and was reckless. Harsh criticism for any scientist.

However, when the history of science is updated, three will be named as the giants of all time: Newton, Einstein, and Armstrong. Before he was 30 he had a Nobel Peace Prize, and the world had new insight into the operation of the brain.

Dr. Max Armstrong's research resulted in three interrogation techniques. Techniques so powerful they allowed a complete upheaval of the system of justice, including universal acceptance of the death penalty. The procedures soon lost their sophisticated laboratory labels and simply became known as S1, S2, and S3.

S1 is the first level of interrogation and the most frequently used. The cocktail of drugs is a general relaxant. Euphoria develops which makes the recipient interested in talking. Talking not only talking about the crime in question but also exposing his complete portfolio; it appears confessing is good for the soul. There are very few people who can stand up to the drug's seductive power, and one session of S1 completes an interrogation.

S2 uses the same drugs but at almost double the dosage. Since, at times, side reactions can be severe, this interrogation requires medical staff to be present and monitor the recipient.

S3 is reserved for capital crimes and entails an intense probing or scanning of the suspect's brain. This interrogation step allows the legal system to access, retrieve and display streams of memory from any individual. This inquiry is mandatory before a death sentence can be carried out. The suspect's mind reveals his role in the crime.

Dr. Max developed the chemical mix which enhanced the scanning and retrieval process and at the same time provided the brain with protection from the severe probing process. Without this protection, it was impossible to conduct a complete scan without killing the participant. The probing action is an irritant which causes the cells to release weak signals, a stream of electronic consciousness. It was Dr. Max who integrated and modulated these fragile signals into an electronic stream which could be processed by the software he developed. The results are fed to regular computer monitors for all to see and hear. The net outcome of an S3 interrogation: guilt or innocence is no longer in doubt.

Dr. Max Armstrong's IQ exploded off any measurable scale; not as loudly proclaimed: his emotional IQ was that of a young teenager. His appearance surprised those who met him for the first time, his extraordinary good looks and physique the picture of a Hollywood stud. Mother Nature, for a few seconds, relaxed the rules and allowed all her gifts to be packaged together in one man. Female companionship was not a problem, his indulgence a legend.

To the chagrin of his employers, a minor genetic idiosyncrasy persisted: he was attracted to the younger segment of the female sex, a character flaw neither humorous nor harmless.

CHAPTER 2: WHERE WAS CHARLIE?

"When we first arrived, she was creeping on the sidewalk, like an injured cockroach."

Jean Hardin delivered each word in a strained cadence; at irregular intervals, she lost all control. The convulsions and tears transformed the attractive woman into a sobbing five-year-old, knees tight against her chest as she rocked in the big chair.

Dr. Sam Taylor, her psychologist, decided it was best to allow her to vent without any interruptions, no questions, and no clarification. He would wait until her hysterical energy depleted. She was an EMT, emergency medical technician. Her prior visits had centered on a horrible traffic accident involving young teenagers. This visit was different. Today's session went beyond depression.

"The patient screamed every time she heard a male voice. Any time a man spoke she let loose with a desperate howl. The only reason we managed to get her into the ambulance is because Detective Zubik was there and she helped me. Karen, that's the detective, even stayed in the ambulance and tried to calm the woman. The poor lady. Oh god, she kept screeching, tossing her head and spattering blood over me and the inside of the ambulance.

I'm still not fully qualified to connect her to all the sensors of the new patient monitoring gear, but the senior EMT couldn't get close, so I wrestled my way through the setup.

No one could understand her. Jesus, her entire face was swollen and bruised, almost shattered, most of her front teeth were missing…"

Jean stopped for a moment the memory overwhelming her. Great sobs wracked her body. Sam touched her shoulder and encouraged her to continue.

"I'm not sure if it was the mild sedative in the IV or if she just passed out but eventually she stopped. Bill, our senior EMT, decided to sit up front with the driver, and I stayed in the back with Karen.

She's the latest victim of that mad man…rapist…..you know he typically kills them but I think she'll live….her face will never be the same…

I can't sleep. Every time I close my eyes I see her. And I'm scared to go outside. When night comes, I lock all the doors and turn off the lights. I'm going to buy a gun even though I hate them. They've given me time off, but it isn't helping. I've got to resign. I couldn't stand the sight of another one ……….oh shit.."

She lost all control again and the crying intensified. Sam was prepared and decided it was time. He was stepping over the line; as a psychologist, he was not licensed to inject medication, but it was a line he crossed before when facing a hysterical patient.

"Jean, let me roll up your sleeve and give you a shot.......just enough to allow you to relax. Now sit back in that big chair and close your eyes. I want you to rest for about 15 minutes. Then we'll talk."

Jean wiped her face dry, closed her eyes and put her head back; soon her breathing became closer to normal, but Sam knew she needed more time. His official recording would start in a few minutes; in preparation, he logged the date into his recorder: Friday, March 26th, 2021.

As he waited, he thought about the serial rapist/killer who was terrorizing the city. Some his new clients were woman traumatized by this high profile criminal and his bragging rants which all the news agencies appeared anxious to report. Even his ridiculous name was established by the press; the damn rapist got tagged as Horny Harry, which implied, even if he was raping and killing, he was just a few degrees beyond normal.

Harry was a brutal killer, only two of his six victims survived his frenzied attacks. If Detective Karen Zubik was at the site, then Sam's brother should have been. At one time his brother, Charlie Taylor, was the senior homicide detective in the Division and acknowledged as the best man in the squad.

Sam knew all the detectives in the homicide section. When Charlie's wife and daughter were still alive, his brother's backyard became the gathering place for summer barbecues; the detectives were a small elite group, all male except for Karen. She was older than the men but able to sustain their pace and match their humor; the men, Wes, Terry, and Manuel, were all under 35 years old.

Sam compared the summer evenings to being with a bottle of fireflies: constantly in motion, at times one would light up with a joke or a story and all would erupt, an explosion of laughter.

Sam and Monk, Charlie's best friend, were the only outsiders invited. But Sam's wife found the humor too black, and she often found an excuse not to attend.

Was the Chief of Police still trying to keep Charlie buried in the Records department? The entire situation was becoming hopeless; his brother would explode if those restraints weren't lifted.

But the Chief believed 'law and order' also applied to internal procedures and codes of behavior; Charlie, an impatient detective, struggled with the forms and office procedures which he viewed as secondary priorities. So the two good men had their relationship defined by the proverbial lament: not on the same page.

Two days ago one of the detectives, Wes, phoned Sam; it was too tentative to tell Charlie but the latest rumor in circulation: the Chief planned to reinstate and promote the senior detective.

So, where was Charlie?

CHAPTER 3: STEPHEN'S BOARD

Would the executions be allowed to proceed? At the conclusion of the meeting, Judge Stephen Miller's Board would make one of the most notable decisions of its brief existence.

A few of the Judge's staff had witnessed the inaugural set of executions which took place at White Rock prison, in Sector 13. Next up: the prison under Stephen's jurisdiction, Fort Green.

At today's meeting, the Board would review any logistical or procedural issues which had been encountered at the historical undertaking at White Rock. There were no legal barriers; the new legislation, Justice Reborn, demanded the decommissioning of all prisons and the processing of all death row convicts, execute or release the directive.

However, at the moment Kate's early morning voice mail message concerned him. He played her message again:

"Stephen, I'm sorry to interrupt your meeting preparations, but this is critical. I'm driving in from White Rock prison; Emma is with me. We've been working all night, but the results are too sensitive to discuss over the phone. Please ensure I'm last on the agenda and only Board members are in attendance when I report; last, it is best if my results not be recorded. Again, I apologize for the mystery, but I know you'll agree when you hear my conclusions. Emma is the only other person who is aware of the situation. It's not good. Bye."

He trusted her and would do what she asked. But now he had to regain his equilibrium and ensure he was ready for the Board; his nervous energy forced him to pace around the office in a brisk fashion, looking a bit ridiculous, he thought. Eventually, he tired, relaxed, stopped and gazed down at the park.

It was a sunny morning, and the spring wind vigorously tossed about loose debris; leaves, empty containers, and discarded paper wrappers rose, twirled and fell back to the ground with each gust of wind. His corner office, via two large glass panels, provided an unobstructed view of one of the city's most extensive green spaces. Bookcases and walnut paneling covered the remaining walls in an office larger than he required but bureaucratically-sized to match his position.

He reminisced about that April, years ago, and his passionate affair with Kate. At the time, both of them married but not to each other, and both in the final year of different work programs at the University. The work programs, associated with advanced degrees, had been fortunate appointments, and a successful completion would see them assigned to prominent positions. The end of the affair had been swift, with no turning back for either of them. His feelings periodically flared, watching her with others, hearing her voice, at times a challenge to his self-control. Had he made a mistake in appointing her to the Board?

He turned from the window, walked out of his office and into the boardroom, a large room with more wood paneling on the walls, dark hardwood floors and heavy burgundy drapes to shield the space from the warm spring weather. The room accommodated a series of small tables arranged in a U-shape with Stephen and Ann, his assistant, at the top and the various Board members along the legs of the U.

Stephen Miller, Judge for Sector 14, was the chair and in control. Although not avuncular by nature, the Judge knew how to keep the meetings loose and still maintain the pace and focus. His four Division Heads, three of them selected by him, made up the rest of the Board; they were already seated, material organized and ready to report, the exception being Dr. Kate, who was still fussing with her presentation material

Their weekly reviews had to walk a fine line between ensuring serious issues were vetted by the Board before the public was informed and still not get swamped by operational details. Stephen was one of the first Sector Judges to be appointed. At 55, the youngest appointment, his tenure would still only be ten years, the standard term established for all Sector Judges.

"Ladies and gentlemen, if we are ready I will activate the recording equipment." Every session was recorded, and the Judge (via Ann) controlled the electronic panel. "I'd like to start with the Legal Division. Doug, please."

"This is Doug Brewster, Legal Division, on Monday, March 29, 2021, reporting." Doug was medium height, slightly overweight, sporting a full auburn beard, and regularly had a mouth full of pipe, which he chewed relentlessly, particularly when under stress. He could develop a cogent legal argument but at times was viewed as a disingenuous team member. An ambitious man, he had been surprised and disappointed when he had not landed a Judge's position on the first round of Sector appointments.

"As soon as the death row interrogations are completed, we'll be left with the rest of the convicts. It would be easy if we could just open the gates and start all over but, of course, that's not going to happen. We're still debating the options. I know everyone is anxious to have this finalized. And, I assure you every free hour is being devoted to the problem. But I'll defer any further discussion because Jacob has the details and will talk about our status. Steve that's it."

The Judge moved to the next presenter. The Chief had a rather insular attitude, but his skill at appeasing the public was enough to compensate for most of his shortcomings. If you selected one word to describe the Chief, it would be: solid. He was a large man, well over 6 feet, a thick body with the start of a pot belly, large hands and feet, nose and jaw too large for ordinary aesthetics. But with his uniform and cap, he presented an impressive image.

"Chief Duncan Stirling, Investigative Division, March 29, 2021. We have two major criminal investigations in progress, both serial killers and at this point no significant progress in solving either one. The first is a team, a woman and a man, who are killing high priced call girls in four or five-star hotels. So far the media has not taken an active interest in this team, primarily because all the girls have been prostitutes.

But, the Tourist Association is upset. If we have another killing in a hotel, I anticipate the Association will be extremely vocal and will pounding on the Mayor's door. These hotel killers are unbelievably thorough and crime scenes are not yielding anything.

The second serial killer doesn't kill all the time, but this is mainly because the girls have been able to survive the beatings he gives them. He rapes them and tries to beat them to death with his fists or some type of heavy wrench; he is extremely vicious and reckless. We have fingerprints and DNA but he has never been in the system, and there are no matches.

This is the man who brags to the press about his prowess as a lover. Unfortunately, they have labeled him

"Horny Harry"; the nickname from a journalist with a sick sense of humor or possibly to mock him. But, I stress this guy is not a cartoon character, and there is nothing humorous about his attacks. It appears his sixth victim will survive.

My last comment. As you all know Detective Browning had to retire due to ill health. I have considered a number of alternatives and decided Charlie Taylor is the best man to head up the Homicide group." The Chief paused, waiting for a reaction; a few loud sighs and grunts surfaced from the attendees.

Doug Brewster could not contain himself. "Chief, you're aware that Charlie has irritated almost everyone in this room. He is a drunk or the next best thing, and last year he threatened to plant my pipe right up my…"

The Judge broke in. "Chief, you know I usually don't interfere with internal Division appointments, but I do have to ask you about this one, particularly in light of the serial killers you just described."

The Chief had anticipated the reaction, especially from Brewster, who Charlie had insulted on numerous occasions. Charlie's last two years of desultory living had gained him a reputation as a recalcitrant and borderline alcoholic.

"It's because of these two cases I wish to appoint Charlie. We are getting nowhere with the conventional approach. I need someone who can take this in a different direction, and Charlie is the best homicide detective we have. I believe he has his drinking under control and regardless of the character flaws, the Division needs him. I confess we are desperate."

The Judge recognized Doug's anger, but it was time to move on. "Thanks Chief. Please see me later this afternoon. It might be best if you could hold the announcement of this appointment until we have a chance to talk. Let's proceed. Jacob, please."

Jacob was the only person on the Board who had not been selected by the Judge, an apparent source of tension. Jacob's hubris had caused problems in the past, but he had a wide circle of influential friends. He was a political animal who was overly aggressive when looking down and the proverbial ass kisser when looking up the organization chain.

The Judge deemed him marginal but he noted most people exercised caution in any exchange because Jacob's inimical behavior was well known. This meant Jacob commanded, if not respect, a healthy degree of obsequiousness.

"Jacob Konahouse, Division Head Prisons, March 29, 2021. Within a few hours, my advance person should be at Fort Green prison to start briefing prison staff; the rest of the preparation team will probably not get started for a few days.

At White Rock prison, some our personnel did assist. There were some logistic problems. First, the lead time to contact the relatives and witnesses, which the convicts are allowed as part of their S3 Interrogation, turned out to be longer than anticipated. At Fort Green, my staff will start contacting relatives and other potential witnesses, the Watchers as they are called, as soon as our temporary offices are established.

Second, the execution process went faster than anticipated, and local resources were not able to cope. A backlog developed. Bodies literally stacked up in the hallways; they ran out of gurneys and body bags, a damn mess. Since we will possibly be dealing with almost 200 corpses in 90 days, we have established contracts with firms from outside the Sector to assist as required.

As far as processing the remainder of the prison population, my staff is working with Legal. But, it has been difficult to find the appropriate amount of time to devote to this problem, regardless of its importance.

Our goal is to have a set of recommendations by the end of May. Public safety will be the significant issue, and this will be the cornerstone to any recommendation. I know the prisons have to be decommissioned in a year and the prisoners processed or released, but a hasty decision has too many consequences. So we will be methodical, possibly a few weeks late.

In conclusion, I would like to register my strong opposition to the appointment of Charlie Taylor. His skills, in my view, don't warrant the aggravation and potential bad press he will attract."

The Judge ignored the comment, but Jacob's presentation triggered more debate about the problems of decommissioning all prisons. Much of the discussion covered old ground, issues which could not be resolved that morning. The repetitive dialogue allowed Stephen's mind to wander, and he thought about the live demonstrations he had witnessed.

Of all the innovations, based on the genius of Dr. Max Armstrong, it was the S3 Interrogation which was the most difficult to accept. This process, actually an involuntary interrogation, was used to confirm guilt, to pronounce the death penalty, and allow the execution. He, along with other senior personnel, had attended a live session; and, he was able to experience the impact of such an interrogation.

At one level it was simple: the accused, restrained, lay on a table, his head covered with a futuristic helmet. The helmet was laced with a mesh of cables: many connections leading into the helmet and one larger cable leading out. The exit cable ran to a computer system which fed a large screen monitor on the wall. A technician, through a probing process, was able to retrieve and display streams of memory from the accused, thus an involuntary interrogation. It was like a TV show, but here everything was unedited and raw. The vivid memory streams often rendered an audience speechless.

When a crime scene, as stored by the accused, was on the screen there was no doubt about what happened, brutal, savage and relentless cruelty often the case. These scenes were the output of an S3 and the innovation which allowed the public acceptance of the death penalty. Instead of legal appeals, this process was being used to clear death row. The retrieved pockets of memory played out on a wall monitor and established culpability.

Stephen focused back on to the Board meeting. He was becoming impatient and was prepared to intervene, but the room sensed his mood, and the prison decommissioning discussion ceased. He was ready for the Forensic Division, which had assisted with some of the executions in Sector 13.

"Dr. Kate, we can proceed. I understand you are going to address the concerns about the ten convicts at White Rock, who were found to be innocent."

Dr. Kate Martinez's Mexican heritage reflected in a soft olive complexion, dark eyes, long vivid black hair which now contained four or five randomly situated white streaks, the hair being pulled straight back, a no-nonsense approach. She was a healthy mature woman, a runner, not competitive, but she did maintain a regular schedule. People described her as slim, but she noticed over the last year the extra pounds had more tenacity. The one consolation, she told herself, an increase in bust size and a softer curve to her hips.

As the new technology emerged, her natural curiosity compelled her to become involved, and she was soon a leader, able to understand the new concepts and adapt. The announced creation of Stephen's Board with the available vacancies stirred her interest. She never applied, old ghosts dampening her aspirations. But, when Stephen called and offered her the Forensic Division, she accepted immediately, only after did doubts resurface. Her emotional churning should not have been a surprise because periodic flashbacks had been with her for years.

"Dr. Kate Martinez, Forensic Division Head, March 29, 2021, I declare a Condition Confidential and request the recording equipment be turned off during my presentation."

Her declaration brought even more focus to the meeting. Kate presented a grim and determined image. She had everyone's attention. A Condition Confidential signaled a serious issue and was only invoked to ensure top level secrecy; anyone who leaked the discussion which took place under a Condition Confidential would be immediately dismissed and charged with a criminal offense.

Ann, on a signal from the Judge, pressed the console button to stop the recording; Stephen turned back to Kate. "I assume this has to do with what you observed during the S3 Interrogations at White Rock prison."

"Yes, and I will get into the details in a minute, but first let me give an overview. None of this is confirmed, and it's all highly speculative. But, it is my observation, and I stress...... only mine. It appears the highly emotional events in a person's life may be stored multiple times in different locations."

Silence. The entire room stared at Kate. Everyone afraid to ask the obvious question; the Judge asked. "Kate, are each of these different memory streams duplicates of the same event or does each memory stream have a different interpretation of the event?"

Jacob, the political appointee, regularly last to understand implications, was fast enough on this one.

"What the hell! White Rock has already executed 155 convicts based on the infallibility of the damn memory streams."

CHAPTER 4: CHARLIE'S LOG: THE TIPPING POINT

It's a shit-face job.

I snuck away earlier this afternoon. Another week in Records and the Chief and I will have our last conversation, something along the lines of:

"Duncan, there's part of my anatomy which is aching for a kiss, why don't you pucker up?"

Well, that's for next week; now it's a few minutes after six. Monk and I are in my kitchen: maple wood cabinets form a semi-circle around a central work island. The blinds are only partially closed, and the warm spring sunshine makes dappling patterns around the kitchen; it's hot, too hot for spring. Monk is starting to arrange the ingredients he needs to prepare his ham on rye specialty, our supper before the basketball game. Today happens to be one of those rare Monday night games, due to some scheduling conflicts.

Even his gentle smile cannot subdue his menacing appearance, a tall man at 6"8", just a fraction over 300 pounds, a shaved head, and hands each the size of a small computer monitor. He got the 'monk' label at University when he was the only regular church attendee on the team. Monk is new to the priesthood, now Father Ed.

We were both young kids when he arrived in my neighborhood as an immigrant from some eastern European country, his assimilation difficult because of language and cultural issues. He claims his transition was facilitated by a friendship with me. The two of us romped through elementary school, next did all the teenage crap, both good students, and excellent athletes, our bonding continued to the University level.

Injuries forced me to the sideline, but Monk graduated to the pros and spent eight full seasons as a defensive tackle, five times named all-pro. During those years, he was a typical young athlete enjoying all the privileges that came with fame and adoration of the fans: parties, women, soft drugs among the pastimes. The big man had his youth, and as long he stayed away from the hard drugs, he could run and sweat out his indulgences. He abruptly left it all behind and today is a Roman Catholic priest.

When he arrived earlier this afternoon, he walked around the house looking for adjustments. On his last visit, he chastised me; he is upset because I never change anything in the house; the kitchen fridge is plastered with notes from Nancy and Linda's drawings. All the same family pictures are on the wall; Linda's bedroom is vacuumed weekly, bed made up and ready for her return. Since my wife, Nancy, and daughter, Linda, were killed, I've had a few problems. It's been two bad years.

I'm on a stool at the island. My Internet connection is reliable, and the beer is ice cold.

"Monk, you know this guy never stops his self-promotion."

"Who and what are you talking about? Find a great site?"

"I'm talking about our glorious leader of the Legal Division, Doug Brewster. He teaches one evening class at the University, and on his website he has posted his interpretation of the history of our evolution to Justice Reborn. He says it's for his student. Let me read you this pretentious shit. He goes on for pages."

While Monk slices the rye loaf, no sliced bread for these sandwiches, I begin to read aloud from the summary on Doug's website:

We live under a radical new system of justice: Justice Reborn. The question is: how did we arrive at the Tipping Point which forced politicians to make this change? The academic debates will probably go on for decades: how did the public's daily diet of fear and frustration morph into uncompromising anger?

The consensus is it started with the years of unresolved environmental issues; the unrelenting matters

of global warming and polarity reversal dominated everyday life. The media's sophistic reporting combined with a searing sun and erratic transmission signals intensified the prevailing tension.

"Charlie, do you remember our next hospital visit?"

"Yes, I remember….. St. Michael's Children's Hospital, the cancer ward."

"Not sure which ward and won't know until we get there. But, I think we'll need Wes; there is a lot to distribute, and the hospital doesn't want us on the ward for more than 90 minutes."

"Not a problem but try and get us some smaller jerseys. The extra-large are more like overcoats, and we look like refugees. Don't worry I'll make sure Wes comes. Toss me another beer. And listen carefully: this is important."

The scale and complexity of these problems meant the public had to depend on the experts. Unfortunately, the war of egos dominated; politicians, bureaucrats and scientists all took turns, resulting in many stalemates, no sustained focus, and no practical solutions. Responsibility and control evaporated in these heated debates.

This time, it's Monk's turn to interrupt. "Is it true you once threatened to shove Doug's pipe up his ass?"

"True. At the time, Doug was just an assistant DA......
still a real asshole. I needed a search warrant and no matter
what I came up with he insisted it wasn't enough and never
provided any ideas or assistance as to how to enhance the
request. I asked him if I shoved the pipe up his ass, would this
clear his mind."

"How much did that cost you?'

"Doug never registered a formal complaint, but it
trickled down and got to the Chief. All I got was one of
Duncan's screaming sessions. Now please, allow me to
continue with this masterpiece."

**By this time our original system of justice had
evolved into a process the man on the street could not
support: defense lawyer flaunting their clever arguments
and judges ready to accept any minor deviations in police
protocol as a reason for dismissal. The inequity (real or
perceived) became the new focal point of frustration,
supplemented with prisons as hardcore playgrounds, and
repeat offenders were laughing at society.**

I stop. "Well, Doug got this right. I remember too
many cases where a judge appeared only to care about the
accused, and we had to prove 'intent.' The fact that a son of a
bitch left a night club pissed, mad as hell, got into his car and
drove right into the existing crowd, didn't matter. We had to
prove he intended to kill someone; two dead bodies didn't

count. For us this was an impossible scenario; his bloody track record didn't even matter. How could I prove he meant to kill and not just do some minor damage? Of course, for me the key point was that there were two dead kids, and this asshole got his wrists slapped."

"You know Charlie, if you had pursued your legal career, you would have ended up as a hanging judge."

"Bullshit, listen to the rest."

Monk continues to drink beer and fuss over supper, careful about the sequence with which he completes the layers of ham, lettuce, onion slices, cheddar cheese, mustard, salt, pepper, and tomatoes.

I drink the rest of my beer and kept reading aloud.

But crime and punishment were an issue the man on the street understood and when Dr. Max Armstrong's innovations burst onto the scene, it became apparent: alternatives were now possible. Here was an opportunity to establish responsibility and take control, a move to soothe the widespread feeling of helplessness.

The guilty or innocent debate no longer required a legal team; if doubt no longer existed, why not execute?

Monk speaks up again, "The more I hear, the more concerned I become that 'mercy' has been deleted from the system."

I know this is his opinion and don't want to get into it with him. "We are lucky in our Sector to have Stephen Miller as the Judge. The entire system needs his type of leadership; some unanticipated events will test all of us.

I know the impact on repeat offenders will be accepted by the police forces; but eventually, the public may wonder if they asked for too much...... ...will it be perfect? Not likely but I am optimistic. Alright? Let me finish.

Armstrong's scientific innovations allowed a dramatic paradigm shift and the associated legislation was passed in ....."

Monk interrupts. "Leave it Charlie. I heard all I want to know about the system."

I shut down, and we tear into the sandwiches. Food out of the way, I open another beer. I'm not driving tonight, and I'm a little careless with my consumption.

"I'm curious about Dr. Max Armstrong. He seems to be a real character. You meet this Armstrong guy at least once didn't you?'

"Dr. Max, as well as being brilliant, is tough and aggressive. You would not want to stand between him and one of his ambitious goals. It was evident many of his colleagues were jealous, but I'm not sure it's because of his science or libido. He was one son of a bitch of an interview; he always tried to stay a step ahead of any question. Always guessing as where a question was leading.

However, I will say, he is one helluva good looking guy, regardless of what planet he comes from."

"Come on Charlie finish your beer and let's go. I don't want to miss any of this game the coach is starting the new kid, the seven-foot center."

As we drive to the game, Monk continues to lament about the rigidity and harsh punishments of Justice Reborn. Monk is silent for a few blocks and then.

"All society must now face an uncomfortable question. Since there is no place to hide, are we seeing man's true nature? It's hard to reconcile and remember we are all selected from the same gene pool."

CHAPTER 5: THE FIVE STAR COUPLE

The homicides always began the same way: a woman, without a companion, booked a hotel room for an extended stay, four or five days.

Unfortunately for the killers, a long term hotel quest spied a man leaving one of the crime scenes, a fortuitous sighting, a fleeting glimpse of an individual with a large scarf and sunglasses. This one brief look allowed the police to declare: it was a couple.

Today, the male half occupied the room, on the second floor of the Ritz. His female partner left earlier in the day, their staggered departures all part of their plan. At times, he brooded at being spotted after the first killing but tried to flush the feeling from his mind. Now the housekeeping, a chore he could not share; he had the expertise.

He was not a large man, very slim, a few inches below six feet. His bare chest signified strength and fitness; his clothing, including his underwear, formed a mound on the floor against the exit door. With his back to the door, he sat on his haunches like a Vietnamese peasant and scanned the room.

After the second murder, the media labeled them: The Five Star Couple. They were pleased with the press name; it reflected each partner's unique contribution to the killings.

His knowledge and expertise equaled whatever forensic expertise the police could muster; in fact, he was a year or more ahead of most cities. His tools, an array of chemical sprays and a miniature vacuum device, were all assembled. Even though he knew the technology and the details, his caution resulted in careful, premeditated moves.

The murdered girl's body sagged against the pillows at the head of the bed, nude and posed in the yoga lotus position. Various body fluids associated with her recent death stained the sheets and floor. The intense and prolonged tortured ended when they broke her neck; the approach meant fewer weapons to transport.

The killer waited for the application of the first fine spray to soak the body, the furniture, the clothing, and carpeting in the room. The delay allowed him to read last night's newspaper, the hotel being one of the old fashion exceptions which supplied printed news to all guests; the headlines blared:

PRISON DECOMMISSION STARTED:
155 DEATH ROW INMATES EXECUTED

The Warden at White Rock prison, in Sector 13, confirmed the first step in the Prison Decommission program, euphemism for "empty the jail", was started by processing the death row inmates. An average of four prisoners has been executed every day for the past number of weeks. S3 Interrogation is being used to confirm the guilt of each inmate: any prisoner found to be innocent is released; otherwise, the individual is executed.

The Decommission Plan is to shut down all prisons within 12 months. Although there is a definite plan for the death row inmates, there has yet to be an agreement reached in how to process the remaining prison population. The simple approach of "just open the doors" puts the public at risk and would never be accepted. An informed source states there are many ideas, and the debates have been intense, but no agreement has been reached.

During death row interrogations, a prisoner may reveal additional crimes. The recent adjustment to Justice Reborn, Amendment 33-2, is in effect at White Rock. This amendment allows for an execution even if the inmate was never formally charged with the newly revealed felony. However, prison officials refuse to comment on how this is being implemented. Our understanding is: when unsolved crimes surface during an S3 memory scan and guilt is

confirmed, the presence of a Legal Division representative is all that is required for an execution to proceed.

The article went on for a couple of more pages, but he did not have time to read anymore; there was a job to finish. The housekeeper used his second spray application to saturate specific spots, next scrubbing and vacuuming the troublesome areas. His creeping anxiety screamed: get out, leave, and leave now. But he relished mastering the tension and exercising his discipline; each square foot required all his attention. He did not rush.

Other thoughts started to surface and challenge for dominance. Was it time to get out of the city? This fifth girl might force a change in police priorities. Because all the girls were prostitutes the public and media outcry remained subdued, in fact, some even treated it as a joke: a recent cartoon featured a prostitute going up to a hotel room and getting a bigger bang than expected. But this sluggish police response would not last.

An extraordinary development generated more confusion, particularly when the idiot started dumping bodies in their target neighborhoods. The media labeled him: Horny Harry. He roamed the streets raping and killing any girls, except prostitutes. The police were furious with the press for the inappropriate name, but the rapist-killer thrived on his notoriety and communicated with the news media using his new identity. His letters to the media were sick announcements about his charm and stamina; unbelievably, he christened himself a 'lover.'

The police would never reveal how resources were allocated, but housekeeper assumed Harry would be their priority. Regardless, he knew with each killing there was the chance of a mistake or an opportunity to leave a clue for a perceptive detective. Best to move to another city? His internal arguments swayed back and forth; first, the risk had increased and then: no, the risk was reasonable.

The vigorous scrubbing produced a fine sheen of sweat, his upper body gleaming, the room silent except for his heavy breathing. When he reached the back side of the hotel room door, he dressed and packed. Before leaving the room, he used the third high power spray whose fine disbursement was able to reach all corners. The chemical mist would slowly settle and cover the entire murder scene. As long as the crime scene remain undetected for the next 24 hours, the combination of sprays would convert the space into a neutral hotel room.

Before stepping into the hall, he carefully adjusted his large sunglasses, a wig, and a hood, all selected to provide an effective cover but still not look suspicious. The enhanced disguise all a result of that one unfortunate sighting. The 'Do Not Disturb" sign would remain on the outside door lever; this sign would buy them time. As well as booking the room for four days, they had booked the prostitute for the entire week.

The more days which passed before the body was discovered, the more difficult a detective's job would be, witnesses struggling with fuzzy memories and security tapes possibly erased and reused.

The hallway did not present a challenge, and he casually strolled to the stairwell, best to walk down to the lobby. The killer descended a couple of flights of stairs without encountering another hotel guest. Overconfidence could be the downfall of the Five Star Couple. The housekeeper knew the dangers, but he could not help thinking the killing was as close to the perfect crime as anyone had ever executed. Not like the imbecile, Horny Harry, who continued to provide the press with clues and brag about his lovemaking prowess and sexual stamina.

As he strolled out of the hotel, he thought back to the beginning. For the housekeeper, violence started early, a frequent visitor, his father, and brother delivering unprovoked brutal punishment. The beatings and pain became a regular cycle in his life, until he matured, gained strength and mounted an offense with his fear converted to rage. His demonstration of explosive anger and the week in the hospital convinced his father, and his older brother then behaved like a well-behaved pet.

The enjoyment and high from random acts of violence became a habit; however, after a couple of incidents with the police, he realized some control was necessary. It was about this time he met his current partner, and he had someone to help him manage the incidents and to share the fun, her analytical mind and poised regime provided a stabilizing dimension. With some proper planning, the cycle of rage and violence could continue, and the intoxicating highs enjoyed.

As he stepped through the front door of the hotel, the suffocating heat delivered a shocking contrast to the air-conditioned hotel. It was not raining, but many people used umbrellas to provide protection from the blazing sun; everyone appeared to be hustling, in a hurry to get to the cooler environment of an office building.

The housekeeper walked away from the hotel at a leisurely pace, his rage satiated, his demeanor like a Buddhist monk. In a matter of days, another cycle would start a slow build, daily ratcheting up the desire for a violent climax. With the help of his partner, he would plan one last assault in this city.

The police investigation continued to stumble along the wrong path; the media was screaming in the wrong direction; unless Providence lobbed some biased missiles, their schedule would not be disrupted.

# # #

Emma Collins assisted Dr. Kate at White Rock prison and helped prepare the Board report concerning the multiple memory streams.

This afternoon she brooded about a recent telephone call. Unable to reach Dr. Kate, she convinced herself a call to Wilson was their best alternative: Dr. Joe Wilson would know some answers and was normally willing to discuss any scientific topic. Wilson, now retired, had been a member of Dr. Max's original research team.

Unfortunately, her call was shuffled to his answering service; her next decision, to leave a message, now appeared reckless. How big a risk was the damn verbal note?

Emma identified herself and labeled the message as 'private and confidential.' First, she set the stage, covering their current status and their time lines, and then she posed the two difficult questions:

"Why were multiple memory streams of the same event not encountered during the initial research work?

Second, are memory streams a real reflection of an event? Or, is stored memory modified by the emotions of the individual at the time of the event? Or, does modification occur later when the memory is relived?"

The message, although labeled as confidential and personal, might be accessed by his wife or an adolescent. There was no way to know how his household handled personal messages; maybe they all used his password. A leak would be a fiasco for the Sector.

If some unpublished idiosyncrasies might taint the original research, why would he tell her? He had nothing to gain. In fact, the revelations could cause problems for the entire research team. Wilson might contact Dr. Max and let him know what was going on, something the Judge insisted not be done. And why had the Judge declared Dr. Max not be contacted?

The Sector desperately needed the answers, but had she made a grave mistake?

Both men sat in the Judge's chambers; both silent and upset, mugs of coffee untouched. They waited for a confirmation or correction call from Doug's senior man, Jessie Lopez. Doug Brewster, head of the Legal Division finally broke the silence.

"Stephen, we can't duck this one. I discussed the issue with both of them this morning; the father is furious……he claims the girl was underage."

A frustrated Judge responded, "I can't believe anyone so smart could be so dumb. Damn it he has women chasing him. Why go for a young teenager? Did he think no one would find out?

He seems to think it's a game. You know he loves to match wits with anyone, likes the high of being on the edge, the risk adds to the affair."

Doug provided more details. "Jessie is researching the family and digging into Max's record. But I don't think it will change anything. The only question is: how outrageous will this mess become?"

Doug's phone rang, causing both men to twitch.

"Alright Doug, you may as well answer it. We have to know all the details maybe there has been an error. Maybe the girl recanted."

CHAPTER 6: CHARLIE'S LOG: THE BASKETBALL GAME

"You grabbed a stranger's bare breast?"

My brother, Sam, was screaming. I shouldn't have answered the phone. It's early morning, and my departure had been delayed by a few dirty dishes and by reading ancient to-do-lists stuck on the fridge door; reminiscing should not be a full-time sport.

Monk must have called him as soon as he dropped me off. Sam is a few years older than me; today, he is a clinical psychologist with some big time clients. We are close, and he enjoys playing the big brother role. Although I am not a scientist, I have established a formula for our dynamic: Sam + Monk= Mother.

Sam has always been the academic in the family. My university experience was dominated by the demands of a football scholarship. By the time graduation arrived, I had collected enough knee damage that a pro career was no longer an option. However, I had accumulated sufficient credits to pursue a legal career but had trouble concentrating for more than 30 minutes. Those volumes of legal texts presented too boring a prospect for me.

After a few undirected years, I joined the police force and worked my way up the ladder. I live with two personality traits: first, a unique sense of humor and second, a tendency to lose my temper. These attributes are a dangerous combination when confronting the bureaucratic bullshit which is ingrained in the regimental mindset of a police department.

Two other characteristics saved me: I've an eye for detail and am able to discern patterns and relationships, not apparent to others. So, even though I was known as a habitual hard ass with a big mouth, I managed to progress up the ladder and solve some notable cases.

It's ironic that an apostate should have a priest as his best friend, but that's what Monk has been since grade school. The problem is that after a couple of beers in the relaxing company of Monk, I revert to a superficial 16 –year- old. Bulletproof, shallow, a joker with the world ready to be conquered.

I try to calm him. "Listen big brother, it's not as bad as it sounds. Relax."

"You crazy bastard. You were drinking, weren't you? How much did you put away?"

When my wife and daughter were killed by a drunk driver, I refused to acknowledge the new reality. I started drinking too much and exhibiting behavior of someone who doesn't give a damn about consequences. As a result, I'm in therapy with a friend of Sam's and have diminished my reputation in the department plus gained a new nickname: Crazy Charlie.

I rationalize by observing if I only have a few drinks, I can remain a humorous drunk or, on occasion, a belligerent asshole, a fun evening with no major harm done. I think I told you logic was not my strong suit.

The rest of the story is going to be difficult. Damn Monk can't keep his mouth shut. I try to be light and funny. "I confess. I had a couple with Monk before the game, but you know our spring dance will happen in a few days. I have to get in shape and be ready for the big night."

Sam isn't placated with that comment. Always the worrier, he'll not let go.

"I'm listening. Tell me your version of events. How does a homicide detective get arrested at a basketball game?"

"Jesus, cool off. I had a few drinks at home while Monk prepared supper. After eating, we rushed to the game. The University men's team is strong, and it was a blowout, a bit boring. We had a few more beers and near the end of the game hunger arrives, an annoying distraction.

Right in front of us are three women; the one in the middle is miss-motor-mouth, and she never stops talking. Her companion on the left is also talking. I don't think either one heard what the other one said. The third woman, on the right, sleeps through all of this. Honest to God she is sleeping. Now in between her and the center talkative blond is a huge barrel or pail of popcorn.

Well, now and then I reach down and get a handful of popcorn. The ladies never noticed, too busy talking. Near the end of the game, I'm reaching down for my last handful, and the team executes one of those dramatic ally-oop slam dunks. At this point, the center blond, for once gets excited and jumps up to cheer, as my hand is going down ……and….and she didn't come straight up. It was more of a tilt right; my hand slips right onto her right boob."

Sam makes some noise. "Stupid, stupid…..this is hard to believe. You son of a bitch. You had more than a couple of glasses."

"Just wait. I'm getting to the good part. She had on one of those very loose blouses that are cut so low it's more like a halter top, and my hand goes right under, and I have a handful of bare breast. The proverbial crap hits the fan. She starts screaming and swearing, and because she is jumping all over I can't get my damn hand out. If I just yank, I'm afraid I'll tear the blouse or flip the breast out.

Of course, the one who was sleeping is now up, and I find out her favorite word is 'pervert.' And this in combination with 'fucking pervert' is what she is yelling. Next, she picks up the barrel of popcorn, and you know how you throw a pail of water to empty it? Well, that's how she empties the barrel, and I have popcorn all over me."

My attitude seems rather flippant to Sam, but I'm far from calm or casual. For the last number of months, the Chief has had me riding a desk in Records and has forbidden me even to come up to the detective floor. The homicide squad has been warned not to discuss the serial killers with me, the ostracism an embarrassment for my old crew and me.

Now this bloody basketball blond is in the queue. If any charges result, it will be difficult to keep out of the news, meaning I'm either fired, or it will be many years before I return to Homicide. Have I reached the end of the line? I should have moved forward, but I keep slipping, living in a different world, oblivious to even the extreme environmental temperatures.

Sam is groaning. "God…goddamn it ….damn it."

"People are standing. A couple of teenagers are cheering, laughing, and one of them provides the wolf whistle. The damn blond keeps prancing with me caught in her bra, a reluctant partner to this embarrassing dance. I use my free hand to wipe the popcorn from my face, thinking maybe clear vision will help. Finally to the rescue…… Monk stands up and holds the woman's shoulder, forces her to sit in her chair and pulls my hand out; he gestures and we slide away."

"Didn't anyone try and stop you?'

"Get serious. Monk is huge and not in a good mood. No one was going to challenge us, and we almost made it. But I had to visit the bathroom. And when we came out the security people were waiting. I explained it all as a stupid accident, and we got lucky. The head of security was one of the Monk's parishioners. He smiled and told us to wait until he has a chance to talk to the blonde one more time. Maybe she might be willing to let it go."

I paused because the rest was not the best part of the evening.

"Dumb shit! Come on Charlie, don't leave me in mid-air. What happened? Were you cleared? Or, were you arrested?"

It's hard to go over this again, but I had to tell him. "I thought we were in the clear, but when the security guy returned he didn't look happy, and I guessed this was going to the next level. He told us she wouldn't let it drop and wants to press charges."

Sam still didn't understand. "What was her concern?"

"She doesn't think it was an accident because she claims, while my hand was on her breast I kept squeezing and stroking."

CHAPTER 7: CHARLIE'S LOG: THE REST

It's known as the Mamma Mia case, and I'm the prime suspect, but not charged.

It turns out the blond at the pool is an Italian tourist. So as soon as the woman surfaced, the Chief took charge and immediately enforced a blackout. Nothing was to get out. Nothing. The last thing he wanted was a front page splash with one of his men charged with assaulting a tourist.

Of course, not many vessels are 100% air tight and enough leaked, so speculation roared around the station. Some smart ass decided that when a strange hand slipped onto her bare breast, the Italian woman probably screamed. "Mamma Mia!" By placing emphasis on different syllables of the two words, it became a day's entertainment for the station staff. Random screams of "Mamma Mia" filled the detectives' workspace, and, of course, this was followed my howls of laughter as one asshole after the other grabbed a breast. Thank god I'm still downstairs in Records, away from the main crowd.

I understand why the Chief may have placated the tourist and smoothed over the incident. But what I don't understand is: why he hasn't ripped me apart?

I have to think about something else and return to Doug Brewster's Web site. Back to where I was when Monk wanted to stop; Monk said he was bored, but I think he hates the death sentence and avoids talking about it.

Doug Brewster's site is complete and well designed. As the Head of the Legal Division, it appears he supports Justice Reborn, but I think he'd flip in a microsecond if it would buy him one more rung up the ladder. If I was the Judge, I would always keep this guy in front of me. Anyway here is some more of the site:

Armstrong's scientific innovations allowed a dramatic paradigm shift, and the associated legislation was passed in record time. The media hailed the new system as Justice Reborn, and the tag became part of a worldwide vocabulary. The basics included:

•   The system no longer had prosecutors, defense lawyers or juries.

•   A judge was assigned a designated territory (a Sector) to administer.is staff consisted of four Divisions: Legal, Investigative, Prisons and Forensic.

•   The focus was on uncovering the actual sequence of events associated with each crime; motives and underlying circumstances surrounding the incident

were not to obscure the fact that there was a victim. Technology allowed an infallible review of a crime, culpability no longer a debate.

- Prison time was a thing of the past; penalties for noncapital crimes were the 30 to 60 days of reorientation at facilities known as Farms.

- Repeat offenders were under scrutiny and penalties escalated with each incident.

- The death penalty was reinstated, encompassing repeat offenders with the three and four strike legislation in effect.

- Criminal investigations revolved around three levels of drug controlled interrogations. The progressive levels of examination were known as Stage 1, Stage 2 and Stage 3 Protocol Interrogations, now S1, S2, and S3.

- The system was based on the fact these interrogation techniques made it possible to know exactly what happened, guilt or innocence no longer in doubt.

Since the entire planet was living with a doomsday forecast, the execution of a few unrepentant citizens did not seem to be an outlandish prospect. The executions were like the human sacrifice of an ancient culture and appeared to alleviate tensions and frustrations.

If it was impossible to control the environment, at least society could manage its institutions. The revised legal system was now a prominent and integral segment of the zeitgeist of our times.

Most of the western world is in the process of adopting the new justice model. The USA has an established infrastructure, and Justice Reborn is operational. England, Canada, and Germany are close behind, developing the legislation to make this a workable system for their countries, with universities scrambling to enhance their science and medical programs. The training of staff is a hurdle to overcome, the new science complex, and the new legal paradigm a challenge. The learning curve is steep, with no room for errors. Date: January 15, 2021.

Let me add a few more details. The Judge and his team of four Divisions met weekly to assess progress in the implementation of Justice Reborn, review crime statistics, discuss any unexpected developments, and revise strategy, if necessary. The Divisions are:

LEGAL: is mainly staffed by the original prosecutor's office.

INVESTIGATIVE: is a revamped police department with all the standard units.

FORENSIC: is technically demanding with a number of medical doctors, physicists, etc.

PRISONS: The challenge is the operation of two parallel systems: old and new.

Some practical details: once suspects are identified they have little choice but to cooperate. The Investigative and Legal Divisions only require a minimum justification to initiate an interrogation; interestingly, this drug-induced grilling regularly uncovers more than the original charge, not a desired outcome for the accused. It's in the suspect's best interests to confess early and avoid an S1.

At this point, White Rock Prison, in Sector 13, is the first prison to execute their death row inmates using S3. The execution of 155 prisoners in a matter of weeks was a shock even to our demanding public. The news media, for once, stayed off the soap box and just reported the events as they occurred.

A second advance team is assembling at Fort Green Prison, debriefing staff, installing equipment, getting prisoners ready. With the S3, there will be no doubt about the inmate's guilt and the execution can proceed or if innocent, the prisoner released.

Oh, I forgot to expand on the dangers associated with an S3; if the scanning exceeds 45 minutes, there is always some degree of permanent brain injury. The damage becomes particularly relevant if the accused is found to be innocent.

Mamma Mia................ can you believe this mess?

CHAPTER 8: THE BLACK ANGEL ARRIVES

"You killed 155 men in 45 days?"

Pat's response was measured. "Warden, as you know, Justice Reborn requires all prisons to be decommissioned within 12 months. And one of the first steps is clearing death row by either carrying out the original sentence or freeing the prisoner. Hence, it would be more accurate to state: we executed 125 convicts by carrying out the court imposed sentence. The only nuance of this process was the additional 30 prisoners who had previous capital crimes uncovered, and they were dealt with under Amendment 33-2."

Five people occupied all the chairs in a large conference room on the top floor of the administration building. A small east window filtered in the early morning sun and faint noises sifted in from the exercise yard below, overall a drab morning. Seated at the head of the table, the Warden acted as chairman. He wore a baseball cap, an old cotton athletic windbreaker with a time-worn crest, the entire ensemble inappropriate for the meeting, the most intense in the history of Fort Green prison.

Labeled as old fashioned, too soft, avuncular, and known in the yard as 'Uncle Willie,' the Warden had failed to keep himself or his staff current. He ignored technological advances and the new legislation which appeared to be changing weekly. There was little doubt the Warden, an anomaly among prison administrators, was not a fan of the new approach, Justice Reborn. But before he could retire his prison had been selected as the second to clear a death row unit.

"Warden, it appears I proceeded too quickly under the assumption everyone was fully aware of what has taken place. Let me start again."

They were huddled around a large rectangular table. Pat, the speaker, although not condescending, was certainly not impressed with the Warden and his senior staff, and she decided to revert to basics.

"To repeat my name is Pat Holdner, and I'm the advance person for Sector 14. My job is to ensure you and your staff understand the details and roles in this first step of Prison Decommissioning; this means clearing death row. During the next 24 hours, members of my team will begin arriving at various times throughout the day.

This team will set up all the equipment required, walk your staff through the process, debrief death row, ensure convicts understand their options and contact the local resources needed. For example, bodies are cremated, and if we don't have sufficient local resources, we have contacts outside the district."

Pat thought her presentation sounded like a computer delivery, but if it seemed rather abrupt and cold, it might be the best approach for this group. The prison population had dubbed her the Black Angel because they said she was preparing the way for their trip to heaven or hell.

"Although the inmates have already been sentenced and some have pending appeals, we are using S3 to confirm their guilt or innocence. White Rock prison, in Sector 13, has completed the process and, as I said, 155 convicts were executed, and ten others found innocent. At White Rock, the death row cells are now empty.

The only complication to the event was that Amendment 33-2 was passed before White Rock started. This Amendment means when we are proceeding with an S3 Interrogation and encounter a capital crime the prisoner may be executed for that particular crime. Since there is always a Legal presence and all records are archived, the entire process is deemed valid. Under this amendment the execution occurs, even though this was not the original crime that resulted in the court imposed death sentence.

Another point to remember, at White Rock we were observers and only assisted when Sector 13 requested additional resources. It is now our turn in Sector 14 to process Fort Green's death row."

The Warden was trying to ask a question and simultaneously control his temper; mass execution based on science was not a process he endorsed. "It is correct that 30 inmates were executed under this Amendment?"

"True but that doesn't mean they were not guilty of the original crime. It just means another capital crime was encountered first, and it was deemed unnecessary to prolong the process. And, I should point out it doesn't matter if the offense was committed before the Justice Reborn legislation was passed. There are no time constraints. To repeat: of the 165 convicts on White Rock's death row, 125 had their original sentence confirmed, that is proven with the S3 interrogation. The other 30 were executed under Amendment 33-2, and ten were found to be innocent of any crime and released."

Jeff Hellson, the Deputy Warden, asked, "Pat, I assume Dr. Kate and her group will be in charge of the interrogations in our prison. Did they get any direct experience at White Rock? And, second, has staff morale become an issue with all those executions?"

"First question: Dr. Kate and her staff were directly involved and conducted 12 of the interrogations at White Rock. The second question, morale has not been an issue, but the workload has been intense, and everyone felt it was best to take a few days off. As well, Forensics wanted time to assess procedures and see if changes should be made.

I should point out the process didn't unfold as most planned. At first, the convicts were excited and ready to participate; most were career criminals, and many thought they could beat an S3, possibly, in the same way, some had confused the lie detector equipment.

This enthusiasm didn't last. The inmates soon understood an S3 Interrogation is reliable, and they we're not going to beat the system. Within days a surprising trend surfaced, most prisoners exercised their option to bypass the S3 and proceed directly to the prison's execution room. It was because of this so many were executed in such a short time and one of the reasons for the need for more resources. I am sure your staff will have to deal with the same issue of many executions in a very short time but ..."

The Warden interrupted. "This seems impossible for my staff to prepare the chambers, contact relatives and..."

Pat recaptured control. "Don't worry. As I said, my team will arrive shortly and will provide detailed instructions on all roles and responsibilities; and, I will be responsible for communicating the process and options to all inmates on death row."

The Warden, still upset, ignored the answer. "Why did so many go directly to the execution chambers?"

"An S3 is not painful, but it can be embarrassing. You have to understand the Watchers, who are relatives, a friend or spouse, will be able to see any part of your life. And many different memory streams will be displayed before the crime scene is located.

And after you have been shouting your innocence for years, your actual history will come as a merciless shock. When it became apparent the memory displays are uncompromising images, most of the men decided the best option was to avoid revealing the ruthless segments of their lives. Remember these memory streams are raw, unedited data; there is no censure and any segment at any time can surface, from the most savage to the most personal. Most of the convicts would have been showing some rather horrendous warts, and it was not something they wanted a mother or relative to have as their last memory."

Uncle Willie wasn't satisfied. "I need some detail as to how this S3 works?"

Pat was tired, and technology was not her strength, but the request was valid. She started.

"Memory research and associated debates have been going on for centuries. For example, in the 1940s a neurosurgeon, Dr. Wilder Penfield, was using weak electric currents which stimulated portions of the brain and resulted in fantastic recollections from his patients and this type of research never stopped.

Around 2008, a neurobiologist in Georgia, Joe Tsien, was manipulating levels of the protein alpha-CaMKII to selectively delete memories from mice. And, for years molecular neuroscience has been researching the nanoworld of the brain, studying the signals sent from one cell to another cell….."

Again the Warden broke in. "OK…….OK …. those of us around this table are not technically inclined, have no degrees in physics, medicine or whatever, nor are we particularly interested in how the atoms and nerve connections line up. Can you give us a comic-book version of what the hell happens?''

Pat understood their frustration. "I think if I continue, I'll just confuse the situation. Later in the week you'll all get to see a live recording. This'll make it much easier to understand the process. But I should explain the Watchers because they will be arriving before any S3 can start.

During the scanning process, electromagnetic signals are blasted into the brain or more correctly are aimed at a particular region. This bombardment is an unwelcome stimulus, and the cells respond or release their contents as a weak transmission; these responses are captured and displayed.

All this probing should be completed in 45 minutes or less. Any longer and, usually, permanent brain damage results.

The scanner, a Medical Technician, works with a small group of people, known as the Watchers. This group consists of three or four people.

As the streams of memory play out on a monitor, the Watchers signal the Medical Technician to move "ahead" or "back" in time. They determine if the displayed memory pocket happened before or after the crime scene. Each new position of the scanner provides a new pocket of memories to be viewed and assessed. Watchers are forced to make rapid decisions; any prolonged discussion about the point in time being displayed will eat into the 45-minute limit.

The mandatory member of the group is the Historian, a government employee, who specializes in historical events, customs, and fashions. Also, it is standard practice to have a detective who was associated with the case and can recognize the crime scene.

Last, the convict will select one or two people. His selections have to be very familiar with his life and are usually parents, siblings, or spouse. They will be able to recognize a family event, like a wedding and know when it happened."

The Warden had enough. "So individuals are going to be executed or released based on their memory of the crime, and now with Amendment 33-2, it could be a capital crime they committed at any time." He got up and left the room. Pat watched the Warden walk away, certainly not pleased with what she had brought to his prison

Her concerns and frustrations grew with each hour. The Board concluded earlier in the week. Where was the green light to proceed? Jacob, the Head of the Prisons Division, was not answering her calls. Maybe it was related to the environmental issue. Transmission problems were common, signals breaking up, calls just abruptly dropped, depending on an erratic magnetic flux. Friends tried to explain it was all related to the bloody magnetic north pole; all the technical terminology was beyond her.

She wanted to keep resending her requests for clarification but was concerned the repetitions might irritate Jacob. His physical appearance and style often deceived newcomers into believing they were dealing with the third string, a grave mistake in judgment which, if they had no trading cards, would cost them. He never paraded his backers, a discretion they all respected. The political world, also, appreciated his willingness to accept the public opprobrium associated with some of their more devious agendas.

Pat was left with unanswered questions. Her plan was to corner Dr. Kate or Emma at tonight's Spring Dance; maybe they'd have the answers. Why no team for the prison? Why no clearance from the Board?

# # #

Back at the Hall of Justice, Chief Duncan Stirling was in a black mood. His session with the tourist still lingered and irritated him. He had to appease and win over an angry blond who claimed Charlie grabbed her breast at a damn basketball game.

The new legislation meant innovation and change at a rapid pace with many issues not covered by regulations; creative decisions were necessary without preordained guidelines. The Chief struggled when working in this gray zone, the result unwanted pressure and anxiety.

This current tension was compounded by problems with Charlie, his best detective, the man he usually relied on when a case proved difficult or unusual. Although Charlie frequently drove him to the edge because he never stayed in the box and regularly forgot to provide the type of obsequiousness the brass expected, Duncan recognized his strength and lived with the problems this brought to his office. Or, he had to this point.

The first few months after Charlie lost his wife and daughter, he appeared to be coping. This solitude quickly disappeared. More and more incidents reached the Chief: bouts of heavy drinking and juvenile behavior, coupled with the occasional burst of anger. All finally proved too much. Duncan assigned him to a desk in Records, out of the public eye, and away from the Homicide Squad. But now this bullshit.

The basketball charge was a valid complaint: Charlie had grabbed and held her breast, a goddamn handful of breast. After his strong recommendation at the Monday Board meeting, what the hell was he to do? Call the Judge and ask for an emergency session? Difficult to describe this as a crisis with the S3 issue hanging over them. This was not the time to declare an error in promoting Charlie.

These issues and a home front with an unhappy wife meant Duncan longed for the good old days where everyone knew the rules. How to simplify his life? That fucking Charlie Taylor needed taming, and their history no longer counted.

####

"Kiss my ass!"

Harry studied his facial expression in the mirror and thought he should be smiling when he delivered the line. Earlier in the week he'd read: John Wayne Gacy, the famous serial killer, the Clown Killer from Chicago, had screamed these last words. He'd shouted at his guards who were forcing him into the lethal injection room. Harry thought this was the way to go out. If he was arrested, he would scream it at the reporters: more headlines for a star, a killer, the way to go out.

On a daily basis, he practiced his delivery. Now with a sneer, rather than a smile, he tried again. "Kiss my ass!" That was it. Perfect. "Kiss my ass!"

CHAPTER 9: CHARLIE'S LOG: THE SPRING DANCE

Jesus, I have to hurry. The Chief wants to see me

My head is splitting, mouth unbelievable, and the rest of the classic signs are all present. What a helluva weekend. I think the Spring Dance was a success. Unfortunately, all I remember is arriving and having a few drinks, after that a black void, nothing, nada.

I'm close to my destination, the Hall of Justice, which houses most of the Investigative Division, including Administration, Homicide, Records, and the Dispatch Center. It's early morning. The Chief said 'early' and made it sound like a few seconds delay would be fatal, and not for him. I think this is the day we discuss Mamma Mia.

The street vendors are setting up. It's bright morning with sunshine bouncing off any reflective surface, but once I go through those two massive front doors of the Hall, the setting will change. Inside there will be long, narrow, dark hallways with rows of offices, some doors opened, others closed, but all blinds will be pulled to ward off the hot sun.

I'm trying to remember the dance, the recollection a frustrating, useless exercise. God, this is getting scary. Best not tell Sam or Monk. I run up the staircase in front of the

Hall of Justice, push through the front giant doors and start for the bank of elevators at the end of the hall; I hear someone calling me. Wes Krause, my old partner and good friend, is trying to get my attention.

"Charlie, I hear the Chief wants to see you. I bet I know why. I'm surprised you were able to dress yourself this morning. Why're you looking so stunned?'

"Smart ass. Tell me. Come on, tell me." I like Wes but he does enjoy playing games, and I'm not in the mood. Wes more closely resembles a 1960's hippie than a homicide detective. He has a dark complexion and is tall, with a long dark brown ponytail, a beard which is occasionally trimmed, black plastic framed glasses because corrective surgery not possible, a relaxed persona. In reality, he's an excellent athlete, with strength and speed, who plays on the same recreational basketball team as I do.

Wes is a follower which makes him a good partner for me, a guy who often moves on instinct and occasionally needs someone to flash the warning lights. He is a close friend, and his loyalty is evident to everyone, even if they don't understand the origin. Around the station he has developed the reputation as 'Charlie's bodyguard.' At times, I find his loyalty embarrassing, but our street bonding goes deep.

"You don't know? You had another blackout. Didn't you? You can't remember the goddamn mess you created. Recall the shit storm which followed? Can you?"

This time I'm uneasy; he's right I can't remember, no matter how hard I try. Wes stares at me, and my response is to look stupid, but there is nothing but a blank wall, almost the entire weekend a vacuum; I don't have to say anymore, he knows.

"I better get you up to speed because you are going to hear about this one. Even with all the booze, you were doing ok for most of the party, until near the end. I thought you were safe, and I wasn't paying too much attention to your wandering. At some point you spotted the redhead and her girlfriend; they were both wearing gowns with a lot of bare shoulder and back which presented a target for…"

"Oh, Christ, don't tell me. I don't want to know!"

"I'm just getting started. Their dates had left them to get more drinks. That's when you arrived. The ladies certainly weren't impressed.

I don't know what you whispered into Red's ear. And, I was still on the other side of the room when you started on her shoulders; it was a combination of licking and kissing her bare shoulders and bare back. Man, this was serious shit; your face was all over her back. I think the only reason she didn't scream was she was in shock."

I can't believe what I'm hearing. The lady in question, Red, is Emma Collins, a senior medical technician in the Forensic Division, a real beauty. I had thought, numerous times, of asking her out but never found the courage to ask. Apparently the other night I had plenty of courage.

She is tall and thin, a typical runner not a classic robust build with pronounced curves. She is a light brunette with a natural pronounced red sheen which she wears as a short crop instead of the current fashion of long straight hair. Emma isn't cute but is best described as handsome with light Saxon complexion and startling blue eyes. At 27 years old she is an urban female whose primary focus is her career, someone not prepared to associate with nits.

As you can see I've done my homework, just never did anything about it. From what my sources tell me, her current workload is massive with the new legislation forcing her to continue to adjust and innovate. Technology is being rolled out at breakneck speed.

Wes sees I'm a blank and continues. "About this time her date arrives with the drinks. He is a sergeant from the Robbery Division, looks about 6' 4''. Looks like an ex-Marine. He pushes you away, and when you persist, he reaches for your neck.

This is where your luck kicks in; I think your wobble and swaying made it difficult for him to find you throat. So even in your state, you're able to isolate one of his fingers. You apply a finger bend on him......son of a bitch ....it looked like you turned the finger down to his forearm.

At this time, the band stopped playing. And in this quiet lull, our ex -Marine, now on his knees, comes out with a Comanche style scream. Of course, the entire hall turns to the wailing; everyone, and I mean everyone, is peering at the scene. There is no one else on the dance floor, except for the screaming sergeant, a grinning pie-eyed ex-homicide detective. Red, close to tears, tried to pull you off. I got there in time to get you away before his friends arrived. Shit, I never knew a man could scream that loud."

"No bloody more! Jesus Christ! The Chief was still there?"

"Listen everyone was there. You have to stop drinking. The blackouts are bad enough, but the behavior will get you killed."

We're almost at the end of the corridor when we both see her. It's Red, and she is coming straight at us. Time for a quick decision. I have to apologize. She's going to walk right by us as if we don't exist. I wonder why. I step in front of her and give it a shot.

"Emma, listen I want to.." That's as far as I got.

She glares at me. "You frigging asshole!"

I try a second time, she beats me to it and belts out —— "frigging asshole"—— and walks away.

Wes is grinning. "That was very smooth. Went well. I think she likes you."

Screw it. I can't fix it. I leave Wes and head for the elevators and Division Headquarters. The reception area is exceptionally large; it allows for staff to congregate while waiting to see the Chief. There is a mixture of small lounges and a few armchairs; the steno's station is vacant, too early in the am. There are few other detectives in the office area, in particular a group from the Vice Squad and their head man, big mouth Webster, who is smirking (what the hell does everyone find so funny today?). I'm not ten feet into the office, and Webster starts.

"Looks who's here. It's lover boy. Is it true you bit Red's ass last night in full view of the Chief? So was it the booze or just really horny?"

His pals get into the act. "Charlie puts a whole new meaning into tearing one-off".

At this point, a few of the idiots slip in sets of large plastic false teeth and start making clicking sounds. This group came prepared——Webster is aware of everything that is going on in the Division. Of course, they know I never bit anyone but it makes for a great story, and I will be part of the Division's oral history for years. As the prank continues the laughter gets louder, some are crying (Christ, it's not that funny), and the giant false teeth keep up the vigorous chomping.

Someone lets out a mock moan and groans. "Bite me baby."

The room sounds like it is full of a bunch of goddamn beavers who are going to chew up all the wooden fixtures. The place is full of the clacking sound, laughter and hooting, clack, clack and more clack….the false teeth an unholy symphony.

I'm no longer amused and step towards Webster. We all stop when the Chief steps out of his office. "Charlie, get in here. The rest of you get moving. Now."

The Chief and I go way back. Once I get into his office, I think about how to apologize. I walk to the empty chair and begin to sit down.

"Hold it, did I tell you to sit? Stand and listen carefully. At the beginning of last week, I convinced the Judge you should be appointed the new head man in Homicide. He agreed but wanted the announcement delayed until he had an opportunity to talk to Doug Brewster and Jake Konahouse, neither one your biggest boosters.

Then a couple of days later I have to talk a blond into not pressing charges because you squeezed her breast at a basketball game. Not my favorite chore, playing a humble servant to a groupie. But you managed to top all that this weekend. I didn't see what triggered the incident with the sergeant, and I don't want to know; the spectacle on the floor was enough.

My problem is: I went so far out on the limb to get you back into Homicide I can't afford to make an immediate reversal and throw you back into Records. But you have to understand this, from here on there are no more free passes; one more drinking incident and you'll be buried in Records or completely off the force. The loss of your wife and daughter started all this, but it's time to move on. Either you move on or get out. Do you have anything to say?"

My mouth isn't going to work. I shake my head. As I said the Chief and I go away back, and I know when he is talking tight and under control that he is furious—— best to sneak out as fast as possible.

"At three pm today the Judge has asked that the Section Heads attend a special Board session. This means you. I can't begin to tell you how disappointed I'm in what is happening with and to you. But the gloves are off, and if you let me down one more time, I'll kick you so goddamn hard you may never recover. Now get the hell out of here and get ready for this afternoon."

###

I leave and almost run to the Homicide department, three floors down. The entrance hall leads into an open area cluttered with whiteboards, filing cabinets and some portable cork boards; we are fortunate in that senior staff also have real offices, with full walls, even windows. Wes is waiting, no longer grinning.

I guess. "You knew about the reinstatement and promotion. Why didn't you tell me?"

"Come on, forget it. The rumor has been around here for the last week, but I thought it best to keep quiet in case it was false. Time to go. You have a room full of detectives who want to bring you up to speed and don't get sensitive if you get an uneasy inspection; you deserve it."

I know he's right, and I think about how to recover the respect of the group. This is not going to be easy. There are three others in the room when Wes and I get there: Karen Zubik, Manuel Moreno, and Terry Patterson are detectives in Sector 14 homicide. They know about the promotion and make all the proper sounds; no one mentions the spring party. We assemble in the meeting room, everyone around the large table, and we start a quick review of all the active cases; most of it's routine, except there are two serious open cases.

Wes is in charge of the first major case: a serial team, known as the Five Star Couple, who kill prostitutes in four or five-star hotels. He starts his summary. "Although it's not confirmed, it does appear our Five Star Couple have been at the Ritz. A body was discovered this morning. If the Forensic team confirms the initial assessment, this will be number five. I haven't been over to the hotel, but if it is number five, the pressure is going to mount. The Tourist Association has already phoned the Chief and the Mayor, and I suspect the Judge will get the next set of calls."

I know he is right. The Ritz is a world class convention center and hotel complex, the hub for many international events held in the city. It will get a lot of video and be an evening news as an exclusive feature. "Wes, once you get confirmation I want to know. I'll get over to the hotel and walk the crime scene with you. In any case, I'm going to put together a brainstorming session. This couple is too damn smart for a conventional approach; we need a different perspective."

I turn to Karen. She is the oldest detective in the squad. Her first years in a patrol car were spent with Duncan Stirling, an exuberant and easy going young man who would eventually become the Chief. He had been protective of the rookie, taking the time to pass on all his street smarts. He was a great mentor and, with his love of the book and structure, made sure she understood the written rules and regulations.

Today she is in excellent condition, a small woman, not a prankster, a face with a few hard-earned wrinkles, more years on her frame than the rest of the squad but still a significant force. Her petite physique means she is frequently challenged; her hours with the martial arts fraternity soon prove this to be a mistake. I've become her champion, as I see tenacity, intelligence and a commitment hard to match, and always allow her maximum freedom on most of her cases. As well, she is the only one on the squad who knows about the sting I ran to help Wes. She never told me how she found out, and she never shared her knowledge with anyone else.

Karen is the lead in the other open case: another serial killer but at the opposite end of the spectrum when it comes to method and attitude. This one is wild and appears completely out of control. He is a serial rapist and killer.

Karen provides a short review. "After his first victim, he started regular reports to various news outlets detailing his physical attributes, the size of his penis, bragging about his prowess as a lover, claims he is so horny he can't help himself. This was when one of the reporters labeled him 'Horny Harry,' an inappropriate name, but one the press won't let go….. maybe because the son of a bitch keeps feeding them material. This rapist craves attention and always contacts the media after an attack. If the girl is strong enough, she survives the beating…… only two have survived: the first girl and our current victim in the hospital. He is not very careful, mainly rather sloppy. We have DNA, some clothing fibers, and hair samples."

Karen is not happy with his ridiculous label because it appears to bring some humor to a situation which is far from funny. Yet, she knows she is dealing with a veteran bunch of homicide detectives, and black humor is the norm.

"Gentlemen, Horny Harry has a distinct mode of operation. Our first victim, who was lucky to survive, remembers almost nothing from the attack but does remember getting into a cab. The next four girls did not survive the assault. And, our latest victim appears to be trying to speak the word 'taxi.' I assume he is driving a cab or what seems to be a legitimate taxi and makes his selection from the cab, ignoring any women that are not his type.

The girl is in the General Hospital and will survive. She is fragile, and I can only get a few minutes at a time with her. The doctors are cautious; they don't want to add to her stress with a series of probing questions. It will be days before we can see her again for more than a few minutes.

I recorded her statement. Actually, I recorded several different bursts of dialogue at various times when she was conscious. But her jaw is broken, she has numerous missing teeth, her lips split, and the inside of her mouth is swollen. It is impossible to understand her, but she insists on talking, and I continue to record her efforts to speak. I'm only able to comprehend a few words, one of which is 'taxi.' "

Wes interrupted, "Karen, I'm sure there is a reason, but why not paper and pen?"

"She can't write. Besides being feeble, both hands are severely cut and swollen, in fact, all ripped up and covered in heavy bandages. She was either trying to protect herself or Harry was wild and swinging and slicing at everything.

My guess: he is not a regular cab driver but has disguised a vehicle to mimic a regular cab; it has to be good disguise because women are getting into the damn cab without any reservations. The cab allows him to cruise in any area without attracting attention. Net? All I have is four different recorded statements from the lady in Intensive Care, out of which I can understand about ten words."

I'm rather abrupt and cut it short. "Karen I need you to participate in the brainstorming on the Five Star Couple, then I promise we will form a different group to review Harry with you. We have a fresh crime scene with the Five Star Couple. I need to start there."

She wants to spend all her time on her case; she is not pleased. Still, I have something to contribute. "Come back to my office after the meeting. I've a contact with an FBI technical group, and they have some gurus who may be able to work on your recordings; the contact owes me. Maybe we can get priority. Maybe get you some understandable phrases or words."

Everyone is starting to leave; I feel I have to say something, but my brain is mush, I almost mumble the words. "People thanks for the reports. I recognize I'm not starting from the high ground, but you all know me and I hope trust me."

There are handshakes on the way out, and no one appears distressed by my promotion; that's about all I can hope. Before all clear the room, the Chief's secretary is at the door.

"Charlie, the Chief asked me to relay this message: the Judge has canceled the special Board meeting today and will reschedule later in the week."

"Thanks, I don't know what caused the cancellation, but it's good for me. I'll be at my desk once I find my new office."

Karen is waiting, and we head out to find my new office.

# # #

Karen is gone, pleased with the FBI willingness to assist and prioritize. I start organizing my small office; it appears someone has already been at work. The place has been dusted, all the little odds and ends are in place, on my desk a new large size monitor connected to central, even my own coffee maker in operation. Since I have all the necessary passwords, I can now dig deeper into both open cases. I'm ok, just fighting a headache and sore throat.

The blackouts are scary. I can't believe I approached Emma in front of the whole Sector and started on her bare shoulders, like a horny drunk. Unbelievable. But then I realize, at that moment, that is what I was: a horny drunk. How depressing. I can't focus on the damn cases.

What's bothering me? Why did I get promoted? I've known the Chief and worked with him for a long time. I understand why he placated the blond and convinced her not to proceed with a charge but why let me off the hook? Me or any other misbehaving member of his force. This is not his style. Second, after the Spring Dance, he has to be worried about me; why take a chance? Doesn't make sense, not for a straight guy like the Chief. Why would he do this?

I drink my coffee. Slowly it begins to filter through, the only thing that makes sense: it's a setup. If he fires me today, there could be a backlash. I could be viewed as a grieving widower who has put in many extra hours for the department and solved some tough cases, then was thrown off the force while recovering from a personal tragedy. But, with the promotion the Chief can prove he gave me a chance.

All the Chief has to do is wait for the pressure of these two open cases to get to me. Then he can ease me out, telling everyone he tried his best but I couldn't recover from my personal problems. Sure: it's a setup. The Chief hates loose ends; everything has to fit and be neat by the book. My approach has always been hard for him to take and the last two years tough on him. Now all he has to do is wait. The next incident and he will be able to clean up the department.

It's early, but I am thirsty. Jesus Christ.

CHAPTER 10: BINARY SEARCH

Leaving the message now appeared reckless.

Emma Collins had a long day ahead of her and struggled with the start. There was still no response from the confidential telephone query she'd left for Dr. Joe Wilson. A decision which haunted her: stupid, hasty, and uncharacteristic.

At 6:30 am, Emma and Janice were the sole occupants, only a few desks apart, but each engaged in her own world for different reasons. The area was part medical facility, part chemistry laboratory, part office, and part communication center, but everyone referred to it as the Combination Room. The space housed an extensive array of specialized equipment, work tables, a multitude of computers, individual desks, and large wall mounted monitors. It formed the primary working space for the Forensic Division and was a formidable site for a first-time visitor.

Emma did not indulge in political intrigue; she was a scientist who had fallen in love with the learning process from her first days in elementary school. At university she blossomed and was recognized as one of the best students in the science program. In her last years, she developed a strong relationship with a young Ph.D. student, Jerry King. Jerry was completing some post-doctoral work and was impressed with Emma's intelligence and creativity. They presented as a natural couple both intelligent, poised, good looking, a good fit. But, before she graduated Jerry got a prestige appointment in Paris, France. For Emma, his unanticipated abrupt departure left a void and a touch of bitterness.

Emma's social skills and associated behavior were not her strong point: on occasion, exchanges resulted in an inappropriate word, an unintentional rebuff, the result a reputation of arrogance. She understood she tended to brood and took on the world's problems.

Today her career was her passion; she only dated on rare occasions, as when a friend needed her to be a blind date. Friends thought the constrained dating and the narrow social life stemmed from the unsettling conclusion of her relationship with Jerry King.

In another corner, Janice Huber endeavored to catch up on her backlog. She was a technician but not with the most senior ranking. Janice graduated with distinction but in this Division it merely meant acceptance as one of the crew. This was a difficult assessment for her to accept, particularly since family and friends had always told her she was the best

This good paying job meant for the first time in her life, Janice was completely independent and earning an excellent salary. Unfortunately, her money management skills did not match her scientific prowess. Her behavior was more that of a lottery winner than a salaried employee. Even though she had a significant unpaid student loan, she proceeded to furnish her apartment with top quality merchandise and used the same approach with clothing, jewelry and all manner of trinkets. The girl loved to shop and show off her purchases, with a few credit cards it was all possible.

Although she resented Emma's lead with the new technology, Emma never seemed to notice; but, Dr. Kate picked up the signals and gently told her to be patient.

This was the first time she had been alone with Emma since the party. "Red, tell me did you get lucky with the monster size detective at the Spring Dance?"

"No, there was no lucky night. After Charlie had bent his finger, we had to go to the Emergency Ward. When the doctor finished, my date only wanted to go home to his own bed."

"You're one tough broad. Charlie has to stop drinking like it's a contest, and he wants the first prize. It's been over two years since the accident. I think he is on the edge of pissing everyone off. He's fortunate the Chief likes him."

"I ran onto the dance floor to get away from Charlie. Then he came after me, and that's why we were in full view of the entire Division. God, I could have died. How he was able to grab the finger and control my giant of a date, I'll never know."

"The worst part was when your partner started screaming. I mean here is this big man on his knees……..in the middle of the dance floor shrieking and Charlie, very calm with a stupid grin on his face, enjoying the show…….it was unbelievable. He is lucky Wes got him out of there before it escalated."

Janice was mouthing words of sympathy, but in reality, she had relished the dance floor screaming and Emma's embarrassment. She thought Emma received too many kudos; she knew it was childish. But, Kate and Emma were tight, and all of Janice's efforts appeared to be of secondary importance. She found it difficult to keep jealousy from disturbing her. However, today a new car, a confirmed exotic summer vacation trip, and a manicure with new nails all enhanced her mood. And, it helped that she knew one of Dr. Kate's buried secrets.

"I don't want to talk about it anymore. The dance, Charlie, my date, the works. Forget it. I have to start collecting all the results from White Rock. Dr. Kate wants me to isolate the duplicate memory streams from every interrogation.

We're to start our analysis with the convicts who were found to be innocent; we have to assess why the scans took longer for this group. There appears to be a problem with the technique used during the S3 interrogation. Dr. Kate did get clearance from the Judge to bring you into the loop because we may need a larger workforce. I need you to run the playback unit while I assess the scenes and take notes."

"I'm certified for S1 and S2 interrogations and now have an upgraded clearance, tell me what happened."

Emma guessed Janice would press for more information about the White Rock S3 examinations. Dr. Kate ordered her: use the term 'duplicate' and not 'multiple' and do not discuss the possibility these copies may be different versions of the same event. If Janice persisted, Kate's instructions were clear; Emma was to lie: the streams were all duplicates, and the extent of the brain damage had not been confirmed.

"I'm not sure what happened because I haven't seen all the results. I'm only familiar with the 12 we interrogated. The appearance of duplicate copies caused delays, and some scans took too long. The duplicates confused the technicians. They spent inordinate amounts of time trying to explain a duplicate scene so they could get to the next memory segment. We're still not sure about the impact on the prisoners who survived. Each surviving inmate was assessed for brain damage, but the results aren't back.

If we can finish in the 45-minute time frame, there are no problems but as the scan drags on the risks increase and there is no way of telling what the complications might be. The scanning is more of an art than a science. We conduct the scanning or probing process as a Binary Search, like a three-dimensional binary search. Once we're focused on an area of the brain, we treated it as if events were stored in a chronological or sequential fashion. This concept works up to a certain point. With a few days of experience, you can maintain a good rhythm as you are probing.

But, there are times when you have to change your perception of the memory scheme. Memory storage appears to be a continuous stream but then individual cells of unique events are discovered in this stream. These are pockets or events which don't fit in this serial time flow........they just appear to be an event thrown in at random. These sporadic memory readouts force changing the probing process and costs us time."

Janice wanted more. "Wait.....wait ..... hang on a minute. I'd like a review of the Binary Search algorithm."

Emma said, "You have our Standards Manual on the shelf; open the textbook, go to Page 15 and read the underlined portion."

Janice took the book off the shelf and read out loud a formal description.

The binary search technique is a fundamental method for locating an element of a particular value within a sequence of sorted elements. The idea is to eliminate half of the search space with each comparison. First, the middle element of the sequence is compared to the value we are searching for. If this element matches the value we are searching for, we are done. If, however, the middle element is "less than" the value we are searching

for, then we know that, if the value exists in the sequence, it must exist somewhere after the middle element. Therefore, we can eliminate the first half of the sequence from our search and just repeat the search in the exact same manner on the remaining half of the sequence. If, however, the value we are searching for comes before the middle element, then we repeat the search on the first half of the sequence.

"That's a start, but more would help."

"Let me take some artistic license and give you the simplified version which in essence covers the process. Think about an old parlor trick where you ask me to guess a number between 1 and 100. You think of a number, and I have to find the number by asking you a limited number of questions. Let's suppose you select 68. Well, first I divide the search horizon in half by asking if the number is 50 or is it larger or smaller. You tell me it's bigger and I now know it is in between 50 and 100; this I divide again and select 75 and ask the same question. You tell me it is smaller and I now know it is between 75 and 50. This guessing goes on until I get the number.

For an inmate's brain scan our horizon is restricted to his date of birth and the current date; from there the search is a very similar process. Once we retrieve the first memory stream, the decisions start.

We jump either forward or backward in time; the probes are series of jumps to narrow into the event of interest. Of course, the schema for memory storage is more complicated than a parlor game, and it's a more difficult assessment to move the probe to a new location, but the general concept is the same."

"Alright, that certainly helps. I'm booked for more training next month and hope I can get certified for an S3. But you still seem upset. Something else is bothering you. Care to share?"

"I'm just concerned about our small window for solving the problem. I haven't had an opportunity to assess what took place at White Rock. I need to review how the technicians reacted when they encountered the duplicates and see if we can adjust the technique for a faster scan. We have to consistently get under the 45-minute barrier. So you and I have a lot to get done in a short time."

Emma took the book. As she returned it to the shelf, she paused when she noticed her old physics text. The book brought to mind her first physics lecture in the massive auditorium style classroom, with a professor who looked like the building janitor but soon destroyed that illusion.

His start had been elementary: units of measure and on to first principles of science. Any measurement made without knowledge of its uncertainty is useless. This was the mantra he continued to stress for the entire first term.

Had Dr. Max ignored first principles and assumed his 'measurements' were always 100% accurate, giving no concern to the fact there are always elements of uncertainty associated with any measurement?

CHAPTER 11: CHARLIE'S LOG: KAREN

Our victim's face looks like a Ford F-150 truck ran over it. Finally, Karen and I are at the hospital where Horny Harry's last surviving victim is recovering, but the lady fades in and out of consciousness.

I've been delayed getting to the hospital. A few months ago when the Chief transferred me to Records, he ignored me, now he insists on making sure I conform to all current Homicide standards. During my absence, he introduced a new set of forms which are a declaration that each detective must sign: Have you read all the relevant JR material? Do you understand the process before an S1 interrogation can be initiated? And, a few others. I'm not skipping one bloody hurdle. Jesus, he even made me go to the shooting range; I understand this weapon's recertification is important: particularly if I encounter Billy the Kid.

I feel rushed; it's my second day without a drink. This is going to be one helluva of a day. Karen is intrusive and demanding; nevertheless, the hospital staff perceives a dedicated woman, and cooperation is not an issue. I know she spends many extra hours near the victim, hoping there will be a lucid moment. Shit, this is a delusion.

The young woman is in the Intensive Care Unit which is one of the floors where money has been invested. The place is spotless, bright, no chipped corners or stained walls, looks like a mission control center. The nursing station is a large circular affair in the middle of the floor with all the patient rooms radiating out from this nucleus like spokes of a wheel. From the center hub nurses can see every patient as well as monitor their vital signs on the multitude of over-sized screens, all very impressive.

Karen, without the demands of a husband or family, has been putting in long hours. This particular case really pisses her off. This guy is cruel, sloppy and a narcissist who doesn't give a damn. He wants a reputation as a great lover and then proceeds to rape and beat the women to death. Only two were fortunate to survive, the last one in the next room.

I didn't plan to interview the victim; I wanted a private discussion with Karen and here is where she spends her free time. I'm concerned about her obsession with the case. Was she losing her objectivity?

Karen is a number of years away from retiring, but has property on the coast and uses her vacation time getting it ready for occupancy. She is an excellent planner and problem solver who will find some less demanding work on the coast. I'm not too sure I'm her favorite detective, let alone her first choice as a supervisor. Jesus, I hope I didn't make a pass at her in the last 12 months. I can't remember!

I'm trying to keep the smartass stuff to myself. It's not proving too difficult. As we review all the victims and each attack, I find myself slipping into the routine, absorbing details, excluding the outside world, full focus on the killings. It's good to be back; it's been a long time.

"Charlie, listen I'm really pleased that you're now in charge. Why are you looking at me like that? I mean it. I know you can be a real jerk at times, but that comes with being a male. I want to catch this guy, and I know you'll be a big plus for us."

I'm a little shocked. "Thanks, you may not appreciate how much that means …I "

She wouldn't let me finish. No time for a private chat with this fireball.

"No more, let's get back at it. We all know your situation, and we're on your side. You see this package? Just came over a few minutes ago. This is from your FBI friend, the sound technician or whatever he does. He told me he was able to clean up the tape and thinks 100% what we hear will be accurate. Almost as unbelievable is how fast he responded; he must really owe you a big favor. One day and he cleaned up the recordings."

She unwraps the package then loads the edited recording for playback. She was able to record four different statements the poor woman blurted. The slurred words sounded like someone mumbling with a mouth full of small stones; a broken jaw and multiple facial injuries will do that. In fact, I don't know how this last victim survived.

"Your sound technician reconstituted each of the four recordings to a point where most words are recognizable. At least that is what he told me. Next, he rearranged the sentences and phrases to develop a logical sequence. He says we now have a recording which sounds like a victim's statement."

She pushes a few buttons, and the small portable unit delivers an excellent sound quality which surprises us both. I think we owe the FBI big time on this one.

The voice is not the girl's but some type of computer generated sound.

It doesn't seem too strange; it sounds like a young woman, under stress, and there are gaps, like she is thinking about the next string of words. This is more than I expected.

" The taxi was a dark color…I think a dark green…..he had on one of those old-fashioned cabbie hats……it was pulled down, and I couldn't see his face…..the cabbie opened the back door …….. I was just settling into the back seat ….I was looking down …a sharp needle or dart hit my neck…. it felt like my head exploded ……….I don't know how long I was out………..when I came to it was dark …really dark...that's all I could see………..he was already on top of me…I couldn't see his face ……….I was face down in the back seat …one door was open because my feet were outside …….I could feel the breeze…………he tore off my pants and held an enormous knife against my throat ………..…I could feel him enter me and then he leaned down close to my ear and whispered very, very softly… I could barely hear him………. if you want to live you do as I say……..when I squeeze your right shoulder you cry out, 'Horny Harry you are the best'……….when I squeeze your left shoulder you cry out, 'I love you'….and you had better be loud and convincing……then he straightened up and started laughing and calling me names, like 'sweetie and lover'…………..he squeezed my shoulders and I cried out as loud as I could and used all the phrases he wanted me to ….he seemed to love it because he got more excited and laughed even louder……..then he was finished and put away the knife and I thought I had

survived……………..he turned me over and start hitting me with his fists ….......it felt like someone was hitting me with a rock….. I passed out ..”

Karen is stunned. “Unbelievable. Goddamn, unbelievable. I thought we would be waiting a couple of weeks to get her statement. She thought she was getting into a regular cab ——that I’d guessed, but all the rest is new.” We play it a number of times. It’s a lot of new information, but I’m not sure how it helps.

There is something bothering me about the recording, and I start my pacing routine. Karen leaves to get coffee. While I am waiting and pacing, I hits me. I know what doesn’t fit.

Karen gives me a coffee and sits on a window sill; I give her my observation. “One of the weird things about this is: he appears to be playing to an audience. Why does he bend down and whisper in her ear? She said she could barely hear him. Why not just tell her what he wants her to say or do? Only the two of them are in the cab. Why not just tell her? Why the soft whisper? Was there someone outside the cab? Someone outside would not hear the soft whispers, just her loud declarations of love.”

“Charlie, you think this guy has a partner, watching and listening, getting off on this charade of a seduction?

You're not suggesting another couple? Or the same two as doing the hotels, are you?"

I leave Karen without any answers. I'm still in running mode, not the best mode for analysis. Not much is making sense. I want to say: it feels like the world is falling apart and then it comes to me. It is: every day the news media reminds us of our environmental hell.

CHAPTER 12: STEPHEN AT HOME

His wife said he looked like a confident pundit, and the public agreed.

Stephen married immediately after university to his high school sweetheart, a girl who almost matched his intellect, but more importantly, for him: Stella was raised in an upper-class home. She knew all the conventional protocols and nuances demanded at this level of society and enjoyed the social and career climbing game.

While Stephen pursued his career, they raised a son and daughter, both now independent and working miles from home base. His legal career was a standard progression: a prosecuting attorney, a criminal defense lawyer, partner in a law firm and finally a position on the bench, with a reputation as a thorough and formidable presence.

With Justice Reborn came his last promotion as the Judge of Sector 14, a position so new and ill-defined even the people who appointed him did not fully understand it. Not everyone at Regional, which was the administrative body supervising six different Sectors, was for his appointment. Some felt he was too quick to look for opportunities to assist the accused, and this was not an attitude which Regional wanted in the new take-no-prisoners world.

After years of dealing with miscreants, lawyers, and detectives Stephen had developed an uncanny ability to read and assess people, often in a matter of minutes. Did this skill fail him when he selected his Board? Doug Brewster, head of Legal, had the legal expertise, but Stephen began to understand the man's ambition could be a problem. The Chief, Duncan Stirling, projected a calm, stable persona, reflecting tradition and firmness but lacked the imagination to deal with the changing world. Jacob Konahouse, in charge of Prisons, was not qualified, but there had not been a choice for his position.

Dr. Kate's appointment had been problematic, and he had not been sure she would accept. They had a history, only known by a few of their closest friends. It had been one of the few times Stephen lost control and took inordinate chances with his marriage and career. The passion had been overwhelming, suffocating any reason he tried to bring to the situation. The affair's whirlwind start, the extreme emotions, and the abrupt ending were all part of his unrelenting memories.

But he had a more immediate problem: the Dr. Max case simmered as Legal meticulously crawled over the girl's accusation and Max's priors. Although the man was a national figure, the incident occurred in his Sector: he would be expected to resolve the issue.

# # #

His house was in the southwest corner of the city. The neighborhood, although not zoned for the wealthy and famous, was certainly a prestigious community. His home reflected his status and matched the community in appearance and size. Stella had supervised every step of its construction and monitored its maintenance and that of their meticulous yard.

She knew what his position demanded and made many sacrifices to keep him on an even keel. Although she felt unappreciated, she knew this was not a novel emotion for most women in her setting. Stella told Stephen he was lucky he had her, and he agreed. Stephen walked in the side door from the garage. "Stella, how much time to I have?"

"Damn it Stephen, don't start multitasking again. Not tonight. There is life beyond your Board. I have the Marshalls coming over before we leave, so hurry and get dressed. This is our Symphony night, and you can't sneak out early. We are going to supper right after the performance, and it's going to be a full night with no shop talk."

Stephen started to reply but thought it would just trigger more comments. He ran up the stairs; his shirt, tie, and suit were waiting on the bed. Steve used to enjoy Stella's organizational skills and her take charge approach to their social life and their home. After his appointment as Sector Judge, there was less time available for a social life. This reduction upset Stella, who enjoyed being with a crowd and all the associated glamor; as the decline grew her frustration blossomed. Stephen knew their relationship was sliding and resolved to make more time. This resolution got destroyed on a daily basis as each new crisis erupted.

As he showered and dressed, his mind raced with the implications of the S3 problems. Maybe he should have informed the Regional Director; instead, he had decided to keep the issue within the Board. If confronted at a later date, he would argue it was a procedural problem which, at the time, he was sure would be resolved.

Besides, to inform the Region would have created alarms which would give opponents to Justice Reborn more ammunition. The reasoning was solid as long as all the S3 issues were procedural problems; but, if the memory streams were not duplicates, the Regional Director would be furious.

Usually, Stephen would have warned the Region, but recent exchanges with the Region left him uncomfortable. At times it appeared the Region already knew about incidents before he reported; their response had been too fast and too well prepared, not a simple reaction. In some ways, this was a test to see if the news reached the Region before he told them. The risk appeared reasonable as long as the science of the S3 interrogation remained solid with no flaws.

While he was dressing, Stella was downstairs giving instructions. The distance between them was too great, and he could not unravel the words. Finally, she yelled up the stairwell.

"Stephen, hurry down the Marshalls are here. We're starting with some cocktails."

He had finished dressing but couldn't stop reflecting on the rapid changes in his life. Justice Reborn provided him with significant power and authority; but, he felt compassion should be part of the equation, and he thoroughly reviewed each recommendation.

"Damn it Stephen, aren't you dressed?"

Steve was already on his way down. "Hi, Marilyn, George. Great to see you; let me get my drink."

They exchanged some local gossip, and the ladies retired to touch up their makeup. Stephen and George took their drinks outside onto the deck. George was a real estate developer and kept a close watch on public attitudes and tastes. His next question came as a surprise. "Steve, are you aware of some of the rumors circulating about the S3 Interrogation?"

Steve's years of experience allowed him to maintain his poise and relaxed manner. "Nothing has reached me. What is it? Is there a sexual component?"

"You think all businessmen are only interested in money or sex. Right? Don't grin at me. No....it was not about sex. The rumor is; some of the interrogations have proven unreliable or faulty. It's a hot piece of gossip all over the office. I heard it a few times. It is coming from our sales staff who work in Sector 13."

Stephen retained his composure, tasted his drink and gave a small chuckle. "Oh, that one from Sector 13. It's been around for the past week. The opponents of Justice Reborn pull that rumor out of the hat about every four or five weeks. It's a tactic which tries to create doubt and confusion without having to prove anything. You can take my word: the memory scans are solid."

Stephen and George were close friends, but nothing would make Stephen leak a Board secret. Friendship seemed to be sliding along with his marriage. Was he prepared to sacrifice everything? Friends and relatives didn't understand he couldn't trust anyone outside his tight legal circle. Had he become too cautious? No, it wasn't possible to share these issues with family and friends. The system demanded a tight lid.

Stella came to get them. The alcohol had softened her, and she leaned on Stephen and held his arm. "Well George, have you been able to get Stephen in the mood?"

Both men smiled. George probably understood Stephen as well as anyone, and he sensed his friend's withdrawal. There seemed to be a regular pattern; any discussion, beyond superficial comments, about Justice Reborn, and Steve quickly changed the subject. It left the impression Steve's friends couldn't be trusted to understand the implications or gravity of the new system of justice.

George thought about Stella's complaint: Stephen was thoroughly entangled in his new appointment, marriage and friendship slipping off the table.

CHAPTER 13: CHARLIE'S LOG: AT THE HOTEL

I'm on my way to the Ritz to meet Wes. And yes, I'm late.

This hotel is confirmed as the location of the fifth serial killing. Although I am sprinting from one place to another, I feel better. This is what I need: a full workload, a challenge, pressure and the company of a team. It's late in the day. I should have been there hours ago.

Wes and I worked numerous homicides; we're close for various reasons, but I think he is most grateful for one unofficial sting. Early in Wes's career, his good looks and a few too many beers resulted in an affair. He wasn't married at the time, but Mrs. Alice Price, wife of the Chair of the Police Commission was. At first, Wes enjoyed the excitement of an affair with an older woman and the attention of someone so close to the top of the pole. The crash came when Alice declared her love and her plan to divorce her husband; she was adamant. My stunned partner pleaded for help.

I forced Alice to meet me, my excuse: I felt obligated to warn her about Wes. I didn't give her a chance to decline but launched right into my pitch. Wes was AC/DC and rather reckless with his sex life, AIDS certainly a possibility for any partner. She became outraged and proclaimed Wes had nothing to do with her, and, in any case, she didn't believe me.

I played my trump card and dumped the pictures on the table. There was a naked Wes and another man as his company, also without clothes. Each image presented a different position or a different angle, the light and focus not great, but the situation was obvious. I pressed. "My recommendation get a blood test as soon as possible. For your husband, best to wait to see if it will be necessary, and be grateful if you are not infected. These pictures and the enclosed note warned about unprotected sex with this detective. I think the anonymous sender is the other man in the picture, angry because Wes found a younger man."

By the next day, she refused to answer any of Wes's calls; he was delighted. It only cost him a few hundred dollars for my friend to doctor a series of photos.

Of course, our relationship goes beyond this incident; he was a real strength in the weeks after the accident which killed my family. Millie, his wife, who was in our car when the crash happened, is still wrestling with depression. Wes rarely talks about her problems. In the days after the accident, Wes, teaming with Monk, took charge. Between the two of them, they looked after the myriad of details associated with these types of bloody disasters.

Wes is the lobby waiting. The place presents as you would expect from a five-star hotel, a large rotunda, opulent with thick carpeting, many plants, bright lights and well-dressed people, representing a contemporary cross-section of the affluent.

In the lobby is a huge fountain, spraying water about 20 feet in the air, the water falling back into a circular basin filled with various marble nymphs, a centerpiece for the hotel. There are numerous staff ready to be of assistance, adroitly located to be available but not obtrusive, most wear the bright gold hotel vests. At the north end is a bank of elevators all with clear glass facing the lobby, providing a view as you ascend to your floor, not for the vertically challenged. Not your first choice as a murder scene but intriguingly close to the location where Horny Harry dumped his last victim.

The forensic team is upstairs scouring the room, the hallway, the elevator and the stairs. At this stage the crime scene is prime. The victim will not run away but once the body has been moved and all the evidence gathered, the scene is lost forever. We only have one opportunity to assess the location as it now exists, hence the extreme time and care with the scene.

Wes leads me over to the reception desk, and I meet the clerk who had registered the woman. He is a young man, well-scrubbed and meticulous in dress and decorum. He has been through this before and has his delivery ready.

"I don't remember a lot about the woman; she was tall and rather robust, not fat but muscular. She wore an enormous, floppy hat, so it was hard to see her face. Dark hair, again the hat covered a lot; I looked over our security tape and this didn't help very much. She said she wanted a room on the second floor close to the elevator because her hip made walking a problem, and she registered for four days."

I reviewed the tapes last night, and he's right the hat is an excellent cover, I ask. "She paid with cash; is this a little unusual?"

"No, it happens often enough; no alarm bells rang. I've been thinking about the registration, and there are a couple of a minor points. She did have a cold, you know a raspy throat with a deep voice and was wearing beautiful white cotton gloves, which almost hid the fact she had ugly hands."

"Ugly hands?"

"My wife and I are both hand models. When an advertising picture displays a limited view, you know just the hands, the hand you are looking at could be mine or my wife's. This happens for example when it's a cream or lotion commercial. I'm very conscious of hands, their size, condition, and shape. I pay attention, and the lady's gloves could not hide her rather thick or misshapen hands."

The clerk keeps on talking, but he is repeating and rearranging the same details: the hat, the build, the voice, and the hands. I'm no longer listening; I've absorbed the details, nothing computes, time to move.

Wes thanks the man, and we take the elevator to the second floor. The murder scene is in a room almost directly across from the bank of elevators; the forensic team is finishing up. The killers were thorough, and there is not much to be gained from this scene. Something does bother me about the scene, as I said I'm great when it comes to detail, and something doesn't fit.

"Wes, do you happen to have the final recording the prostitute made back to the agency?"

"Sure, you want to hear it?" I nod and he starts the tape. As we stand in the hallway, it's a female voice, not frightened, not stressed, in fact sounding very routine.

"Hi gang, this Sherry, I'm in room 272 at the Ritz Hotel and should be here for a few days; everything is AOK."

Wes explains. "The AOK is the code they use; this means she feels safe."

I'm not listening to Wes and am not satisfied. "Again, play it again." We listen again and then the anomaly strikes home.

"Goddamn it Wes, get the tech team back here. This is crazy. Didn't you hear she said room 272? And we've been analyzing room 212 where the body was found. How the hell did she get from room 272 to room 212?"

He closes his eyes and shakes his head in disgust. "Shit! You're right. Goddamn it. I missed it. Suppose this two room routine was part of the other four killings, and I missed it each goddamn time."

Wes and I stare at each other, both probably thinking about the same issues. Do we have two murder scenes? Why kill in 272 and then move the body to 212? Why risk moving a body through a busy hotel hallway? And, I'm sure when we check this will be the pattern in the other four killings, a killing room, and a dumping room. This doesn't make sense.

This couple is too goddamn smart. How in the hell are they destroying all the forensic evidence? Why two rooms? How are they deceiving the prostitutes into thinking they're safe? After four well-advertised hotel killings, they're still able to fool a fifth victim.

Jesus Christ, I'm back.

CHAPTER 14: WAITING AT FORT GREEN

Now she understood why they called him: Crazy Charlie.

Pat Holdner, the advance person for Sector 14, worked most of the weekend except for the one evening to attend the Spring Dance. She enjoyed the dance and the opportunity to reconnect with friends and colleagues. The preposterous episode had been Charlie and how he forced the massive sergeant to his knees, the screaming an extreme and disconcerting spectacle; Emma didn't deserve that intrusion. Everyone said he was the best homicide detective in the Sector, but she didn't understand why Chief Duncan allowed this behavior in his Division.

At Fort Green Prison, Pat and her advance team slogged their way through the day. The old building and associated infrastructure made preparations difficult because even with all the advanced technology they still needed considerable cabling, sound proofing and a multitude of other modifications.

Tomorrow she planned to debrief the death row convicts, all options open for discussion and legal requirements satisfied. The convicts were already knowledgeable, thanks to a grapevine, which was surprisingly accurate as well as swift. An insidious jailhouse rumor worried Pat: no death row processing this week.

It was near the end of the day, and Pat was impatiently waiting. All the concrete, all the security gates, all the guards, all the rifles, and all the buzzers left her anxious and ready to leave at the end of the day. Even the brightly painted walls couldn't stave off depression. Someone had dimmed the corridor lights, the dull ambiance another downer.

John burst into the room, apologizing for being late. John Hellson was Deputy Warden and now operational control for the Death Row project. Pat decided to concentrate her efforts on him and hope this would create buy-in and fill the current leadership vacuum. Uncle Willie had forced the issue, obstinate and uncooperative, not the ideal Warden for such a pioneering process. She started slowly, wanting to ensure she didn't overpower John and cause more tension.

"John, I've a video of an actual S3 interrogation in progress. But first a few comments: you should understand all Watchers are given a thorough orientation. Time is the issue, so we want to ensure they stay focused and not get carried away with seeing this technology. Even after orientation sessions, it's quite common for people to be jolted when the first live feed plays on the screen, but they are pressed to make quick decisions. The 45-minute clock is always with us."

"I'm still struggling, trying to visualize the entire scene."

"Patience. I know it's difficult.   All the Watchers are in a soundproof room with a large wall mounted screen plus smaller individual monitors. Each screen is connected to the memory scanning process and displays the results. Also, there are a series of different switches to allow the Watcher to signal the Medical Techs; they signal to move the probe further into the future or to step back in time. Last, there is a unique audio link between the Medical Techs and Watchers; this allows direct verbal communication if required.

The decisions are based on the scenes they see playing out in front of them. When the technician positions the probe and activates the scan, the contents are played out on the individual screens for each Watcher. The decision becomes: what time frame is being reflected in this memory stream? Can they recognize this segment of the convict's history?

All Watchers don't necessarily agree on the time frame being displayed. In these situations, the Historian's opinion is usually the critical factor. He has undergone extensive training, including all aspects of our history from women's fashions to sports statistics, and typically can quickly recognize the time period of any scene.

A few points to be aware of: first, even if all Watchers agree to a change, the playback cannot be stopped instantaneously. Think of a car moving at full speed. Even when you decide to brake, it takes some time to stop, this along with the technician's reaction time is what we call: the one minute lag. It can, of course, be longer than one minute; this depends on the contents of the particular memory cells and can be embarrassing.

Assume the convict has selected his mother to assist with recognizing early memories, and we hit a memory spot where he is masturbating. Mom wants this to stop. But, the display can't be stopped instantaneously. In fact, Watchers are instructed to keep watching because often these acts are associated with a violent crime. The Watchers have to keep their eyes on the screen, regardless how it disturbs them, and confirm no crime has been committed."

The Deputy stared straight ahead then. "Christ, if I am a Watcher, I may have to watch this guy play with himself, and .."

Pat cut him off. "It gets worse. Remember most of these convicts have been around for a long time. As a watcher, you'll be seeing brutal footage; there is no editing. These are the rawest images you'll ever see. Let's watch."

She pushed a few buttons, and the screen filled: an S3 Interrogation, the first view a group of elementary school kids playing pickup baseball. A Watcher pushed a control knob 'ahead,'and after 1 or 2 minutes the screen went blank. Then a voice was heard in the Watchers' room.

"This repositioning may take a few minutes, and the screen will be blank while this happens, a warning buzzer will sound when the next image stream is ready."

Shortly the screen filled again. This time, it was in a prison cell, and the Watcher reacted by requesting a leap backward and the cycle repeated itself a number of occasions. Some of the scenes were disconcerting, and the Watchers were given reminders to concentrate. A large clock in front of the screen maintained a countdown, and at around 30 minutes the screen filled with an armed robbery. The scene was chaos, screaming, and gunshots. John could see the Watchers were distressed but did signal the end; they arrived at the target memory stream, the crime scene. The video stopped. The technicians removed all the connecting cables and wheeled the convict out of the room.

Pat started before John could ask. "He's being rolled down to the execution chambers. Since he's already been medicated as part of S3, there is no need for further sedatives. As well, there is always someone from Legal Division present to watch the proceedings. When the session is stopped by the Watchers, the legal representative reviews the result one last time. He confirms the scene.

John, your staff will be part of the execution crew, but the actual release of the fatal injection will be carried out by the Citizen Team; these are regular citizens selected from a pool, in the same way, we used to select jury members. This Citizen Team functions as the old fashion army firing squads in that they all push a button, but no one knows which button delivered the fatal mixture. There are three citizens in each Team.

A new Citizen Team is assembled for each execution. You'll need to provide space and meals for about 15 to 21 citizens each day. Since we don't know how many executions will take place, we always bring extras for the Citizen Team selection, like a jury pool. We'll bus them in and out daily; actually, they're bused out immediately after an execution."

John was momentarily speechless. The demo had been overwhelming. Most disturbing: the unedited contents of personal memories, the blunt honesty of each image stream. Was this what would be revealed by the men he had been guarding for years? Brutal unforgiving violence from men who had now found Jesus.

"John, when I explain the process to the convicts and tell them about their options, I think I'll use this video. It'll better than any verbal explanation and will demonstrate what they are facing; I'm sure they already know, but a full description is a legal requirement. John, you OK? Comments on the plan?'

"You're right they should know exactly what they're up against. It's needless punishment for them or relatives to go through this unless they're innocent. I'll bring the Warden up to speed. It appears you're going to need at least a few more days to get everything ready. I'll leave now and meet with the Warden. See you in a couple of hours."

Pat watched him leave. She had not shared any of her concerns with him. Her staff had finally arrived, but no official authorization to proceed from Judge Miller's office. And where the hell was the Forensic crew? Where was Emma?

She was getting stonewalled. At the spring dance, Dr. Kate had tried to be reassuring and talked about some vague procedural issue which sounded like double-talk, not something to be expected from Kate. Jacob didn't even try to explain, his only comment: press on and get ready. It was only Emma, after a few drinks, who hinted that it was significantly more than a procedure issue which was slowing down authorization.

What the hell was going on? And why was no one talking?

CHAPTER 15: CHARLIE'S LOG: CHINESE SUPPER

The Chinese Supper is a tradition, an annual event in the late spring.

Almost everyone in the Investigative and Forensic Divisions attends, with people arriving at different times during the evening. As shifts end, they wander in wearing uniforms or office garb. It's very informal. The recent disturbing Spring Dance continues to be a hot item on the minds of many people; I avoid such discussion groups but am aware of my notoriety.

The reason for the short time between events is the Prison Decommissioning project. Once it is fully operational, there'll be little time for staff to attend full-scale Sector events. The Executive decided to establish an earlier date rather than cancel the supper.

I'm still thinking about the damn hotel room and wondering how or why the prostitute gave the wrong room number to her agent. But she didn't, her controller sent her to room 272, and her audio stated room 272. Wes is upset because he never recognized the room switch at the first scene.

The noise is escalating as the booze starts to loosen everyone up, and the mode kicks in. I'm sipping, and I do mean sipping, a cold glass of cheap house wine, my one and only for the night. The two Divisions have the entire place reserved, and it's like a large family gathering, good news, and bad news. The place is your typical Chinese restaurant with lots of red and gold, a few dragons hanging from the ceiling, and staff bustling around with steaming bowls of food for deposit on the large round tables.

Wes and some of the gang begin to settle on one spot. But table membership is rather dynamic as people wander from one group to the next; gossip is a great mixer. The table is loaded with food, and the carousel has a variety of dishes, some of which I can recognize, but many are just a mass of something or other; someone asks the question. "What kind of meat is that?"

It's dark meat, cut into thin strips. I can't resist; it's not original and not very funny. "It's Lassie but don't worry the collar was removed before the preparation started."

Groans and moans. I look over to the right, and there is Red; she doesn't say anything just shakes her head, not impressed. Next, she surprises me and comes over and sits next to me.

"I thought since we're going to be working together it's better if we're able to talk."

"Sure, I'm all for that." I know it isn't a brilliant answer, but I'm rather nervous. The food starts disappearing from the carousel; the chatter is continuous and louder, as the wine is consumed everyone becomes more animated. Red and I are cautious, and the conversation is a little awkward and stilted, on both sides. My phone rings; it's Karen, and I have to answer.

"Karen, where the hell are you? We've saved a seat for you; the food is good but disappearing."

She is excited. "Charlie, I'd been thinking about your question, you know……. 'why did Horny Harry bend down close to her ear and whisper his instructions?'…….. I don't believe he has a partner. The son of a bitch is too self-centered. My theory is: he is recording everything for the future. He wants to replay, and by whispering his instructions so they are not heard, her comments will play back as voluntary. A quiet whisper will not be heard. The video plays like she is sincere, and all her comments sound spontaneous, coming from her without any coercion. On playback, he comes across as a great lover."

I think she is on to something, and she is pleased. I minimize my challenge. "You think Harry may be creating a library of his love conquests for a replay? The problem is your victim remembers it was dark, really dark; this is not a great setting to produce a porno video."

"Yes, I know. I chased down the one tech who hasn't left for Chinese supper. He tells me it is possible, for top quality you need to get some specialized equipment. It comes in a miniaturized version and can be mounted almost anyplace. The good news is: it's expensive and only a few shops in the city handle the gear. If our lover boy purchases locally, we may be on to him."

"You might be right. Harry is in love with himself. Great thinking. Now come on down, and I'll buy you a drink. You know the food is good."

"I'll be there in 20 minutes."

I hang up. Red and I are alone at the table; the others have all finished eating and have moved on to the bar or dance floor. I'm feeling good because I think Karen may have made a breakthrough, and I get carried away. "Well Emma, do you want to have the first dance?"

She looks straight at me, speaks real soft to ensure no one else will hear. "Charlie, you and I are never going to dance; we're miles apart."

"What does that mean?"

"This Justice Reborn is made for you. Compassion minimized. You see everything in terms of black and white, guilty or innocent, right or wrong. I live with a lot of grays."

"Sounds like an introductory psychology course review and still doesn't explain anything."

"Your reputation is a hard-nosed guy who pushes staff; a man prepared to use his weapon, a relentless pursuer. How many people have you shot in the course of your career? I understand during your time on the force your record is littered with entries related to use of excessive force, unprofessional conduct and a series of sessions with Internal Affairs. No one else has come close to that record."

"Sounds right and your point is?"

"I'll bet you never lost a minute's sleep over any of these incidents and next day arrive early at the station to receive the applause from the gang. No tears, no remorse. No doubts about any shooting, just another criminal off the streets."

At this point, I lose it and am not in the mode for this liberal critique. "You got that right lady. When it goes down, I don't ask questions. And I never worry about any asshole who wants to kill me or member of our group."

This is a lie, but I wasn't about to share my problems with her. On occasion, I do react violently, at least to some crimes, a gut reaction like a reflex. Remorse sets in after, and when I close my eyes, I still see each asshole in living color. It's an irritating aftermath which I can't shake and don't share, although it appears Sam and Monk are too perceptive and understand what is happening.

"There you are. We're miles apart. I hope you have a delightful evening." She gets up, turns and walks right out of the café, an abrupt explosive departure.

I'm not sure what that was all about. One minute she wants to talk; next minute she is pissed off because I don't have enough empathy for the criminal set. Well, screw her. I don't need some left wing academic analyzing me and judging me.

I start to reach for the bottle of white wine when I see the Chief over at the bar looking right at me. I adjust my reach and convert it to a wave, and he acknowledges me; he must have come down to cheer up the troops.

First I deal with Red, now I have the Chief; I know what he is hoping to see. Well, that's not going to happen. My hand never touches the bottle.

Jesus Christ, what a night.

CHAPTER 16: A PRISON VISIT

Last night Monk dreamt he stood in the hallway of death row and listened to the plaintive cries of 'Lord Jesus save me'. The convicts' voices rang as a powerful, melancholy harmony and echoed all around him.

This morning the Fort Green request came from a Ron Bowen. Since the man was on death row and time was short, Monk made a point of responding quickly, anticipating a heartfelt confession, one of many he expected to hear in the next few weeks.

It was an easy morning drive to Fort Green prison. It gave Monk time to reflect. But his frustration nagged him; the issue: his failure to convince Charlie to stop the pointless drinking and face the fact his family was gone. It was time to move on. Whenever reality stepped in, Charlie turned to booze. Monk knew his strong feelings for his friend made it difficult to be objective.

The traffic was light, and the road had only a few gentle curves. The cloudless sky with the hot sun in the clear blue sky made it very comfortable for someone encased in an air conditioned car. On the far horizon, he saw the foothills and the mountains, a peaceful scene, relaxing, with just the hum of his tires as company. It gave him a chance to think about his recent transition.

It started at the end of Monk's eighth professional football season. He attended the regular team wind-up party; next morning he woke up in a motel room with an unknown woman snoring on the other side of the bed. He dressed quietly, not wanting to wake the lady. He left the motel and started walking, first down to the river which was blanketed by a light fog, then along the river bank, his mind a turmoil of dissatisfaction. Monk followed the river for miles, oblivious to time and his surroundings, the fresh fall air a comfort. Finally, he walked on to the bridge, across the river and towards St. Michael's Cathedral.

The church doors were propped open to catch the fresh river breeze. His midweek early morning visit meant a near-deserted church. Monk rested at the back, listening to the organ music. The early morning light shining through the stained glass danced across all the rows, a magnificent interior.

He sprawled on one of the back benches for the remainder of the morning and most of the afternoon. For some time he felt his life was bereft of any significant meaning or purpose. Today, a replay of his mother's words occupied his mind: 'you are meant for the church'. He thought it would be too grand to say he had an epiphany, but Monk realized he was home, and this is where he belonged. His path now clear, the internal struggle over.

This large gentle priest, now Father Ed, became known as someone with a sympathetic ear and an understanding of the real world, patience, and compassion his strengths. Monk managed his transition very well; his excess physical energy found outlets with Charlie and his athletic crowd; the elimination of soft drugs from his life was not difficult, only alcohol a recurring issue. He thought his alcohol habit was under control until Charlie started to ramp up his drinking, and today it seemed they took turns initiating a session. At times, he felt he was on the same Ferris wheel as Charlie.

His daydreams brought him to his first days at the new primary school. Monk remembered his embarrassment as he struggled with the English language; the entire family were recent immigrants, all learning to read and write at the same time. His classmates were relentless, and if it wasn't recess, it would be an ambush on his way home. They imitated his speech patterns but because of his size kept out of his reach as they taunted him, his mannerisms, his clothes, and his big feet. His unhappiness at school changed when a kid with a quick smile approached him.

"Big guy it's time you learned the game. What are you looking at? Show up after school at the south park grounds. You understand? Yes? Shake your head. OK, we're on."

It turned out the game was football, and the kid was Charlie. He was recruiting for an upcoming match, Southside versus Northside, no trophy just bragging rights.

As organizer and coach, he assigned positions and made up plays. The first few practices were a blur for Monk but watching the televised games helped with his understanding of the game. Before kick-off, Charlie gave him a set of shoulder pads and a large sweater, all borrowed from his older brother's closet. There were few rules, no helmets, some had pads, and, of course, there was no referee. Monk was surprised at the number of hard hits which took place and even more surprised: he enjoyed it. All his anger and frustration had an outlet, and as the game went on, it became apparent the big foreign kid was special. They lost, but he and Charlie walked home together; from that day on they became a pair, and Monk no longer had any concerns at school.

It progressed, and in the winter it was basketball. Then nature took over and they were looking at girls; the girls had changed shape, and some of the older boys were already bragging.

As he turned off the main highway and into the Fort Green prison's parking lot, his mind reverted to the present. As Father Ed, he had been to the Fort Green prison numerous times and knew his way through the various gates, security checks and the long hallway to the visitors' room where the convict was waiting. As sports fans, most of the convicts knew him as Monk, and this is how they addressed him; he didn't mind. It seemed to make the conversation flow, particularly when he was willing to discuss some of the old games.

It was a small room, one table, and two chairs. The guard stayed outside observing, not particularly concerned; he knew both participants. Ronald Bowen, a resident on death row for almost 20 years, was the last one scheduled for an S3 interrogation. Ron understood the process. The convict grapevine distributed most of the details before the Black Angel and her advance team arrived at Fort Green.

"Good morning Monk. Thanks for coming. I'm sure you don't know why I requested this visit."

The tall man's body reflected hours of weight lifting. Monk sensed someone who was unpretentious but now a determined man. Monk's limited research uncovered part of Ron's story: a sensitive young boy who had made some mistakes during the turmoil of his teens.

It appeared these errors dominated his emotional life for years to come, and kept him on a path of self-destruction and eventually ruined most of his adult life. In a story-book progression, his intelligence and demeanor might have carried him beyond his environment and to a lucrative profession with all the perks of a family and home. But for Ron, this was not the case, a severe penalty for teenage hormones.

He looked to be in his early 50s, but Monk knew he was in his the late 30s, in another age probably called 'white trash'. His underprivileged housing and upbringing (one grandmother to fight for him but too timid to mount an aggressive defense) were all too familiar a story of many in prison.

"You're right I'm curious. I gather you know about me because I visit and talk with some prisoners, including a number on death row."

"Yes, and through the grapevine learned more about you than you might imagine. I'm the last man scheduled for an S3, and since I'm innocent, I'm going for the full show. I'll undergo the complete scanning probe. I know the risk but am innocent and that's all that matters."

"That still doesn't help me understand why I'm here?"

"S3 allows me to have one or more Watchers to assist with the memory search, and I need you to convince a witness to be my observer, my Watcher."

"Alright let's hear the rest."

"I understand you and Detective Charlie Taylor are close friends. You guys go way back, played ball together. You were best man at his wedding. He is the man I need."

Monk was baffled. Years ago, this robbery/murder had been a high profile news item, with strong public opinion that

Ron was innocent, the arrest and trial an example of a harassed prosecutor and justice in a hurry. The outcry had been intense but didn't change anything and here 16 years later Ron was being queued up to be executed.

"You want me to get Charlie Taylor to be your Watcher for the most important event in your life. This doesn't make sense. Does Charlie even know you? Was he even involved in your arrest and conviction?"

"I know this is a gamble, but the way I see it this is my best bet. I'll tell you a story and how this all has to play out. I just need you……..need you, to confirm that this is covered under the confidentiality vows."

"You have my word "

"Then here is my story and here is my plan. It's a long shot but I think necessary."

Ron started slowly and maintained the pace throughout his presentation and pitch. He had thought about all the issues and understood what had to be said. What this convict was asking could wreck careers if the scheme was uncovered; it went beyond bold. Ron knew he needed Monk to convince Charlie.

# # #

Monk could scarcely remember the long walk back to his car.

He limped most of the way back, the curse of two bad knees, today being an arthritic flare-up day. Maybe he should have stopped football sooner or maybe it wouldn't have mattered. A surgeon was on his hold-and-delay list.

He rested in the car and waited for some of the tension to fade. Charlie was the issue and Monk did not want to add to his problems with this scheme of Ron's. There're too many unknowns. The question was: how to approach Charlie and put the proposition to him? It was only because Ron had suffered so much, and there was no doubt in Monk's mind that he was innocent of the robbery/ murder. The man's life had been ruined by a false conviction; he deserved help.

Monk had faith in Charlie; he was an outrageous individual, but he had more grit than most people realized. It wasn't smart to push Charlie. But this scheme went beyond physical courage. Then again one might argue maybe this challenge might help; it would indeed require discipline and a cool head in an unfamiliar setting, provide Charlie with a focus beyond his own demons.

Monk eased his car out of the lot. The plan Ron had in mind was bold and dangerous; it could ruin them all. They would have to beat an S3 interrogation.

He knew Charlie was physically strong, muscular, with a rigorous workout schedule which up to this point was his defense against the heavy drinking. For the most part, Charlie maintained his grooming except some of his wardrobe was showing the need for replacement, a woman's touch would help. His brown hair was short without any streaks of gray, his face symmetrical, which some women found attractive but in total nothing extraordinary, easy for people to underestimate his native intelligence and tenacity.

Before the accidental death of his wife and young daughter, he had always been able to move on. When one door shut, he was able to recover and look for the next opportunity. Monk remembered when the pros passed on Charlie, a knee too problematic to warrant a draft choice. Charlie took the rejection in stride and surprised everyone by not pressing or trying the European or Canadian league. He walked away and went on with life. But the loss of his wife and daughter had been too much. The psychological impact a burden he couldn't appear to shake for more than a couple of weeks at a time.

On the return trip, Monk ignored the blue sky and the mountains on the horizon, his driving on automatic, passing cars, smooth on the curves, and handling aggressive truckers without any conscious thought. Compassion was all right, but the risks in Ron's idea seemed immense; even the planning seemed dangerous and perfidious. Could they be charged with collusion to manipulate an S3 interrogation? No, it was worse: the plan would be perceived as an attempt to free a convicted killer.

Should he tell Charlie? What he meant was: should he recruit Charlie?

CHAPTER 17: FIRST BRAINSTORMING SESSION

It was early morning.

The squad occupied the largest incident room available in the Hall of Justice. The facility contained numerous electronic whiteboards which served as perimeter fencing around the central conference table. No windows. A perfect room for their wireless network and the isolation the group needed.

Charlie drove the process and used his tablet to capture key words or terms as they surfaced, occasional a phrase but rarely a full sentence. His efforts reflected immediately on one of the electronic whiteboards and would be there for all to see. Charlie believed a visual array of word and phrases with a variety of colored fonts would stimulate creative thinking and encourage people to speculate. If his contribution triggered an entry onto one the whiteboards, a detective was secretly pleased.

The large room allowed participants to get up and wander around. Ideas and challenges flowed freely; the intent was to have new avenues of thinking surface. A couple of paper flip charts rested in a far corner, but they were only used if the discussion became so convoluted they needed a series of diagrams to follow what was being proposed.

Wes arrived early, distributed relevant paper, ensured the network was operational, tested the recording equipment, and made sure the coffee arrived on time. He would kick off, and Charlie expected a first rate summary, would interrupt, correct and aggressively pursue any loose ends, their friendship didn't count at this point.

The 24-hour delay, in getting this session going, annoyed Wes, an entire day since they had been at the hotel; but Charlie insisted he needed a specific outsider. He wanted the Sector's busy Historian whose schedule didn't allow attendance until today.

Wes knew, even though Charlie at times appeared to be a joker, when it came to criminals the senior detective was a hard-liner and expected his team to reflect that attitude. The outlook a surprise to many because Charlie's quick tongue mislead them into thinking he was flippant and casual.

Early in their careers Charlie's family, his wife Nancy and daughter Linda, with Wes and his wife frequently escaped the city. Camping, picnics, hiking, even some fishing and many campfire suppers. It was one large family, and the young daughter had two sets of parents which she enjoyed and learned to manipulate to everyone's amusement. The accident left two dead, Nancy and Linda, and the third occupant of the car Wes's wife, Millie, with some broken bones and some permanent facial scars.

The impact on Charlie was dramatic and visible, for Wes and Millie the situation less open. Wes didn't discuss Millie's depression with anyone, afraid the gossip would get back to Charlie, already on edge and struggling for too long. Maybe it was because of her inability to conceive, maybe she just loved the vibrant youngster too much, for whatever the reason, Millie's mourning was a regular part of their marriage.

The two workhorses, Terry Patterson and Manuel Moreno, had been first to arrive and first to the coffee. Both could be tiresome jokers, but they had bulldog tenacity and knew the streets.

Karen came in on their heels. She excelled in these sessions, prepared to think out loud and go off in odd directions. Wes liked her and was glad she could be there, but her appearance surprised him. Her black jeans and leather jacket appeared a trifle harsh for a senior detective. Was she trying to beat father time? Some nasty rumors, including the Chief, were making the rounds. Wes had a problem with that innuendo.

The last participant appeared to be an out-of-place middle-aged man. He nodded his head to Wes and said: Charlie invited him. He strode in and introduced himself to each member of the group as: John Wojecki. A humorless man, his distracters said 'cold fish', who was able to bring logic to even the most highly charged emotional scenes: a tall, slender man, nondescript face, long sleeve flannel shirt and corduroy pants, a thin goatee, and bedroom slippers. In many ways, he was the archetypical university professor, able to live in whatever time zone he chose, his concentration intense.

This gifted man could read a complicated technical manual and understand most of the material after the one reading. And, his phenomenal memory stunned the uninitiated; but, history remained his first love and given an opportunity this is where he spent his time, in a different century or era. This was the man they'd been waiting for: the Historian.

Finally, Charlie arrived with his recording tablet. "Good morning group. Make sure you have your coffee, muffins or donuts. We need this brainstorming session. I want some wild ideas. Something that will get us.. "

An interruption from the end of the table. "Charlie is it true you are on record as saying that the brain is your second most favorite organ?" Lots of laughter filled the room, even Charlie laughed, although he recognized the line was stolen from Woody Allen.

"Good start." He typed on his tablet, and 'organ' appeared on one of the whiteboards in bold red font. "Let me point out I asked Karen to attend."

This was greeted with a whistle, a wolf howl and a rowdy cheer, just what to expect with Terry and Manuel. "She hasn't been working the case, but we need fresh eyes. And that brings me to John Wojecki. He is the Historian for the Forensic Section, again someone without any preconceived views.

No questions? Good. We'll start by Wes giving us a summary and the latest status. Once he is finished everything is open. Wes the floor is yours."

Wes didn't stand; he used his notes for a careful opening. "There is an old classification system created by Richard Walter which establishes four personality types for killers. Our Couple fits category four, the most difficult to catch, the Anger-Excitation killer, the AE. This AE type doesn't engage for any tangible achievements, like money, power or sex, but just kills for the sheer pleasure of the torture and the kill. This sadist type doesn't stop, unless caught or the killer dies.

In our situation, the first move appears to be the blow to the head to daze or knock her out; then she is dragged to the bathroom and her head held under water until she is close to drowning. According to the experts, the water enhances a killer's sensitivity and pleasure.

I'm not making this up. The struggle under water result in a series of currents; these bathtub currents create tingles on the small hairs on the killer's arm. This tingling sensation evokes an erogenous zone.

The one deviation is AE killers generally work solo. Everything else fits the pattern. The couple is smart and has done their homework and understand chemistry and biology. I think they enjoy the game and thrill of being chased; they believe they're in control and smarter than the cops. I don't believe that they will move on unless we get a lot closer.

The case has taken on the label as the Five Star Couple. The operation is rather straightforward. The woman checks into a room of a four or five-star hotel. The man joins her later; they call up one of the high escort services and have a girl sent up. They systematically beat, almost drown her and torture her. You can see the pictures on the wall.

Finally, the girl's neck is broken, not much deviation in any of the cases; they clean up the room in a fashion we've never seen before. They must bring their own vacuum cleaner and cleaning fluids. Even our new forensic tools have not detected anything of value.

Hotel video is useless; the woman always wears some type of large hat which hides her face. On the first killing, a hotel guest saw the man leaving the room, again not much help, just a glance. Her male partner is spotted with large sunglasses and a hood over his head. Not much from the witness. Just a glimpse. Nevertheless, we were lucky; since the man is never present at the registration desk, this sighting is how we established it was a couple.

The latest twist in the case is the room number. These high-end escorts try and protect their girls, so once the girl gets in a room, she calls. She has a code signal if she is safe or is concerned. If she sounds an alarm, a bodyguard, who is still in the lobby, gets up to the room asap. If she signals she is safe, the guard returns to the office for the next assignment. At the last killing, this service had a recording device on all incoming calls, and we can hear the girl call and provide the safe word code. Please listen:

"Hi gang, this is Sherry, I'm in room 272 at the Ritz Hotel and should be here for a few days; everything is AOK."

"The AOK is the code they use. This call means she feels safe and the bodyguard may leave. It sounds like a useless clue but here is the twist: she was killed in room 212. I had the tech team go over this hotel door, and they found evidence of four dabs of a soft putty. This putty is the kind that teachers, and others, use to hang objects on a wall. The stuff can then be rolled off after use, and if the wall has a high gloss finish, there is almost no evidence left on the wall. This is how they established room 212 as 272; the couple only hung a sign over the real room designation. Room 272 was never used.

None of the other agencies have recording devices, but they do record the room numbers. And yes, in every case the girls were killed in a different place than the one they were sent to and the one they called in with the safe code.

The mystery lady has always registered in the killing room. The second room was just a complete red herring. So what I am saying is the killers registered in room 212 where she was killed. But the request for a woman comes into the agency for someone to come to 272 and the girl calls back saying she is in 272.

The killers can disguise the room number and get the girl into the room; why bother? I'd like to spend a few minutes on this room and door issue. Alright, let's started. Any thoughts?"

There was no hesitation, and Terry started. "If the idea is to fool someone into accepting a wrong room number, this couple must have some carpentry or artistic skills......you know … to be able to match the room numbers….. they'd have to match the colors and texture, the font, etc. To do all this, they must scout the hotel and get pictures of the style, size, and color of a room's numerals."

"A lot of work for what? Just to develop a false clue?'

The Historian was next. "Here is my take: all the killings were in rooms next to the bank of elevators and the wrong rooms at the far end of the hall or around a corner. Am I correct?'

Wes looked at his diagrams and after a few minutes. "Son of a bitch you are right. Everyone follows the same pattern: the girl says 272 which is way down the end of the hall and the killing room 212 is right next to the elevator and the stairway. Son of a bitch, they were establishing an exit. If anything blew up, the bodyguard would be around the corner or at the far end of the hall, and they would be two steps away from the elevator and the stairs."

Karen was ready. "They don't have to be artists. Let's try another scenario. Let's assume they use an 'under construction' approach. The sign says something like 'temporary room number 272 during maintenance period'. It doesn't have to be up very elaborate. The prostitute's directions are to call from the lobby when she arrives.....remember the killers provided a cell number in every instance. On arrival she calls..... gets the OK to come up and at that time they slip the sign on the wall. The special putty is already on the wall. The sign comes down as soon as she is in the room; it is only up for a few minutes, and it doesn't have to match the other room numbers.''

Charlie was happy with this development; this was a feasible scenario. "Let's leave the room number and focus on the lady."

The word 'lady' set Manuel off. "My bet: she is the leader.....a hard-nosed bitch, looking for some bizarre, wild debauchery, completely out of control action."

Terry couldn't contain himself. "Jesus, I am getting horny."

"What? You're always horny. It's your natural state." More yelling and laughter.

The Historian got them back on track, "I read where the hotel clerk described her hands as ugly. What did he mean?"

"He describes himself as a 'hands man' and says even the white cotton gloves couldn't hide the fact that this woman had large hands and what appeared to be large knuckles. I don't know what he saw…. this was a bit confusing……. maybe he didn't like the shape."

"Maybe the hands were large for a woman or swollen, like some martial arts fighter; they can hurt their hands and over time, develop some misshapen hands."

"It's a bit of a stretch but let's follow this. How many clubs are there in the city for female martial arts fighters? Or why would she belong to an organization?'

"Yes, I think she would belong. A club gives her an opportunity to continue to be on top of her game, and since these two are so meticulous, we have to assume they are perfectionists. I would be prepared to canvas the clubs but what the hell would I be looking for? We have no pictures or prints. I don't think she would be dumb enough to wear the dress and hat to the club."

Manuel started. "Let me go in a wild direction. Gloves to cover battered hands. Horny Harry is clubbing women. Also, he appears to be picking his victims from the same general area of the city any closer, and they would trip over each other. Ok hold on ..here is my thought..............what if we are only dealing with one person."

"Jesus Manuel that is wild........your suggesting that one of the Couple morphs into Harry."

"Why not? A psychotic who is directed by inner voices might have more than one set of directives or drives. Or multiple personalities......different one dominating at different times."

"No Manuel that one is not going anywhere. You have three; you're going to turn into one? I don't think so. Jesus, the crime scenes are too different; the hotels leave no clues whereas the rapes have all the evidence we need. Too different. One too many characters."

Manuel didn't argue. Charlie called a break. "Time for the bathroom and fresh coffee and a new roll. Take 15."

Everyone got up, stretched and walked the room. The whiteboard was full of single words or one-liners: sign, expertise, escape route, hands, martial arts, big hat. Numerous words which, regardless of the sequence Charlie entered them, always became rearranged into a random pattern on the whiteboard. Would any words trigger more ideas?

Once they were all back in their chairs, Charlie turned to the Historian. "John, would you like to ask the crew some questions or do some speculating?"

The Historian started. "Thank you. I would. Let me try my way. First, assume I'm a perfectionist; where would I get the knowledge to know how to clean up and what to use?"

Charlie replied. "Well, there is the obvious Goggle search with many on-line experts willing to share, the public library and the University library, with some excellent books written by experts in various fields. And, of course, if you had access to the FBI material, there should be tons of stuff."

Karen added. "And all the libraries have records of who was accessing this material."

John continued. "I want to keep going. The couple also had a thorough understanding of the way the high-end escort agencies operated."

Wes responded. "This would not be difficult. They just had to try a couple of them to ensure they had the pattern, but it would have been recent visit. The Couple had to be sure the agencies had not changed their operating practices………
how girls are assigned and protected.

What I'm saying is they must have conducted some dry runs, dialed up for girls and had one or more delivered. But I afraid this leaves us nowhere because we know so little. What could we ask any girls who may have been part of a dry run? Except, since none of our victims were raped, maybe on the test run he didn't want sex with the girls or maybe his partner was there, and they asked for some weird action. I know it is a long shot, but if this happened in the last year, possibly a girl remembers a strange encounter."

Everyone started kicking in, and numerous suggestions filled the air simultaneously; Charlie had to step in and regain control. During this intense exchange the Historian just sat, deep in thought then he started again. "These new forensic tools to analyze a crime scene: what are they and when were they first introduced?"

Terry was abrupt. "Look we are way beyond luminal.....the latest techniques started about two or three years ago. The forensic team now have special sprays and lights. Listen after they get through with a room they can tell you the guy is 6'2" and when fully erect his penis is 6.25 inches in length, and he had been shaking it around before he left the room." Manuel was the only one who laughed, Terry was wearing thin.

Charlie intervened. "Terry's description is rather vivid but close to the truth. None of us knows the details about the technology. The development and field testing took place, by

Special Victims forensic units, in a different Sector. It took months before all the bugs were out.

This testing and trials ran in a couple of cities on the west coast. Today, the process is a part of all crime scene investigations, but this is very recent, and our techs are still not fully up to speed. I mean, they can use the tools, but I think their in-depth understanding will take some time."

The Historian remained focused, silent and stared at the desk in front of him; the room, for once, was silent, a couple of people up for a coffee refill. Finally, the Historian spoke.

"If I add everything up, the only logical conclusion is that one or both members of your couple are on the police force."

CHAPTER 18: CONDITION CONFIDENTIAL

He tilted the glass and drained all the scotch.

It was too early in the day to start drinking, but he had to reduce the tension. The extraordinary Board meeting still permeated his thoughts; but the chaos of the last week had not provided an opportunity to review, in privacy, the confidential recording of the meeting. Today secure in his office, he ignored the luxury of his surroundings, generally a source of pride, and focused on what he was about to hear. Locked doors and no secretary.

The audio player was loaded and ready. Still, he procrastinated. The fear and anxiety associated with this outlandish act seemed to control his hand. The schemer knew he had taken a tremendous risk in recording the confidential sessions. His reason: if any questionable decisions resulted during these classified segments, he might be able to put pressure on the Judge or use it in other ways to further his career. He knew the Judge had enemies.

As soon as Dr. Kate declared Condition Confidential, he turned on his recording device which he was assured was undetectable and cost accordingly. He drained the remaining scotch and positioned the machine to begin at the central part of Kate's presentation. Although he had been present when she first described the problem, this afternoon he wanted to hear it all again. It was like reading a book for the second time and finding the parts to savor. Her voice filled the room:

"Let me start by saying that Emma Collins and I assisted Sector 13 with some S3 Interrogations at White Rock Prison. Although there were 165 convicts eligible for the process, a surprising number elected to proceed directly to the execution chamber. It appears once the prison grapevine became convinced they couldn't beat the process, only the innocent or real hardcore cases challenged the interrogation.

Sector 13 did most of the processing; Emma and I conducted twelve of the scans and observed another seven. I mention this because my conclusions are tentative and based on this small sample. All the sessions were recorded, and Emma is collecting every session; once we have isolated all the duplicate memory cell segments our in-depth analysis can begin.

As you know the scanning process is a variation of a three-dimensional Binary Search, at least it starts that way. But, then literally depends on the Medical Tech to use her touch to feel her way around the emerging patterns of memory.

I know how ill-defined this sounds. However, there is no point asking the Medical Tech why she moved to a particular point; the answer is like asking a visual artist why she used Hansa Yellow instead Cadmium Yellow on one particular spot on the canvas. The answer will not satisfy you.

Once the Tech develops a rhythm, their moves and decisions are ineffable. The problem with the duplicate memory scenes was: it took some time for us to figure out what was happening. At first, we thought it was an error in the equipment. The probe had been moved to another spatial location, but we were still projecting the original memory stream.

The question became: was the probe back at the original physical location? The Techs develop a certain rhythm and maintain a pace with their visualization. The appearance of the duplicates completely disrupted their rhythm and with the 45-minute clock we couldn't afford these disruptions.

Each appearance of a duplicate caused confusion. The Watchers thought the Techs had not heard their instructions and were sending back the same event; the Techs thought the equipment had not responded properly. All this meant recovery time and time was not available to deal with continued retries and repositioning of the probe.

Why the duplicates? My theory is when an incident is very emotional, it tends to be stored multiple times and in different locations. Why? I don't know. Maybe the multiplication makes it easier to remember some events or so difficult to forget some events……….. their greater quantity dominates, and they surface easier and more frequently.

The other unfortunate aspect of the situation: innocent men appear to have significantly more of these duplicate memory cells. This means these prisoners became the most difficult to process. My guess: if you are innocent and falsely accused, your life will be filled with lots of emotion; in particular, some special events invariably come back to haunt you. Maybe there is some credence to the old adage that a cold blood criminal will not be haunted by recurring memory flashbacks, brutality not an emotional hang-up.

As you know, Sector 13 did find ten men innocent. Of this group, five were sent home in good condition with a minimum impact as a result of the S3 interrogation; they only lost a few IQ points. Three other innocent men had significant losses, close to 15 IQ points. The impact depended on their starting IQ, but they are being held, not released; more testing is necessary to see if, after a rest period, there will be some recovery.

The last two inmates will have to be institutionalized; there is no way they can be looked after by their families. They are bedridden, the classic vegetable. Again there may be some recovery in the future, but it is very unlikely.

In all cases, it was the time issue. During any probing, there is always an outside chance of some minute brain damage, and beyond 45 minutes the risk significantly escalates, and the individual will be fortunate to escape unharmed. In all cases, it was the duplicate memory cells which caused the extensive searching and restarting.

This is leading edge technology. And now, I even wonder about these men who appear unharmed; do we really know what may develop later in their lives?

I recommend we suspend the Fort Green process until we get all the data and have a chance to review the material."

"Dr. Kate, are these extra memory cells exact duplicates, exact copies of each other or do they provide a different version of the event?'

"Judge, I can't answer that question. Everyone assumed it was an operator problem, and we all focused on getting the probe into a better position. There was no time for comparisons.

My other concern is: when individuals remember and review past events, they may be modulating memory as it's being perceived. Why? Again, I don't know. Maybe this is where our emotions override. Do we selectively block out actions that are too painful? Do we turn ourselves into heroes?

The fact is there are multiple streams of some events in a person's memory banks. And unless we understand and can deal with them, it is impossible to keep our scanning under the 45-minute barrier. In conclusion, I repeat: all the recordings from White Rock are on the way to our Combination Room."

"Does anyone have any questions?"

"Alright let me summarize. There are three fundamental questions which must be answered, and I'm afraid Dr. Kate...... you and Emma will have to provide the answers:

First, the obvious: are these true duplicates or different versions of the same event?

Next, if they are true duplicates, how will the process be changed so as not to confuse the Medical Techs or the Watchers and keep us under 45 minutes?

Last, why was this situation not uncovered in the early work? The pioneering work was extensive with many top scientists taking part, and our current legislation is based on their results. What is different between the original research and our current situation? Was something overlooked in the original studies?

I'm not concerned about discovering who is culpable. At the moment, all that is secondary to knowing what is going on with a process which was to be our foundation.

Kate, I'm going to ask you to restrict the research team to yourself and Emma; Dr. Max is not to be contacted. I'm not trying to make this difficult, but there are other developments which can't be revealed today; they make it impossible to utilized Dr. Max.

I'm going to adjourn. And, let me repeat the obvious: you all know the nature of this discussion and the consequences of any leakage outside this room. Please be careful, and I will see you all very shortly, hopefully with many answers."

The recording ended. The schemer sat rigid in his chair stunned with the news and realized the entire system was in jeopardy. Different versions of the same event: what a mess. The question was how could he take advantage of the situation and be part of any changes which may have to come?

The stark image of Dr. Kate persisted. During her presentation, she appeared confused and frightened, trembling hands and her eyes flitting from one corner of the room to the other. Was the Judge's confidence misplaced? Throw in the

Dr. Max's situation, another anomaly. Our best scientist barred from participating. What the hell was that all about?

He vigorously shook his drink causing the ice cubes to rattle against the glass. The ricocheting ice cubes were the only sound in the room.

CHAPTER 19: CHARLIE'S LOG: AT THE ABBEY

The session halted with the Historian's conclusion unresolved: one of our own is the killer.

It was a helluva of a time to stop the brainstorming session, but everyone had other commitments, including me. I'm driving to the Abbey where Monk is helping with an upcoming charity concert; he says it's critical to meet. The sun is burning and the sky cloudless.

As I drive to the monastery, my mind wanders as much as the road. And yes, I am thinking about the Chinese supper and Emma Collins. What a bitch, she has a lot of gray in her life; isn't that nice. She wouldn't survive one shift out on the street. I've better things to do than debate with her.

The Abbey is a good 90-minute drive on a winding road which climbs out of the valley to the top of our highest hills, almost mountains. The Abbey is a seventeenth-century edifice built by a sect of monks whose origin I can never remember. It's a series of interconnected buildings of various sizes and shapes. Since the buildings and the grounds are diligently maintained, the result is a magnificent piece of architecture and a perfect setting for someone seeking peace or just a quiet environment to walk and reflect. The path from the parking lot is constructed of old bricks and weaves its way through shrubs and large trees which are getting the full attention of some of the junior members of the Abbey. No doubt our early spring is ready to depart and make way for another searing hot summer.

It's been a few days since I've seen the Monk. Today he wears the collar of a Roman Catholic priest, Father Ed; nevertheless, it's always a relaxing time when we're together. After many years, there is not much we don't know about each other. Monk was a great friend of my wife Nancy, and I think loved young Linda, my daughter, as much as I did. He arranged to have them buried in a plot outside the east wall of the Abbey, looking over the valley with the city on the distant horizon, a fabulous view.

"Charlie, Sam tells me you're still getting yourself into various layers of deep shit."

"Oh, you know Sam. He is always letting these little incidents get him upset."

Monk nods his agreement, looking very much like an understanding priest. I never discovered what made him take the vows, but his commitment was evident throughout his life.

"I know you you've all sorts of dragons prepared to burn your ass, but I want to tell you a story and need your opinion."

I stare at Monk and wonder what the hell is this all about; the guy is always straightforward, and now he appears to be dancing and uncomfortable. "My friend, the coffee is hot. The view is excellent. Fire away."

Monk's preparation is solid, and the story flows. "Once upon a time in the far south a young athlete, who was being raised by his grandmother, became difficult to handle and started to hang with the wrong crowd. He maintained good grades, in fact, maybe things were too easy for him, both in the classroom and on the hardwood. Once all the teen hormones kicked in, he kept looking for more and more excitement.

His frantic grandmother begged him to stay away from two high school drop outs who had earned enough money to acquire a car and raise hell most nights. One night, grandma's begging failed. Our young teenager jumped into the car with the two jerks, booze, and pills the diet for the evening. They cruised around whistling at girls, yelling, drinking, and getting high. Later that night they picked up Gail who was known as a fun girl, an easy lay; she started drinking with the boys but had a way to go before she matched their condition.

They drove to a secluded part of a municipal park, and they all got out to rest in the grass. The guys tried talking Gail into taking her clothes off or to a do strip tease; our young athlete was not a good drinker and passed out.

When he woke, the two jerks were swinging thick tree branches at Gail, who was on the ground trying to defend herself. It seems they both had sex with her, and then for some reason, they decided to tease her with their knives. She started screaming and the bigger guy, in a fit of anger, grabbed a fallen branch and began beating her. The other idiot decided it was fun and decided to help his friend.

Our athlete, a recovering drunk, tried to stop the beating, but they just brushed him aside. It didn't take long. The screaming stopped, and it was all over. All three finally silent, the only noise their heavy breathing and the odd car roaring past on the other side of the park. After 15 minutes of accusations and curses, they decided to escape and leave the dead body in the park.

They drove out of the park and back onto the main strip where all the action rolled on, fast and loud. Our athlete couldn't stop crying, and the other two were sick of him. They threw him out of the car, with a warning: shut your mouth.

He was not far from home and started staggering to his house. He didn't get far when headlights of a patrol car found him. There was only one officer in the car. This sympathetic man saw the teenager was harmless. He barked: go home. The other occupant of the police car stayed rooted to his seat.

Just as everyone prepared to separate, a loud crashing sound filled the night, and the patrol car tore off with the siren blaring. It turned out our two heroes decided they needed more booze. When the owner refused, they threw a rock through the vendor's plate glass and tore off down the road.

The cruiser accelerated, on their tail, and the chase was brief. They two jerks were in no condition to drive, let alone proceed at high speeds. At about 110 mph they slammed into the concrete abutment; various auto and body parts flew around the highway. After their DNA matched the semen found in the girl, the cops wrapped up the case. Our athlete escaped, in one sense, but in reality never recovered.

He graduated from high school. But his sensitive nature never allowed him to forget that one night. The dead girl became a set of recurring nightmares and daytime flashbacks. Booze and drugs didn't help. One incident followed another, mostly penny-ante stuff, and some minor jail sentences to provide him a warm winter residence, a chance to dry up between events."

Monk stops and starts drinking his brandy-laced coffee. I'm trying to figure out where this is going because I sense he is waiting for me to respond. "Would this happen to have anything to do with your visit to Fort Green Prison the other day?"

He doesn't even bother to ask how I know about his visit. "You always were a smart bastard."

"I also have an excellent memory. Let me fill in the rest of the story, which I am sure you know. When in grade 12, I wanted to be a cop and had a cousin in a small southern community. Because the police force had a rather laid-back attitude, my cousin, Mark, was able to get permission for me to ride in his patrol car. The trips were restricted to some quiet periods when his unit wasn't a first responder, more like a roving paddy wagon. I never left the car unless he signaled it was ok.

And, I remember your athlete, never knew his name; he was a sorry looking mess staggering down the road. My cousin thought he was an accident victim. But once he talked to him, Mark understood what he was dealing with and told the kid to go straight home. I just stared through the window and watched as the boy tried to put one foot in front of the other.

When the crap hit the fan, my cousin yelled: get that belt on. And we went flying down the road. I could see them ahead of us. The weaving car tottered from one side of the highway to the other. Within minutes, they smashed into the abutment. The mangled mess was too much for me; my stomach heaved, and I splattered the side of the police car."

Monk grunts; he can roar but today it is more of a soft rumble, and I can see he's very subdued and nervous, which is rather strange for him.

"Charlie, I don't know how to put this to you. It's about a convict preparing for an S3 interrogation. He thinks if this incident surfaces during his memory scan, he could be in serious trouble. With Amendment 33-2 and all officials in a hurry to clean out death row, they could easily interpret this incident as his participation in the girl's killing. The way they are processing convicts.......one quick decision and it would be over for him."

"I don't know him or his record, but I agree it could happen, and I'm still waiting."

"From here on, I trust you to either accept or forget my proposition. Yes, I drove up to Fort Green Prison and spent time with Ronald Bowen."

"You mean Ron of the liquor store killing? He's the kid I saw on the road 15 odd years ago?"

"Yes, he's the one. You're the original lead at the liquor store robbery; you brought him in for questioning along with a few other characters. After you were reassigned to a task force, Ron was arrested and found guilty. A large segment of the population believe your successor was too lazy and the DA in too much of a hurry. The guilty verdict shocked the public, even the press. Of course, this was before JR. The consensus: Ron had been railroaded and never did receive a fair trial."

"I know all that, and if he's innocent, he'll be released after the S3 interrogation. I do feel sorry for him, but I can't get involved in some plan to beat an S3, and that's where I think this is heading. Right? .... Best we leave it before it goes too far."

"I'm not asking you to help him beat the liquor store rap. The issue is this teenage party and the dead girl. If the wrong segment of this teenage drunk appears on a monitor, and if someone is trigger happy, he'll be executed. Will you at least give this some thought and let me describe the plan?"

I drain my coffee and stand up. "Monk, I'm going to walk in the gardens and visit the grave site, and I'll forget our conversation; it's a great spring day. I'll see you on the way out."

I know he's disappointed, but I have to be abrupt. Monk is too good at talking me into helping with one of his projects, and this is the last thing I need. I walk away and think about the dramatic change in Monk's life. The training for priesthood is an eight-year affair after high school, four years of university and then four more at a seminary. But Monk was able to reduce the eight-year stipulation because he already had a degree, with biblical studies as his optional courses, whenever possible.

Once he decided this was to be his life, it only took three years to be ordained. I am not sure how he reduce the time demands. They say maturity and years as a prominent believer were the main factors. I suspect the Church saw him as a blue-chip recruit, all-star pro football player, ready to work the streets as a priest; this is the stuff of movies. I'm sure the Church didn't want any obstacles in his way.

My goal is the grave site, but I do enjoy wandering around the Abbey, this religious labyrinth of buildings and greenery. Some monks from a monastery in Russia are here for the early summer benefits concert. They're practicing, and their voices fill the halls. I walk outside and then under the shade of some stone arches which border the east wall. These ancient walls and the melancholy chants of Russian monks set the mood; it provides a medieval atmosphere, pensive, but relaxing.

I have got a few flowers and place them in the small vase I'd anchored to the burial plot headstone. The intense rays of the sun bounce off any reflective surface, but at this altitude, the air still has some lingering winter crispness.

I perch on the edge of the nearby bench. I never speak out loud to the two of them, Nancy and Linda; the conversations are all in my head. I close my eyes. It's time to relax with the voices of the singing monks as an embracing powerful spiritual force, like a hypnotic spell. The plaintive music funnels through the halls and seems to target the grave site. A melancholic mood. Relax, ease off.

Before long, images are coming at me like an old fashion slide show, one grainy frame at a time. There are only a few of them, but they continue to repeat, play like a carousel, one after the other, taking turns filling my consciousness.

The first image is the accident scene: bodies are sprawled at the side of the road and standing by the wrecked cars, the drunken driver with blood pouring down his face. Then images of the morgue surface: each body on a metal gurney, draped with a sheet. Last I see them leave the house that morning: they are waving and smiling, Linda giggling with excitement because of a day of shopping with mom.

My eyes stay shut; this is an internal show, all in my head. One frame after the other jerks its way to the front of my consciousness; it doesn't stop. Finally, all the images morph into dancing lights, like a wild set of aurora borealis, violent exploding lights. They flare and die down. There is one last explosive flash and then nothing but darkness. The images are all gone. God, it's true: they are gone; it's over. I feel the vacuum; they're gone, and I know it; God, it's over and I accept it. I'm surrounded by emptiness.

The Russian monks are becoming louder, more emotional, and as they reach their climax, the singing overwhelms the entire yard. I don't understand a word; the acoustics are such that the voices arrive from every direction; the damn music plunges straight to your soul, the anguish, grief, and despair all surface. I feel the tears pouring down my cheeks. I can't stop them and the next thing I know: I'm sobbing, hard gut wrenching stuff which has me off the bench and on my knees. I don't know and never asked, if I was screaming and shouting or for how long this lasted.

It ends with Monk: he picks me off the ground, wipes my face and leads back to his office.

"Charlie that should have happened two years ago. You had to let go sometime." He doesn't say anymore and hands me some brandy. I'm completed wasted. I drain the brandy and stare at him, my best friend. I know it's an exaggeration to say I went through a catharsis but certainly I'm not the same guy who walked into the Abbey a couple of hours ago.

"OK, let me hear it."

The Monk smiles, not smug, just a grateful look on his face, and then he tells me how we are to save Ronald Bowen. Compassion rules my friend's life.

Jesus Christ, will I ever learn?

CHAPTER 20: FORENSIC DIVISION PROBLEM

The arrival of the weekend was of no consequence to the two women.

At one end of the room, Dr. Kate slumped at the laboratory counter, struggling to maintain her focus, the workload, pressure, and late hours taking its toll. Her mind skipped from one vignette to the next; her mental drifting stopped at her one illicit love affair. It happened years ago when they both attended a Friday night campus beer-fest. Before the fest ended, they left the building together, both well beyond their usual alcohol intake. When they found themselves alone in a friend's apartment, primal lust destroyed any inhibitions. From there on it was a rocket launch, with each secret meeting escalating in passion and intensity. They became reckless, and a mutual friend warned them rumors had started.

Once warned, each recognized the decision point. Fiercely ambitious, logical, and conservative by nature, knowing the impact a divorce would have on their careers, they walked away from the relationship. There was no looking back, no unwanted calls, no gut-wrenching reconciliation attempts, all public contacts conducted with professional decorum.

In her corner of the Combination Room, Emma continued to return to one question: why hadn't the duplicates surfaced during the original work? Hours and hours of basic research by some of the top minds in the world developed the techniques and confirmed the safety of the interrogation.

She studied all the research documentation, the published work, and even news articles; at the time, the original researchers became media stars, and the press coverage had been extensive. An explosion of information existed, thousands of words, except for three: duplicate memory streams— absent from every source.

She had narrowed her focus to one man: Dr. Joe Wilson, a brilliant scientist, was a critical player at the beginning of the project and then disappeared from the scene. Emma met and talked to Dr. Wilson, years ago at some forgotten conference. This was the man she phoned and used his answering service to leave a desperate appeal for assistance.

Why hadn't he answered? Why not at least acknowledge her call? Joe was one of the pioneers in the field. An outstanding scientist but a maverick, with a reputation for candid explosive comments to the press. The

Wilson-Armstrong debates became acrimonious, no holds barred yelling matches, both unyielding egos.

Was he out of date? He had been the oldest in the group and left the research program some time ago. Was he current? On the other hand, the gossip in the scientific community was: Dr. Wilson harbored many secrets and declared his willingness to share if it shafted Dr. Max.

A skeptical Emma resisted the idea Dr. Max was culpable. It was unthinkable a scientist of Dr. Armstrong's caliber would risk his reputation and suppress information of this nature. Although many labeled Max a womanizer, he was one of the top scientists in the world. He would not allow a process to proceed with this type of flaw.

She couldn't turn to Dr. Max Armstrong because Kate said other developments put Dr. Max temporarily out of the loop. The Wilson option seemed an extreme long shot, and she felt embarrassed to discuss it with Kate. But, if she couldn't turn to the Nobel Peace Prize winner, an old timer who may have been there when duplicate memory streams appeared seemed a good choice.

The Combination Room felt like a sterile operating room with banks of equipment the only company for two desperate women. Their working partnership had begun years before S3 became part of the justice system. As a team, they had tackled and solved many problems; they rarely wasted time with mundane preliminaries. When the duplicate issue erupted, they both understood it would be their most significant challenge, the enigma of the decade.

In the past, when dealing with supervisors, Emma found herself to be a rather diffident participant; this all changed with Dr. Kate where her real intrepid character was allowed to surface and flourish. She understood Emma, trusted her, and recognized her ingenious nature.

"Kate, I now have all the questionable recordings; I think I know what took them so long to get the material to us. I'm afraid I made some enemies at White Rock, and this delay was payback. I'm sorry. I could cry.

Regardless I have been crawling through the details of one case, frame by frame. The problem is the amount time it takes to review and analyze. It'll take hours to ensure there are no significant differences in the duplicate streams. I've almost finished one case, and the multiples appear to be duplicates and not a different version of the event, but there are subtle differences which give rise to some doubt. Did I miss something? I'm still not sure. At this rate, it'll take days to assess all the White Rock records."

"Well Emma, I have some good news. I reviewed the problem with the head of Information Technology and discovered they have an old program, apparently part of the original memory research project, for analyzing memory streams.

Over the past few years, various summer students had been given the task of upgrading the software; numerous research grants funded the work. Bottom line: in about one hour we'll receive a technical team from the IT department. These two analysts are familiar with the software and are prepared to view our complete White Rock inventory; and, they believe they can complete a review by the end of the day.

They think it'll only take about 30 minutes to make some modifications which allow multiple streams to be compared against one standard. So we'll use the first retrieval and compare all others against it.

Apparently, the differences in colors, shading and so forth will not be a problem for the software. They can isolate which streams are true duplicates and which ones are not. If this works out, we may have all the answers by the end of the day. But I confess, I'm afraid of what we are going to find."

"This is the best news we've had in days. At this point I don't care what the result is; I just want answers. In my frustration, I began pursuing a different line. Do you remember Dr. Joe Wilson one of the original researchers? Yes? You do? Good. He's retired and living miles from here, but I found him and left him a long message about our problems.

I thought if anyone knew about these kinds of issues, it had to be Joe. Many felt his contributions were second only to Dr. Max's, but Joe couldn't stop criticizing the financial sponsors and irritated the wrong people. I know it's going back rather far, but I'm told he's the guy who knows the details. The problem is: he has not responded, but I'm hoping he'll call us this morning."

"Sure I know him, and I agree we might have to go that far back to solve this issue. Joe always was a bit of a radical and did manage to get himself forced into an early retirement. But let's not waste time speculating. While we wait for his call, tell me about the duplicates that you have reviewed."

"It appears your theory is correct. I've examined a dozen duplicate streams. Some contain a crime scene, but there are a variety of events: the birth of a baby, scoring the winning touchdown, a brutal dog attack on a young boy; all are emotional events in someone's life. The innocent prisoners have about three times the quantity of duplicates. I don't understand why. But this issue is confusing the scanners and Watchers and pushed us over the 45 minutes for many cases."

"Emma, my theory is: as a prisoner convicted of a crime you did not commit, your life tends to be very emotional, and this poignant state spawns these duplicates. Possibly, you continue to remember and replay events. Maybe it's those incidents which mean the most to you, whether they are failures, or a success, or just a happy afternoon. In any case, these multiples are there and part of our job. I don't know; maybe the multiplication allows the events to surface faster.

This is just useless speculation, another research paper. Right now we have to figure out how to deal with the multiple recordings. Emma, why don't you start organizing all the records for the IT analysts who will be here shortly? I have to one more loose end to track down. Thanks."

It was an abrupt ending to the exchange, but Kate was not in the mood for an extended dialogue. Kate had always been an honor student and had a Ph.D. in biochemistry and a medical degree. Before joining the Board, she was the lead scientist on numerous research projects at the University Medical Center.

Although intelligent, her success benefited from hours of grinding work, and her last degree, acquired while married, had been particularly challenging. Possibly this accounted for her less than sympathetic demeanor with colleagues or students who she perceived were not committed.

She was now back in regular contact with Stephen but knew any reconnection was out of the question. His marriage appeared stable, and she knew he took his duties too serious to jeopardize his position for an affair. On the few occasions, they had been alone there was some careful reminiscing, but he never made a move to touch her or give any indication that he missed her.

Besides, her daughter, Sonja, depended on her. For the last few years, Sonja maintained a grueling study pattern to produce the necessary grades for admission to medical school. Kate's support was unlimited, and she did everything possible to assist Sonja with her dream. Then yesterday, after acceptance into medical school along with a prestigious scholarship, Sonja's first move was to call to her father with the good news. This phone call upset Kate; she couldn't control her emotions.

Her ex-husband did little to assist Sonja, had not been around to contribute during the tough economic times, and yet Sonja turned to him immediately with the good news. It appeared Kate's extra efforts and dedication were taken for granted, and father came across as the good guy who provided the positive feedback.

An external sound disrupted Kate's thoughts. The soft ringing filled the room, and Emma answered her cell.

"Hello Dr. Joe. I'm sorry to pull you away from your golf game……………. yes I know you're not always on the links………..may I put you on the big screen and make this a conference call with Dr. Kate?……………. just give me about 30 seconds." Within a few seconds, the wall screen was filled with Joe's face and upper body. He looked trim, fit, tanned, and presented a big smile.

"Hi Kate, I won't waste words. You two are into something, and you're lucky to have found me. I've been on a remote beach with no connections to the rest of the world. It was great. I just got back this morning and reviewed my message service.

And Emma I apologize for the delay; you must have been worried. I think I know what some of the problems are. I'll provide background which may explain what is going on and why it has been difficult to find out about the early days of the project and the reticence of people. All the research was viewed and, probably still is, as pure academic research emanating from a university campus. In reality, private industry controlled and financed the work.

As the research progressed the potential for truckloads of money became apparent. A pharmaceutical company wanted control of all of the drugs; next, there was hardware, circuit design, and software to be patented and monitored. To be part of the research team, all of us signed secrecy and working agreements with monster financial penalties for those with loose lips. This is still in effect and does cover pensions and any other future cash flow you may have been promised. Control was absolute with Dr. Max editing all research papers or presentations."

"Joe we wouldn't think of telling on you, so please open all the doors, and let us know what was going on in those early years."

"Ladies, I do trust you both. As you know, the first probes were only able to retrieve and play audio pockets from the brain. It was a massive step to get a decent picture to accompany the sound. First, we were only able to retrieve low-grade images; the quality was so poor you couldn't be sure what was surfacing.

Dr. Max was a fucking bear, and I mean a fucking bear. He would not accept anything but complete success; he was convinced this would work. He lived in the lab and personally harassed anyone who wasn't getting the results he wanted. Naturally, we solved all the issues associated with getting a clear screen image; memory mapping and developing searching strategy became the next hurdles. Did a chronological pattern to a memory schema exist? And where to begin a scan and how to move the probe?

Dr. Max decided to use the Binary Search as the basis for starting each scan, but each scanner still decides where to move the probe as he visualizes a schema. Emma, you know even today, it depends on a good scanner to get a feeling for the pattern, much like geologist has a vision of the underlying folds and layers under the earth's crust.

Oh sorry, I'm off the central issue and getting carried away. At that time, the probe was controlled and physically moved by hand. And yes, we started to see the same event appear on the screen more than once. After some passionate discussion, the conclusion was: the technician was not able to hold or control the probe correctly. You know, the technician's hand only had to slip fractions of a millimeter, and you would be back in the same region, retrieving the same memory stream."

Both Emma and Kate were quiet, concern growing the longer Joe talked. This was one of the rare times Kate heard Emma swearing, but now she mumbled, quietly and softly, swearing a steady stream.

"Repetition of an event was obviously not acceptable. Max worked with the IT group, working as project leader, writing a significant part of their code. They designed a program which analyzed each scan and compared the results to previous scans. They came up with an algorithm to assess each pixel in a memory stream. The objective was to develop a numerical value for each display. This depended on the detailed analysis of each pixel. To simplify: they added up all the pixel values for a numerical total of the memory pocket or read out. The calculation was called a D Value.

If any scan came up with the same D Value, it was not shown on the screen. That is, it was deemed a duplicate readout due to either to the unsteady hand of the operator or limitations of the probe apparatus. These D values didn't exactly match. They rarely had the same numeric value. We had an acceptable range, and if they fell within the range, this was deemed satisfactory; they were considered duplicates and filtered out of the feedback."

"You developed a software filter which blocked all duplicates as you worked your way through a brain scan?'

"Yes Kate, and once we had the filter in place, the results were amazing, and of course, we could complete under the 45-minute limit. And, it's my understanding numerous versions of this software have been developed; the research funding has allowed summer students to create and modify more rigorous versions to allow for in-depth analysis of memory streams."

"Yes, we know about the student software and will be using it today. But, back to the comparisons. You said the comparisons were not necessarily perfect. Can I assume just because two events were within the same D Value range this didn't automatically prove they were identical?"

"That was my contention, but Dr. Max overrode all the opposition. He said it was good enough. He fell back on FAPP......you know the John Bell abbreviation meaning: for all practical purposes.

Max stated that the differences we were concerned about were not material to the results. The sequence of actions and the players in the events were the same; the different hues, black and white images, the shading, and superimposed images were insignificant. Of course, I pushed too hard and was forced to take an early retirement."

"Joe to your knowledge did anyone do a manual frame by frame review of all the duplicates to ensure Dr. Max was correct?"

"I'm not sure. Indeed we reviewed a lot, but I left before they finished comparisons on many of the streams. Did anyone compare every duplicate scan? I don't know. Dr. Max assured everyone he had conducted a complete review, and no one was left to challenge him. Besides the results were so fantastic, and as time went by, I think, this was all forgotten; as well, any press releases were controlled by Max.

And remember, at that time it wasn't to be used to execute people, no one was that prescient. FAPP was not an unreasonable approach."

Emma was afraid she would become physically ill, and she could see Kate's face was drained of all color. "Joe, if the duplicate issue was taken care of years ago, why did start showing up the minute we worked on death row convicts?"

"I've been thinking about this ever since I listened to your morning message. I called some former colleagues, to understand what's changed; they are suspicious, which means you better solve it fast because too many people know about White Rock. Anyway, this is what I know.

A few days before you began the Prison Reform project a major revision became operational, modified equipment and software. A new model scanner was used for the first time; here the probe is housed in the helmet device, out of the direct control by the operator. Although the technician still monitors the direction of the move, the physical movement is under computer control hence there is no danger of slippage back to a previous location. The prisoner's head is shaved, and the helmet is fitted for best transmission."

"Doesn't this improve the process?"

"Yes, it does. But the designers made one assumption. Because no slippage could occur, they assumed they would not have to deal with duplicates and didn't bother trying to include the filtering program into the helmet design. The software was discarded.

Now, for the first time, it's obvious the multiple versions are not due to operator error or equipment limits because the probe is not slipping back to a previous location. Multiple copies of memory stream do exist. Now confirmed. No doubts. Listen I'm sorry.

This is as far as I go and will not be available to testify or whatever else may be required; the financial penalties are too severe. I've been through enough with Dr. Max and his crew. No more phone calls, the rest is up to you. Kate, you have a helluva problem on your hands; I don't have any suggestions but do recommend you keep Dr. Max out of this as long as you can. I just don't trust him to come up with a solution which doesn't first serve his reputation."

They continued with some minor chatter, which was a little ridiculous given what they had just heard, then all signed off. Two apprehensive women filled their coffee cups and started pacing the room, neither speaking, the only sound the scuffling of their footwear. They walked around the entire large sterile room. Up and down the lab, round the tables and chairs, a short pause to look out a window and then back to the rambling. Emma started.

"Kate, I think I can solve the problem of the duplicates appearing during the scanning. I need some time to test my solution with our current equipment and a little help from IT.

The more critical question is: what is in those multiple memory streams? Are they true duplicates? Can you work with IT team and get that question answered today? Did Dr. Max review ever incident of the copies encountered? Did he go beyond FAPP? Joe certainly is doubtful."

Kate was shaken by the aggressive nature of Emma's outburst. "Yes, I am prepared to work with IT, for as long it takes. And we will have answers by the end of the day, but

- 186 -

tell me how are you going to keep the new scanner from delivering the duplicates?"

When Emma told her, Kate laughed for the first time in a couple of days. "Sure it might work. No, I'll go further. It will work. It normally is the most obvious solution which is the answer.

And Emma, for a change of pace. I have one for you. Are you ready for this?

Charlie Taylor is on the list to be the one and only Watcher for one of the convicts, the last one in the queue on death row at Fort Green. What do you think about this appointment? To me, it's almost as mysterious as the Chief Duncan promoting him to head up Homicide."

Emma thought about Charlie as a Watcher: it didn't make sense. Was he ordered to attend? She struggled to forget him but reluctantly admitted there were times when she smiled about the incident at the dance, funny in a weird sort of way.

Charlie was tall, an olive complexion, average looking guy, almost handsome with a rugged appearance and an athletic build. She heard he worked both sides of the street, hard drinking played off with intense workouts. She knew his family history and his reputation, fast mouth, hard-nosed, excellent detective, fearless. He upset her. She grudgingly acknowledged, to herself, when she saw him, there was a visceral reaction but knew she would always keep her distance. She was not getting close to a man many in the Sector labeled a reckless maverick.

"This doesn't make sense. If this convict thinks Charlie is going to help, he must be desperate. I'll keep a close eye on that scan. I don't know what's going on, but my guess is: Charlie will try to pull something."

CHAPTER 21: BRAINSTORMING CONCLUDES

The Historian's original conclusion triggered the argument.

Terry refused to believe that one or both of the Five Star Couple was a cop. Charlie allowed the loud debate to continue, hoping the emotion would eventually drain and logic return. Could John convince the group? John Wojecki developed a reputation for being calm under pressure, his role as Historian for the S3 memory scan demanded that temperament. As one of the smartest people in the Sector, the Historian often searched for atypical activity to keep himself amused. When Terry stopped his rant, John started in a soft voice, very confident.

"Let's go over some of the clues: first, one of these individuals or both has extensive practical knowledge about forensics, high-class call girls, and police procedures. It is extremely unlikely even a gifted academic could acquire this information and the associated practical knowledge by merely researching the subject areas.

Second, some of the forensic tools are so new only a restricted number of technicians are trained and able to use the innovations; then I say it had to be someone who saw these tools and sprays being used and knew how to apply them and the business…"

Terry interrupted. "OK…OK…..I've changed my mind; someone definitely had street experience. The way they dealt with the call girl agencies means either a frequent user or someone who knew the business, but for an active cop or a recent resignation, the risk of exposure is too great. Vice cops are known around most hotels. Shit, even the escort staff might recognize them. The street people certainly know most vice- cops, and we have to assume it is not a rookie."

Manuel stood up and looked at Charlie. "It's a fucking Hybrid……….a fucking Hybrid."

Charlie stepped in. "And John before you ask: for a few years Investigative Divisions created and experimented with a unique deployment of staff. A specialized unit worked with Forensics in gathering evidence at a crime scene; Forensic still supervised and managed the scene, but the assigned police personnel did a lot of the grunt work.

Because these guys work both the street and Forensics, they acquired the Hybrid tag. The experiment didn't pan out, and people were absorbed back onto the force. But with this type of exposure an intelligent individual could absorb the science and the technique."

The room fell silent again as everyone absorbed and accepted the conclusion. Even Charlie's tablet remained silent, and the electronic board only carried his list of words from the initial session. Wes walked to the window and stared at the river; Charlie took the time to grab a donut and coffee.

Karen kept on doodling, then broke the silence. "There were two west coast cities who experimented with those forensic tools….........numerous months before our city, in fact well ahead of any city. If someone from one of those cities is a member of the Five Star Couple, it would explain why they were not worried about being identified by street people or hotel staff."

Charlie interrupted. He wanted to move. From experience, he found fresh ideas often came when a new direction was started. "Let's go with that …..assume we are on the right track. What the hell is motivating the pair of them?"

Terry was impatient. "Christ Charlie, you don't have to go that deep on these two. There is no logic; both are fucking crazy. In the old world a defense lawyer's dream for instant notoriety, temporary insanity, just a couple of mixed up kids, take your choice,"

John didn't miss a beat. "Let's assume one or both are crazy or borderline wouldn't something show up on their records? Like the excessive use of force? Or the unjustified use of a weapon? These are people who enjoy violence. If they were on a police force, I don't see how they could have resisted using violence on some of their arrests or on an encounter in the street. There had to be cases where a criminal would be an easy victim."

Charlie intervened. "I agree these tendencies would be hard to hide. Let me try this on you: suppose an incident happened which forced a resignation. Now our aggressors are really pissed and ready to step it up. The small taste of violence they've had up to this point just became a start, the appetizer."

Karen jumped in. "We can search records. But if an incident or a blow up occurred, there's a good chance it may have been hidden or worded with so much double talk you would never recognize it as a forced resignation. Otherwise, that department is announcing they are responsible for turning them loose, and the incident would have received prompt media attention. Hence, the official record could show up as a mere resignation to pursue avenues of greater interest and not a firing for cause or a forced resignation."

Charlie's instincts convinced him they'd broken through and he summarized. "This is good. Next step, each of you has to think about any contacts you have in those two cities, of course, a Human Resources connection would be ideal. It may appear to be a strange way to start, but I share Karen's concerns that an official reply to a formal request may be sanitized.

I'd like to try the back door first........unofficial......station gossip which tells the tale about someone who enjoyed the heavy hitting too much.....was frustrated by rules and was gently pushed out the door. We look for off the record sentiment that points to someone who was too much, even for the hard-nosed types.

I suggest we keep the search parameters broad and loose. We focus on a man or woman who was employed as a Hybrid. The individual was fired or resigned in the last 12 to 24 months..... hands-on experience with the new forensic tools...... has moved out of that city, and possibly, had some street time with Vice. And if all this doesn't work, I'll approach the Chief and we'll proceed with an official request and get pressure from the top.

Any questions? No. Good. Please get on the phones but be careful; if our target department wants to cover its ass, staff may have been threatened to keep quiet and will be wary of any requests. If word reaches the top, they may freeze us out.

Wes, I want you to coordinate this search. In the meantime, I'll bring the Chief up to speed. When we catch this couple, we'll see how good our logic was.

On your way out, help yourself to any of the left-over donuts or muffins.....and...John... Karen...thanks for the help."

A successful end to a difficult brainstorming pleased the entire group, a sense of fulfillment, satisfied with a tough session. Although they were close, in the end, there would be another surprise waiting for them. As with science, logic was not always foolproof.

# # #

It was late Saturday night.

Stella asleep, Stephen in his study. The house was silent, all dark except for the small lamp which shone onto his monitor. Before he settled into his study, he'd taken the time to mix an extra-large Irish coffee, one of his favorite drinks.

For the last time, he read the query from Regional: two questions demanded an official response: first, since White Rock had completed death row clearance, why wasn't he fully staffed at Fort Green? Second, was he aware of the rumors circulating about flaws with the S3 interrogation?

Stephen knew his delay option had run its course. His original plan assumed Kate would have resolved all the issues by now. Should he be open about the dilemma and try to explain why he had not been frank at the beginning?

He felt the Irish whiskey warm his empty stomach, soothing and relaxing, maybe too relaxing. Stephen pushed the 'send' button and Regional headquarters received their reply. Years later he still could not understand why he did it, a brash move for a conservative man.

His response, although rather academic and ponderous, matched the style Regional preferred. But his summary was short and to the point: the delay existed because Forensic, after the observations at White Rock, wished to develop some procedural adjustments to S3 interrogations which should enhance the efficacy of the process. Last, the underlying science for S3 remained sound; rumors were to be expected with all the changes which were taking place.

His position now official and hard wired. If S3 proved defective, he would probably be asked to submit his resignation.

His original rationale had been to buy time, and he decided not to change course. If he allowed the doubts about S3 to surface, Dr. Kate would be swamped with questions, other experts and specialists contending for attention. Dr. Max would demand control, something which would only multiply the complications. His confidence in Dr. Kate remained high; if she had time and no media circus, she could solve the problem. He had to buy her time.

If the S3 Interrogation proved to be fundamentally flawed, at least she would not have to pay the penalty. But, he couldn't give her more than a few more days, and then he would travel to Regional and make his explanations in person.

CHAPTER 22: CHARLIE'S LOG: CONCERN

Every week or two, my brother, Sam, visits for breakfast.

We finish the main course and are enjoying a coffee at my kitchen island counter. Herbie, Sam's dog, lounges at my feet, hoping I'll have an extra piece of bacon or toast, anything will do; he loves my cooking. He's a mixed breed and, although a large dog, is a gentle creature.

I'm getting a little hot. "Jesus. You're a clinical psychologist, certified or whatever, surely you can provide a little assistance."

Sam hesitates; we have been down this road before. "There are numerous reasons why I'm not the best person; the main one, of course, is I'm your brother and too close to be objective. But since you persist I'll give you two essential truths which will save your life. First, have one beer, then stop because I know blackouts aren't stopping; second, chase the red head, I mean chase her and be nice."

I smile, thinking Sam will eventually fold. "I won't even tell you how I screwed up with Red and burnt every bridge which might have existed. So forget that path and listen to me. I've a concern, stupid stuff, but I'm just asking for your opinion, no head shrink shit. Alright?"

"Bring it on, you stubborn bastard, and by the way, I know about the spring party."

"Forget the bloody dance. My promotion means more contact with the Judge's Board, and regular mixing with senior staff, like Doug Brewster and Jacob Konahouse. I will have to attend some of the weekly meetings, reporting and taking questions from Division Heads or their specialists. Senior staff often attend and are expected to participate with probing questions and opinions.

Anyway, my concern is the amount of additional exposure to all these people when I prefer to minimize contact. These exchanges mean stress and you know what happens to my vocabulary and temper when I have to deal with self-serving questions."

I pause to give Sam some time which he doesn't need; it helps if you have a thorough understanding of your patient and have grown up with him. "Let me guess. You've allowed the feud with Jacob to fester. The situation is ridiculous: two adults at odds because of an incident dating back to high school."

"OK true. But I also hear Doug Brewster has his sights set on my ass."

"Is there anyone on the Board that you've not pissed off? You insult the Judge yet?"

"No, I think the Judge likes me. Not sure about Dr. Kate and Uncle Willie. I have to.."

Sam interrupts. "Slow down; you haven't even attended a meeting.

To summarize you're worried one of these senior staff members will take a run at you, and you'll respond like a pit bull. I suggest you let it play out and see what transpires. Unfortunately, I think you're right: a smart individual who knows you can set it up. His best strategy will be to trigger a hostile exchange to diminish your status and position, to demonstrate your presence at Board meetings is not appropriate.

You'll be alright when you're giving a report which you have prepared and are in control; the problems will occur when the questions and the give-and-take start. Here you had best remember your breathing routines and take your time in responding. Don't rush, it may feel like hours, but it's only a few seconds delay, and you can regain composure. Don't react, don't jump.

OK? Let's go at this again after the first couple of meetings. Just don't react, when you perceive a threat or insult. Play statute, be still. Play statue."

"Alright, alright. I don't like any of this, but I want to stay in Homicide and out of Records, so I have no choice but to attend the damn meetings. Thanks Sam."

Sam is rather economical with words. He says he gets paid to listen. "No problem brother, and shouldn't you be running to your first Board meeting?"

"The Judge's assistant called and said the meeting was canceled until further notice. This is strange; the Judge keeps canceling meetings. You know there doesn't seem to be time to think. Today there are twists, subtleties, and nuances which almost have me spinning. If I ever fall off the wagon, I will be gone for a long time."

Sam doesn't understand what I am talking about, and I don't explain. I don't tell him about a cop as a possible serial killer, about my suspicions that the Chief is trying to set me up for a fall, or about the wild rumors the Interrogations have failed. Sam laughs, gives me a hug and then is out the door, Herbie at his heels.

These goddamn Board meetings, on and then off, then a canceled emergency session. Stir in grave doubts about the Interrogations, combine all this with my two serial killers and I feel like I'm breaking the speed limit on the freeway and chaos has just merged in from the on-ramp, a potential collision at any moment. This last sentence is my attempt to avoid some more basic terms like shit and fan.

I'm up and pacing at 2:00 am in the morning.

We've very little on that bastard rapist/killer. Karen and I both know it's only a question of time before his next strike. He won't stop. We've issued a warning to the public, but earlier in the evening I cruised some of the target neighborhoods, the hot spots. From what I saw it appears our warnings are being ignored. The streets were busy, many girls on their own, looking for adventure, easy pickings for a psychopath.

I feel I'm not much help to Karen. Does it mean we have to wait for one more rape/killing and hope he makes a mistake or is spotted? A helluva way to solve a case.

Jesus, the house is empty, only the hum of the refrigerator for company.

CHAPTER 23: CHARLIE'S LOG: FIRST MEETING

I'm nervous. I can feel a tremor in my hands. My imagination?

Finally, I get to attend a Board meeting. And just my luck I run into Jacob Konahouse, head of the Prisons Division. He's a nasty mouth, and he starts on me immediately.

"Charlie….Charlie. World famous detective and shit disturber. Hope you can behave yourself for a solid hour, and don't embarrass your Chief."

I know what Jacob is hoping, and it isn't for my good fortune. I give him a shot. "Jesus, Jake, you're out. I see the hospital reinstated day parole. You must've been a good boy. It's always nice when they let sex offenders out for a few hours. Just remember to take your meds."

He ignores me and goes to his seat. The Chief sees me in the doorway, waves, and points to a chair next to him. It's a large rectangular room, arranged to accommodate the four Divisions with chairs and tables for all in attendance. The front is reserved for the Judge and his assistant. There is an emergency exit at the side and a series of large windows filling the east wall. The other walls are covered with some type of wood paneling, elegant, impressive, an intimidating scenario.

The Judge and the Division Heads are all comfortable with each other, the rapport obvious, the Judge first welcoming all the seconds and deputies who are in attendance. I try not to look over at Emma, who is with Dr. Kate. Since our rather hostile discussion at the Chinese supper, I have learned something else about Emma. Her empathy for the less fortunate runs deep, and she is quick to take umbrage with comments which exhibit a hostile or unsympathetic attitude toward the underdog. Her stance is often seen as naïve and not realistic for a professional in the modern world.

I scan the room one more time, nodding my head to acknowledge people. I know everyone but have never seen them perform in front of the Judge. There is Doug. I'm sure he remembers the time I almost grabbed the pipe out of his mouth; the guy is smart but is always calculating the next move in his career.

And of course, there is Jake. Jacob as he likes to be called.

We have a long belligerent history. Money and ambition rule his life; law and order are only a means to an end. He has built an extensive political network. A persistent rumor is: the Judge never selected him, but he was forced onto the Board by the political masters.

Next, is my boss, Chief Duncan, who promoted me for some strange reason, well maybe not that mysterious. He likes rules and order; he would have had a great career in the military where life revolves around a solid core of regulations for all occasions. The Chief does have a fierce temper, most of the time under control.

The last Division Head is Dr. Kate. She's a great looking lady and possibly the hardest worker of the lot. I think she's the star of this group; she has worked long hours to get her team ready and thoroughly familiar with the tools and chemistry of all three Interrogations. On occasion, I encounter low-grade gossip: Kate and the Judge used to play house, but if true it must have been many years ago.

This could be a creepy meeting. Hope I'm not asked to report.

The Judge is in control. He doesn't waste any time with small talk. "I called this particular meeting and requested other senior personnel attend because we have important issues to deal with this morning. First, I want to address the problem we encountered at the last meeting and will ask Dr. Kate to report on the situation. Kate, please proceed. And, for reasons which will become apparent, I am declaring a Condition Confidential for this meeting."

Kate is well prepared and launches into her report. "Thanks Judge, during the White Rock Prison project we encountered some cases of multiple memory pockets for the same event. The concern was: possibly the brain was not capturing the event as it occurred but was interpreting events and logging any number of different versions. Another theory was: when individuals relived or remembered the event, they unconsciously modified their memory. If either theory were correct, it would destroy the base of our reformed justice system.

We have finished our analysis of all the White Rock data and confirmed for some events, or points in a person's history, multiple copies of memory streams do exist. Comparisons were conducted to determine if the copies were duplicates or different versions of the same event. Fortunately, we discovered existing software to do the bulk of the comparisons, but for a couple of brutal crimes, we also conducted a manual frame by frame comparison. After an extensive review, I am pleased to announce that the multiples are true duplicates. By this I mean the sequence of events, the individuals, the action, in other words everything of significance, are the same in all the memory streams.

The differences are entirely irrelevant; the differences are inconsequential, minor variations such as a switch to a black and white stream, some unusually lighting or shading or images morphed into sepia monochrome. We have no idea why this is happening or why there are duplicates. All questions for the future. More food for the next research project. Bottom line: S3 interrogation is a valid test of guilt or innocence."

I look at the Judge; he's trying to suppress a smile. I'm sure she briefed him before the meeting, but with this announcement it is understandable he is having trouble with his composure. I wondered if he and Kate ever did get it on; there certainly seems to be something special between them, but then maybe I'm sex-deprived or beer-deprived or both, a case of faulty judgment.

The Judge interrupts. "Kate since many people in the room aren't scientists may be you could provide a short explanation of how the duplicates impacted the 45 minute limit of the memory scanning."

"Yes, I was about to get to the second problem. The duplicates were causing Sector 13 to exceed the 45 minute limit for some the convicts. In the problem cases, after a probe was repositioned a copy might appear on the monitors. The screen was displaying an event that Watchers had already viewed; both the Watchers and the Scanners were confused.

The Scanners scrambled to make adjustments because they thought the scanning mechanisms had malfunctioned and the Watchers were confused, thinking they had provided the wrong instruction to the technician. It might not sound like much but when many of these duplicate packets were encountered it quickly added up. And 15 to 20 extra minutes are too much, particularly for a difficult search.

These duplicate packets surface during the final stages of Dr. Armstrong's pioneer work but were deemed an operator error or equipment limits. The solution: software to analyze each memory stream before it displayed. If any packet proved to be the same as a previous flow, it was discarded.

When Sector 13 started at White Rock Prison, a redesigned scanner, which used a computer to control the movement and position of the probe, went into operation. Since operator error was eliminated, the software filter was not installed on the new scanners. And, of course, the duplicates started to reappear and cause all the confusion for Sector 13.

Emma has been able to install the filtering software into the redesigned scanner. This means we will be using the software, which over the years has been maintained and upgraded, to stop the duplicates from appearing. We'll still dump these memory pockets to archives in case there are ever any future challenges; however, I'm extremely pleased to say: Fort Green death row can be scheduled for interrogation."

A standing ovation from the crowd, except for those of us who were never aware of the problem existed. The Judge is in a hurry and pushing.

"Thanks Kate, excellent and you know what a relief all this is for us. I'm going to ask the rest of you to hold any questions until the end of the meeting. We have to move on. I apologize for this abrupt shift. More drama is not what we need, but there is no alternative. We have a situation which has the potential to explode on us. To repeat...... this issue has the potential to severely shake the system.

I will start this explanation, and Doug can finish as required. About a week ago, Dr. Grovernor, CEO of Allied Scientific, requested a meeting. I know Dr. Grovernor from various charities and similar event, but we are not friends. Given all our problems I was not anxious for a meeting, with no particular purpose; however, considering his position in the community, I decided to honor his request.

A furious Dr. Grovernor demanded immediate action. The reason for his anger: his 15-year-old daughter's relationship with a man. Grovernor claims the seduction occurred when she was 14 years old, and, therefore, is statutory rape. His high profile family will ensure this will dominate the news for weeks.

He continued, and the accusation exploded. The reason: Dr. Max Armstrong is the accused rapist, our Nobel Peace Prize winner, designer of the various interrogation drugs and protocols we are currently using."

There is shuffling and a variety of sounds coming from around the room, as people try to absorb the accusation. Jacob is the first to speak. "Judge, we can see this will be a bit of a nightmare, but we should acknowledge celebrities are always getting into trouble and within a few months the press is going after someone else. I don't understand why this is an agenda item for an emergency meeting.

Surely this will blow up and then die down, and as long as Dr. Max expresses his regret and behaves, it should be out of the public mind rather quickly. The good Dr. Max already has a reputation of chasing many skirts at the same time."

The Judge looked over at Doug Brewster, head of the Legal Division, and Doug started. "Yes, I concur with your analysis; however, as we researched all the parties and their backgrounds, details surfaced which make this significantly more complicated.

First, when Dr. Max was in Grade XII, and legally an adult, he connected with a 14-year-old girl, and they had sex on a regular basis. The girl didn't complain, but her parents laid the charge. The presiding judge was very sympathetic. Max already had his university scholarship, without a doubt the best student in the district. The girl was very mature, in every sense, and was very much on Max's side. The future Ph.D. got off with community service and a stern warning.

Throughout his university career, Max chased and caught many girls. One summer when he was finishing up his Ph.D. thesis, he earned extra money by working for one the chemistry profs. The job included mostly lab work, and that's where Max was when the tour group arrived.

The touring crop consisted of various graduated grade 12 students; the intent was to provide early orientation about life on the campus, the location of the parking lots, the use of different buildings, and all the rest. Love or lust discovered one tall blond prospective student and Max. And soon they were engaged in many sexual romps.

It appears Max is unlucky in love. Although mature and sexy, the tall blond had never seen the inside of a grade 12 classroom. This girl, only a grade nine student, had been allowed to tag along with her sister. When Max found out, he backed away as quickly as possible. Unfortunately, the young teenager loved and missed Max, the result a teary confession to her mother.

A different judge heard this case. Fortunately, a man was known to be tolerant and lenient. Max already won almost every academic prize the university offered and apparently slated for a brilliant career. The girl's family admitted they allowed her to masquerade as a grade 12 graduate, and, again, the girl pleaded for Max and stressed her part in the romp. The legal system exercised its wisdom and Max returned to community service for statuary rape."

Most people in the room were beginning to understand where this was going and why a Condition Confidential had been declared at the beginning of the meeting.

"Under our existing legislation you all know about the escalating punishment for repeat offenders, in particular, those dealing with sex and minors. All previous convictions, regardless of the penalty imposed and regardless of when they occurred, are counted. This means: Dr. Max is a classified as a repeat offender of sex crimes with a minor. And, if found guilty of the statuary rape of the Grovernor girl, this will be his third conviction.

He is not a routine repeat offender. Sex with minor means one less chance to rehabilitate. The death sentence is mandatory for the third offense. This is the reason Dr. Max was excluded from Kate's research on the duplicates."

The entire room is in shock, too much to absorb, the implications profound. I'm aware of Dr. Max's reputation with women, but this one is hard to believe. My mind is spinning, and I think: we are looking at the possibility of the death sentence for a Nobel Peace Prize winner, an international celebrity.

Jesus Christ.

CHAPTER 24: DR. GROVERNOR

A solitary figure slouched in a webbed lounge chair next to the pool.

The sun, high and bright, created a glaring shimmer on the pool surface and heated the concrete surroundings. The remnants of breakfast lingered on the table. He was a heavy-set man, between 50 and 60 years old, dark stubble on his face, his hair disheveled; he was under the shade of the large beach type umbrella, oblivious to his surroundings.

Months ago, his CFO announced the bad news. Dr. Vince Grovernor reviewed the numbers, again and again; nothing changed and no matter how he tried to twist and turn, the conclusion survived, the financial picture grim. A competitor drastically reduced production costs and flooded the market with comparable products at almost half the price. Grovernor's sales volume plunged, and only loyal customers continued with his company, the results reflected in a disastrously small revenue stream.

A few years ago when the trade journals first reported his chief competitor hired two top flight chemical engineers, he guessed they would tackle the production costs. At that time, Max was no longer with the company, but Grovernor turned to him. A four-year absence from the manufacturing process didn't trump ego, and Max dove in with a multitude of suggestions. But, he refused to leave the University; he said, he was on to something new which Grovernor translated as: on to someone new.

However, Max did spend time with the company's scientists and technicians. Never shy to demonstrate his superior intelligence and undeniable talent, he presented many ideas and alternative solutions. He provided his best arm's length analysis.

For a time Grovernor's staff made progress, small but steady cost reductions. Unfortunately, his senior chemist died from a heart attack, and the rest of the crew floundered without strong technical leadership. The cost reduction program stumbled and flat lined.

Again, Grovernor turned to Max, pleading for him to leave the University for two years so they could solve the problem and get into a revised production cycle. Max refused; his new research was too exciting, and he feared losing his advantage. It was at the University where Max's career had skyrocketed and where he knew future glory resided. Grovernor begged.

An unyielding Max couldn't understand: Grovernor was a multimillionaire. Why not just walk away and sail around the world? Grovernor didn't try and explain. Money

- 213 -

was not the issue; he didn't like to lose; damn it he was a competitor, and Max should have known.

After the financial situation had become desperate, he told Max not to come around; the scientist was no longer welcome at the house or any of their functions, all open invitations canceled. Max, living in his own world, found this hard to believe and showed up at some parties where a brusque escort showed him the door. For some reason, he still wanted to be part of the family and didn't seem to be offended if a security guard forced him out through the front door.

Grovernor's daughter compounded his stress. He was not naïve and was not fooled by his daughter; in fact, they were very close. Building a company from the ground level, organizing a group of sensitive academic young scientists, which had included Max, meant his time had always been a precious resource. But, Grovernor ensured he made time for his daughter and enjoyed her transition from toddler to beautiful teenager.

Her academic record became a source of pride, and he was pleased to hear the drama club chose her to play the lead in the wind-up production later in the spring. She surprised everyone with this acting gift; the drama director labeled her a 'natural'. Grovernor thought this would not be a wise career choice and already planned how he could curtail any moves in that direction.

Today, he second guessed himself. He had known about her attraction to Max. Damn it, the infatuation started early, at times embarrassing. If she knew he was coming, you could sense her excitement, and within minutes she would be up the stairs to find a better outfit to wear. She always attempted to sit next to him or at least be close. Grovernor knew Max understood the attraction; her interest was evident to all and Max didn't need much to pick up the scent; the bastard was the master.

Although Grovernor and his wife discussed the issue, he refused to intervene and decided to treat it like a school girl infatuation which would dissipate with time. The unspoken reason was: in those start-up years he needed Dr. Max and didn't want to irritate him. Surprisingly, Max had developed a sensitive about his relationships with teenage girls, too much innuendo spilling onto his workbench. And, it had appeared the good Dr. was exercising some control.

Grovernor spoke to his daughter many times and even told her about Max's reputation. Hell, the revelation seemed to intensify her interest and make him more desirable. His wife tried to reason with Sally, but that was even a bigger failure.

The situation, as his wife liked to call it, presented itself when they were forced to return early from a European trip. Within minutes of walking into the backyard, he knew something had happened.

The birthday party concluded a few days ago; everything should have been smiles and laughs. Instead, he found his daughter alone, no friends at the pool, furniture strewn around or broken. Sally upset. Damn it where did she get that swimsuit, might as well be naked. After he spied the empty bottle of Champagne and recognized the quality, he guessed the source. They started to talk, a brutally frank discussion. He would not let this slide. Grovernor resolved to put an end to the situation.

That son of a bitch would not stop; once Max focused on a girl, it appeared only a bullet would stop him.

# # #

Back at the Judge's office, Ann and the Judge had a rare coffee break together.

"Stephen, sometimes I can't believe where we've arrived and how fast we got here. Do you think the pendulum will ever swing back?"

Ann and the Judge had evolved into an indomitable team, each crisis another challenge to be resolved. She knew more about the nuances of his moods than he realized and understood the pending mass executions and the body counts would cost him many a sleepless night. He was guarded in his reply but did not adopt the didactic style he often used with the legal staff.

"Abrogation may occur in the future, but I fear that the sun will roast the entire planet before that happens."

"It appears as if there is no mercy left in the system."

"We do provide for a first-time offense: a generous opportunity for the individual to prove this was one mistake which will not be repeated. But, as you know, the penalties escalate, and any incident which involves a serious injury or death is covered under the repeat offenders' legislation. This law gives you three chances, but on the fourth event, it is unlikely you will avoid death by lethal injection. No excuse is accepted. Whether it is a motor vehicle accident or a bar fight, it is immaterial. You have exhibited a violent pattern of behavior."

While the Judge gathered his thoughts, Ann remembered the first time a woman was sentenced to death because her drunken driving killed a pedestrian. At first, the public reacted, but after her record was published, sympathy disappeared, and the prevailing mindset quickly accepted the sentence.

"This extreme approach is balanced with the emphasis on rehabilitation, and we have invested a great deal of money into Farms and appropriate staff. The Farms have been a success, to the surprise of many of us.

The Farms, at first glance, appear to be summer resort camps, but they operate like a six week Marine camp, emphasizing physical conditioning, proper diet, and an extensive outdoor work program. Also, they identify social skills which requiring upgrading: for example, someone who is illiterate is put into a reading program. The Farms can't deal with all the issues in six weeks but do identify the major problems, and they provide the outside contacts for follow up.

This emphasis on rehabilitation continues even for the second and third-time offender. The motivation to succeed is driven by the knowledge that the penalty for a recovery failure is severe. When restoration fails, we have concluded it is best to remove the individual from society. What makes our situation unique is: there is no longer any doubt about guilt or innocence. Once established the rules are firm and clear."

"Does this make your job easier?"

"In some ways but there is still an element of judgment and discretion. For major crimes and repeat offenders, my job is to review the offense, assess Legal's recommendation and make a decision which will reflect society's demands. I'm the final authority for our Sector.

But I'll just be a spectator as the Prison Decommissioning work unfolds. Since prisons are to be closed, the prisoners not on death row will have to be released or moved to a Farm. If inmates are subjected to S1 interrogations, officials will undoubtedly uncover different crimes; each revelation leading to a possible lethal injection which was never part of the prisoner's original sentence.

And, the repeaters will be a more convoluted issue; as they are uncovered, it's a certainty the body count will mount."

She could sense his concern and watched him retreat into his office. Earlier that morning Stephen had explained: he wanted her to approach Charlie. It was now Ann's turn to prepare for a lunch with Charlie, a person she liked but wondered about the Judge's confidence in the man. To her, this assignment demanded an investigator who had a record of discretion and was able to operate with limited resources under a top secret security clearance.

Today, Charlie was an unknown; his earlier history included a string of spectacular successes, but in the process, he gained a reputation of an iconoclast, an unpredictable force. She understood why the Chief had to be by-passed, but Charlie's flamboyant style didn't appear to be a fit for this assignment. Since she rarely challenged Stephen, tomorrow she would lunch with Charlie and give him the job and possibly some advice.

###

Monk walked the paths at the Abbey. He was pleased with Charlie and Wes, the detectives' participation in the recent hospital visits; the kids loved all the attention, and the men seemed to be buoyed up by the energy and optimism of the children. A small bald, very young, boy took to Charlie and hung around his neck the entire visit at St. Michaels' cancer ward. The homicide detective smiled for the whole tour, a dramatic change from an average day.

But it is hard to think about that success. The planned attack on the S3 interrogation continued to worry Monk, a pressing issue. He rehearsed his next debriefing of Charlie; Ron Bowen, the convict on death row, provided Monk an in-depth review of the entire week prior to the incident. The accused killer tried to remember all the details from the daily weather to the clothing his grandmother was wearing. Then Monk and Charlie would walk through each day of that week. They wanted this detail firmly implanted in Charlie's mind

The plan was: as soon as one of these early scenes surfaced, Charlie would be able to recognize them and order a jump AHEAD. They hoped the jump would be far enough to get past the drunk killing in the park.

Charlie appeared to be coping, but Monk wasn't convinced. He thought about all the issues: Horny Harry, the Five Star Couple, Emma, the basketball game and the Chief.

Was there more? How could Charlie concentrate on Ron Bowen's history? There was no room for error.

Maybe he should have Charlie pull out; maybe just play it straight and hope the scene never surfaces. But this could be Ron's death sentence.

CHAPTER 25: HARRY AND THE HOTEL COUPLE

The last girl was still alive: an error, not to be repeated.

He was an ordinary looking guy, average build, average appearance, and average in almost any way you cared to describe him. The biggest surprise was his near genius, which surfaced when he repaired sophisticated, specialized equipment, any computer controlled device or audio/visual apparatus, his intelligence conspicuous at the work bench. The original design was not his strength. But, he repaired and modified existing equipment to allow utilization beyond anything incorporated in the first model.

His current employer understood his value and deflected the criticisms and complaints, lost a few female staff because of him but considered that the cost of doing business. Harry, not his real name but paradoxically the nickname his coworkers gave him when the media created the Horny Harry tag, was well aware of his value. He tried to control himself at work because he wanted a low profile, but on occasion the temptation became too much, and he rationalized a little incidentally contact should not be an issue.

Harry knew the value of an apology and developed into an excellent confessor, and tears of sorrow came fast and easy. This worked the first couple of times, then the lament and admissions sounded rather hollow, and it was time for the girl or Harry to move on; most of the time it was the girl.

Early in his life, the fascination with electronics consumed him, and his late physical maturity meant more hours at the workbench in his parent's garage.   By the time all the hormones started to take over, he was nearly 20 years old, with the dating expertise of a 12-year-old. His first rape happened at a party organized by a couple of like-minded university students. He didn't know where they got the drugs, didn't ask, and just went for the ride which, other than the excitement of the first time, he did not particularly enjoy. The drugs made his victim an uncaring participant, this diminished partnership not to his liking.

His first solo unrolled during a routine date. He and girl had been drinking most of the night. Although he did not batter the girl, he still used his strength and fierce temper to achieve his objective, which proved much better than his first experience. To his surprise and relief, the police never showed up at his door.

His first violent rape, of an unknown victim, occurred almost by accident, certainly not because of a comprehensive plan. The girl, after hours of heavy drinking, decided to wrestle with him, an aggressive warm up. Things got out of hand with fists flying, and soon the blows from both parties were landing with full force. He beat her to unconsciousness, raped her and left, hoping she was too drunk to remember him or any of the details.

The police report detailed the crime with one omission: the girl couldn't remember his name or his appearance, an alcoholic fog prevailed. The pattern was now set. He proceeded with great care, meticulously selecting victims, many weeks between encounters, the incidents often not reported. He never thought he would lose control, but each incident seemed to demand a higher standard of brutality and blood. A few months after receiving his degree, he developed a more elaborate plan.

Periodic employment as a cab driver financed his early university years. Scholarship funds grew with each semester, and by his third year, he dropped this temporary work. But, the prior experience made it easy for him to rig a disguise for his car and himself, monitor dispatchers and identify the action streets.

When he communicated with the news media, he used his technical skills to keep his identity hidden; the notoriety was magnificent. The DNA and fingerprints he left didn't matter because if they got close enough to him, he would not get past an S1 interrogation without spilling everything. They were wrong when they called him reckless and sloppy; he knew exactly what he was doing and how he wanted to do it.

The surreptitious nickname he acquired at work provided an unspoken satisfaction. This backstairs tag, only spoken when he was not present, was meant to mock him, but he loved the recognition. It was almost as good as the public acknowledgment and fear that Horny Harry generated. His arrogance made it difficult not to strut around work each day with a self-satisfied grin.

His injured left hand enforced patience. His best guess: in another week it would be healed.

# # #

The Five Star Couple started planning for their last attack in this city.

Remnants of their police training and experience were evident: a city map taped to the wall, red pins marked their strikes, blue pins for Harry's attacks, and related spreadsheets documented dates, days of the week, and times of each attack.

Initially, they only recorded their kills but recently, as his activity escalated, started tracking Harry. The reason for their interest: some his assaults were close to the upscale hotel district. Harry's last attack within a few blocks of the Ritz hotel. They tried to ascertain a pattern or frequency to his activity. He appeared to regularly cruise or dump his victims, close to their preferred operating zone, which meant drawing police surveillance to the region. The best hotels were located adjacent to the large city parks, but Harry didn't leave his victims in the parks.

This afternoon they focused on the wardrobe changes, everything to be new and different: dress, hat, gloves, wigs, and no physical resemblance to previous attacks. The planning a painstaking process, detail by detail. The male partner always the most vocal, paced the floor, verbalizing new ideas and potential problems, his female partner a more composed, calm, and deliberate participant. Neither drank or used drugs, sex with each other or their victim not part of their world, unlike Harry, who was driven by his lust. But the demand for violence grew, and they both knew their demon would soon take control.

For this city, their goal became one more girl. After, they would move to a different and larger city, farther north. The target hotel was selected, but their analysis software flashed troubling correlations: Harry kept showing as a possible visitor in their area. Also, from their assessment, they concluded Harry would strike soon, too much time had gone by since his last attack, and they understood uncontrollable urges.

The female partner urged caution and wanted to leave the city immediately: any unanticipated or fluke event could be their downfall; the presence of Harry could flood the region with police. The Housekeeper was adamant they could do this, and they could move before Harry's next attack. Worst case scenario: Harry attacks and causes chaos in the area. The risk seemed to add to the excitement and pleasure; it was a challenge to a disciplined mind and superior planning.

The housekeeper decided to make this a unique send off and settled on the ritziest hotel in the district. Then he planned to engage the most upscale escort agency in the region, in total a great going away present for both of them.

After reading the latest media summary about the Five Star couple, his confidence soared, the inaccurate reporting and the floundering police a bonus. The most fundamental characteristic of their operation still eluded the cops. The housekeeper laughed and enjoyed the duplicity, his partner more subdued. The plan detailed a brief, violent encounter and then a rapid exit from the city.

The misanthropic couple never understood or appreciated the limits of man-made plans; before they left the city, fate would provide an unanticipated explosive challenge.

CHAPTER 26: CHARLIE'S LOG: THE ASSISTANT

It's been about ten days since my reinstatement, and both investigations have stalled.

First, our search for suppliers of specialized recording gear didn't yield anyone of interest. However, a local distributor volunteered to assist with a wider search pattern, and no, we didn't tell him the gear was used by Harry.

The real bitch is getting cooperation from the two west coast cities, the ones who developed the forensic crime scene investigation tools. Our attempts to tap the gossip circuit failed. Next, I tried a formal approach: filled out all the forms and requested access to their personnel files. Neither city has responded to my request.

My guess: they are afraid of a lawsuit. Why and how I can't understand; before replying, the west coast squads must have run it by their legal team and received a warning. Their reluctance appears to confirm our conclusion: someone was forced to resign, a cop with a history of using excessive force. Since these cities refuse to cooperate, the Chief has finally agreed to become involved and if need be, ask the Judge to help. We're running out of time, and this roadblock needs clearing.

This lunch stands as a unique experience for me. Ann, the Judge's assistant, is a special person (my opinion), generally reserved and on occasion intimidating. For her to request a luncheon meeting, and further, I keep the appointment to myself, turns into another mystery. She's certainly serious about the secrecy. This restaurant is miles from the Hall of Justice; the interior is dimly lit, and there are red and white checkered tablecloths. My imagination takes over, and I wait for a secret service agent to emerge from the back door.

But I keep my mouth shut and try to relax. This smart, attractive lady controls the situation, but I can't help feeling I'm about to get a lecture on the rules of good behavior. Next, I wonder: is she really gorgeous or are my standards slipping? Then, again: what the hell is the business about standards? I skip the wine and am rather pleased with myself. Being able to set limits is good.

She continues to eat, well more accurately she nibbles, and she talks about the great team, the Board, that the Judge has put together. I try not to talk with my mouth full, not to use my fork as a shovel and all the right stuff I know about but regularly forget or ignore. I know eventually, she will get to the reason for the lunch. I know it isn't because of my natural charm and sex appeal (you may not agree). She's finally finished her nibbling and begins.

"I have to inform you: this conversation is covered under the Security Act, and any disclosure of this conversation carries all the associated penalties. Alright?"

I nod an affirmative and wonder what the hell is this all about.

"The Judge needs you to solve a security problem, well actually a breach of security. He thought it best if the assignment came through me rather than you getting called to his office. This being a security breach, everyone on the Board is a suspect, including the Chief.

First, a revelation: in Board meetings when a Condition Confidential is declared the recording is to stop. Well, it doesn't. This fictional 'stop' exists as a psychological ploy someone dreamt up.

The intent or objective: a confidential declaration makes the situation more acute and reinforces the sensitivity of the issue under discussion. This fake Condition Confidential approach and the associated severe penalties significantly reduced the premature leaks which were occurring."

I'm not surprised, think it's excessive but what the hell, if it works, all the better. I don't have much time to think, let alone comment; she is pouring the stuff on me.

"Recordings are reviewed, cataloged and stored every evening. After the last meeting, when Dr. Kate declared a

Condition Confidential, our sound technician picked up some electronic disturbances. This was the third time he'd encountered some suspicious noise patterns......now don't look at me like that Charlie, I don't know or understand what he picked up. Alright?

Anyway, he went back and conducted a more thorough review of some earlier meetings and told the Judge he thinks someone on the Board is recording the Confidential sessions. As I said, this behavior carries severe penalties. Whoever is doing this is taking an enormous risk." She stops for a drink of water, and I sit there trying to look intelligent but am really concerned because I know how hard the Judge has worked in an attempt to make the Board an efficient team.

"To continue, the technician says this must be the latest and the best recording equipment on the market, a custom made job, and he was lucky to catch it. Whatever the design, the detection stations, which are built into the Board room's front entrance doorway, did not detect the extraneous hardware. The Judge needs you to find out who is doing the recordings, but you can't start grilling the Board or accusing individual members.

To start, I have background material on each Board member and can get more as you need. Of course, any wrong accusations or the news of this activity will be a terrible blow to the prestige of the Board."

She finally runs dry, and I have an opportunity.

"I understand the sensitivities and assume this means there will be severe limits on the men and resources to be brought into the case. You're nodding …meaning I might be on my own? Jesus, Ann that's an impossible restraint.

OK, first question: your technician said your built-in detectors, at the entrance door, have not been able to sense this recorder?"

She confirms the failure of the detection equipment. We both drink our coffee. She is quiet, and she waits, naturally accustom to these kinds of situations and knows when to wait. I think about our technical staff but doubt they will be any better than the group associated with the Judge's office. I don't see how I can get technical assistance without sending out some tip-off signals. Whoever sold or put together the device must be a well-connected technical guru, and if any in-depth queries start, the grapevine might transmit a warning. I go at the dessert, and she changes the subject.

"Charlie, while you're thinking I'll tell you something else. Jake Konahouse has been to see the Judge and requested your promotion be stopped or you be barred from attending Board meetings. He insists your track record proves you're not ready to participate in the dialogue and interchange which occurs at these meetings. The Judge told him he would consider his request. Jake's connections and many political allies make him difficult to ignore. I'm just telling you this in case your promotion gets reversed, at least you will know the source."

I'm upset but try to appear calm. "Thanks for the warning I'm not sure there is anything I can do about it."

She pays the bill, and we wander into an adjacent courtyard and stroll around some magnificent flowerbeds, a surprise for this shit hole of a restaurant (you can see my attitude is deteriorating). The hot sun pours through the transparent plastic dome roof, a great afternoon except for my head. She remains silent and gives me space, a good tactic at this point. After about three rounds in the small garden, it comes to me. The plan is risky, but it appears like my time on the damn Board may be rather short in any case.

"Ann, the other door in the Board meeting room, the one marked for 'Emergency Use', it's a standard door and could be used as a normal exit, if someone turned off the alarms? Correct?"

She confirms this is correct. I'm on a roll.

"I need you to confirm where it leads. I think it exits into the hallway on the south side. Right?" She confirms the exit.

"I need some time to round up equipment and staff. Don't worry; they'll not come from our police staff. When I am ready, I'll contact you with instructions, but the basics are:

the Judge will have to declare a Condition Confidential early in a meeting. This is to give you time to let me know if the device is in the room. If it is, at the conclusion of the meeting, the Judge will ask all Board members to exit via the 'Emergency' door. I'll have my equipment and staff set up and ready; the Board will pass through a revised detection system."

"When did you become a technical expert? I just told you our equipment failed to detect the recorder."

"You have to trust me on this one. I have a plan and know lots of different experts and characters. Tell the Judge I have accepted the assignment and have a plan."

She doesn't look convinced, but since the Judge wants me to tackle the problem, she doesn't have much choice. Of course, I don't tell her how I'm going to detect the recording device. If she knows the risks, she'll go back to the Judge and tell him I should be pulled off the project.

Before leaving, she asks. "Is it true they call you, Crazy Charlie?"

I laugh. "Yes, but not very often when I am present. In my line of business, it sometimes helps to have a street name that begins with 'Crazy'. If the accused knows of your reputation, it immediately provides a certain edge to any discussions. Don't worry for the most part I can decide when to allow Mr. Hyde to appear." She walks away, apparently unconvinced.

An attractive woman. Maybe I should ask her out. Screw it. Wait until I get kicked off the Board.

What the hell is going on? Right after my first Board meeting, I got called to the Judge's residence, not his office but his home and there I'm forced to accept the first secret assignment, directly from the Judge. I'm at his house in the middle of the night, a midnight job outside my scope of expertise.

Stephen appears desperate: even Ann doesn't know about the first assignment. And now, I get another secret assignment from Ann but again for the Judge.

I have the serial killer cases to solve. Plus the Judge dispenses two assignments which are not to be discussed with my boss. I can't wait until the Chief finds out.

In a matter of days, I've been escalated from clerk to super sleuth. And oh yes, I have Monk's plan for the guy on Death Row.

Jesus Christ.....I really need a drink.

CHAPTER 27: STATUTORY RAPE

Even his extensive preparation did not alleviate his anxiety.

For most of last night, Jessie reviewed the initial complaint recordings made by Dr. Grovernor. This morning he still procrastinated. Finally, Jessie pushed aside his fears and forced a start. Jessie opened the door and walked into the reception area; he held out his hand and introduced himself.

"Dr. Grovernor, my name is Jessie Lopez, and I'm a senior deputy in Legal and have been appointed project leader for your case, and this must be Sally...... hello."

They all shook hands and exchanged a few superficial comments. Jessie continued.

"Before we begin I have to explain our change in procedures. Usually, the police would conduct this S1 interrogation, but as you know, these are exceptional circumstances. Judge Miller insisted that Legal and Forensic be involved from the beginning.

Dr. Grovernor, I'm going to ask you to stay in the reception area and allow me to interview Sally. And after, when Sally proceeds to Forensic for the S1 interrogation, she'll also have to proceed on her own."

Dr. Grovernor nodded his agreement, and Sally followed Jessie into the interview office. Maintaining a professional demeanor became an issue for Jessie. The girl was a stunning model. He could not believe she was a teenager; her physical appearance was that of a 25 years old, a tall brunette right out of a fashion magazine; no wonder Dr. Max had been unable to resist.

"Mr. Lopez, my Dad explained the entire process to me. There is no need to go into a lot of details."

"Unfortunately it's these details I have to make sure you understand and, by the way, this conversation is being recorded and will become part of the official record of your case. Please sit down. I have to ensure you understand what will happen as you proceed and what will be expected of you.

First: you'll have to tell me what happened and the background of your relationship with Dr. Armstrong. After this discussion with me, there will be a short break while the Forensic team studies your comments and prepares for the S1 Interrogation. During this break, staff will take a blood sample to ensure there are no drugs in your system which may influence the Interrogation medication. Last, you will be given the Interrogation medication and encouraged to relax on a big couch. It takes a few minutes for the meds to take effect.

You will feel a little drowsy, and it's best not to get off the couch. Finally, Janice will ask you a series of questions, and you will get a chance to expand, fill in all the details of the event. When she's finished, you will have to stay on the couch for about a little while. In a small number of cases, there are some minor side effects for the 24 hours after an S1, dizzy spells, and some stomach upheaval. It is best to stay home and close to your bathroom. Any questions?"

Sally nodded and sat, relaxed in the big chair. If she was nervous, it certainly didn't show. Jessie thought her confidence and calm manner rather strange; he didn't understand this level of poise in a 15-year-old. "Alright, Sally go ahead. I may interrupt for clarification, but I'm not trying to challenge you, only trying to understand."

He didn't mention that Janice Huber, the Forensic team member who would be handling the S1, was on the other side of the mirror watching the entire process. Janice would modify their planned approach, based on Sally's recitation. Jessie also didn't tell her that the blood sample was not a standard part of a regular S1 interrogation. The blood analysis was something the Judge requested, specifically for Dr. Max, but the decision was made to keep both interrogations identical in every way.

"Dr. Max is a friend of the family and has been for years and has been in our house many times, especially when he and Dad worked together at Allied. The seduction happened a few days after my 15th birthday party; I was alone in the house….."

"Wait a minute, Sally you said the rape happened a few days after your 15th birthday. This means you're past the age of consent and no longer classed as a minor."

"I know, but my real birthday was a week later. Dad and Mom had to go to Europe on the birthday weekend, so we invited everyone early and had a big bash a week earlier than my actual birthday. Dr. Max wasn't at the party. Dad wouldn't let him attend any of our parties or dinners.

He showed up later after the celebrations ended. I was out at the pool, alone, Mom and Dad had already gone. He carried a bottle of champagne and said now that I was a grown up, I should be able to sip the cool stuff.

It didn't take long to finish the bottle, and with the music playing, we started some close dancing. Max said he should be allowed a birthday kiss. I liked the way he kissed, and it never stopped; we did it on the lounge near the pool and a couple of other times before he left, and I thought I was in love."

She paused for a moment, and Jessie asked, "Where you a virgin at that time?"

"Yes, I was. He overwhelmed with the attention and technique. Max is world famous and a great looking guy. Only after he left my doubts started. A friend happened to call, and we talked about the boys we knew and our plans for the next day, then I became depressed. I never told her what had happened."

Jessie was impressed with this recitation. "How did your Dad find out?"

"An emergency forced him to left Europe abruptly. Late the same day they got back. I was still at the pool. I just didn't feel like getting dressed and making supper. When he spotted the empty bottle of champagne, he guessed who brought it to the house.

By this time my depression and tears made him suspicious, and I told him everything. He was furious. His yelling frightened me, and I was afraid he would hurt Max. Mom was there to keep him under control which she usually does, and I tried my best with a lot of crying and begging to have him forget the whole thing. But he never cooled off, and within a few days, he went to see the Judge."

Sally, of course, had been through this presentation before, and her Dad had prepared her for an intense review. The careful delivery of each sentence and the lack of any extraneous verbiage confirmed her preparation. This was a smart, mature young girl.

"Good. I don't need anymore; the full details will be recorded during your S1 interrogation. I'll take you down the hall and introduce you to Janice Huber, who will be conducting the examination. She's an experienced technician, and you have nothing to fear.

One last warning. For serious accusations like this and under the current legislation, the consequences escalates as we proceed. If this moves on to an S2 interrogation, you should be sure you are prepared to continue."

She was abrupt and displeased with what she perceived as an insinuation. "I don't know what that means. I told you what Max did. Why do Dad and I have to keep on reviewing it?"

"Sally, it's a standard warning I'm obligated to give anyone who is making accusations which force an S1."

The preliminaries completed, Jessie escorted her out of the room, past her Dad in reception, and over to Janice Huber. On the way back to his office, his mind stayed focused on Sally, a beautiful woman, calm and self-assured.

He wondered if Doug assigned him the case because he was gay and, in theory, would not get overwhelmed by Sally. On the other hand, the case was a political nightmare, and this would be reason enough for Doug not to take a leadership role.

After Sally's interrogation, Jessie and Janice would go through the same process with Dr. Max Armstrong, Nobel Peace Prize winner, innovator, the man responsible for all the science used in Stage 1, 2 and 3. No doubt a genius resided in the university research laboratories, but campus gossip divulged: every beautiful young skirt was a potential partner.

Concern permeated Forensics; the confusion and worry revolved around one question: how would Dr. Max beat the system?

The bastard created the demoralizing, confidence-shaking ambiance which now flooded the Division.

CHAPTER 28: UNCLE WILLIE WANDERS

"Mario, the Sector team will be up to full complement by late afternoon; then they'll start executing the prisoners on death row. Maybe, just maybe, they'll uncover a few innocent men who will be able to walk out the front door."

"Warden, once they start clearing death row, I'm not sure it'll be safe for you to continue wandering, at any time of day or night." Mario, a guard at Fort Green prison for 12 years and the man in charge of the exercise yard, worried about Uncle Willie.

"The prisoners know about White Rock and the results of the executions, not many walked. Everyone knows legal appeals no longer exist. It all comes down to an S3 interrogation to prove innocence or guilt. Even the guys not on Death Row know that, eventually, their turn will come for an examination of some type."

The Warden listened to Mario and didn't stop him even though this was not news to him. He wanted to hear grassroots concerns. The rapid introduction of the new system and Amendment 33-2 fertilized the rumor mill. Where they on the edge of a prison riot? He waited, knowing Mario would eventually tell him any unpleasant news.

"Warden even the guards are worried. No one has defined our new roles. Where will we fit? Are we going to have jobs? And if so, where and what? Or, are we going to be deemed unsatisfactory for the new system. Not having the proper education, too indoctrinated in the old approach to be of any value. If we're not careful, the guards could strike or develop some work protest, work to rule, or whatever; it would be ugly."

"Mario, you can pass the word. I guarantee it won't happen. There'll be a place for everyone. My retirement doesn't start until you're all looked after." The Warden meant what he said, but he knew his promise would depend on his immediate supervisor, Jake, the son of a bitch.

Today, at 67 years of age, Willie reflected most of his years: almost handsome, short and round, with a pug nose, the beginning of jowls, a full head of curly white hair. The wrong crowd dominated his early life; the whole spectrum of trouble was on their agenda: fast cars, alcohol, drugs, early school dropout and a few petty thefts. As the group aged, they became bolder, the result being more high-risk crimes. At this point, Willie accepted the time had arrived for him to move away and change direction.

He returned to finish high school, got a part time job as a corrections officer because it allowed him to attend afternoon classes at a local university. The longer he worked in the prison system, the more comfortable he became, and he began a slow, methodical progression up the ladder. The prison population recognized someone with empathy, not cruel or vindictive. The Warden believed everyone could be rehabilitated and never changed his approach, regardless of the number of times he had been disappointed, an unapologetic straight shooter, hence his nickname: Uncle Willie.

Justice Reborn and all the preceding political debates disgusted him; he stopped reading about the evolution of the legislation, of the miracle drugs, the technology of no interest. He'd met the criteria and was legally able to retire before the full impact of the reform hit his prison. However, Jake insisted that he stay on until the first phase (Death Row) was completed.

Willie knew enough about Jake and took the demand seriously; Jake played for keeps. Although Willie's lack of a degree had hindered his career potential, he was recognized as one of the most competent administrators in the system. The Sector needed Willie's kind of experience to deal with the convict population as the prison decommissioning evolved. Some people complained the evolution was equivalent to jumping off a cliff without knowing if the water at the bottom was deep enough. Willie became the best hope to deal with any unknowns which might surface in the prison population.

Although only a few weeks separate him from full retirement, he refused to be a stationary object tied to his desk. The solitary wandering relieved the tension. His life had been a long journey and struggle, but he had enjoyed his tenure, in particular, his climb from guard trainee to the top of the heap. He knew the inmates and his staff referred to him as 'Uncle Willie,' and he was perceived as soft or too liberal and a push over for a sob story.

These halls triggered memories, and they flowed through his mind as he wandered from one location to another. The guards monitored his wandering but didn't try to engage him; their sole task: opening the security gates as he wandered, occasionally stopping to talk to a long-term prisoner or a senior guard.

He would have to be present when they cleared Fort Green death row; the thought of so many executions and bodies flowing out of this prison each day revolted him. But, Jake warned him to keep out of any debates and to allow this to happen without incident or he would find out how serious the politicians viewed this process. Jacob hinted bureaucratic errors could delay pension checks for months.

Today was not an aimless wander; he had a particular destination: to talk to Ronald Bowen. A random draw had Ron as the last prisoner to be assessed with an S3 interrogation. The Warden believed Ron was innocent, a conclusion reinforced by numerous chats with him over the years.

Since being in prison, Ron dried up, upgraded his high school marks and completed three years of University, making full use of the Internet facilities provided. His new maturity and confidence were now evident; his native intelligence, which got derailed years ago, flourished on death row. The Warden stopped at his cell.

"Good morning Ron, I see your interrogation position is set, and you've named your Watcher."

"Good morning Warden. Yes, I'm trying to get ready, but there's not much I can do. I have neither family nor any possessions so that part is easy."

"I understand you've named a homicide detective as your only Watcher. It's not my place to advise you about this policeman, Charlie Taylor. But you should be aware he has a reputation for being a hard-nosed cop. I doubt his primary objective will be to help you, and I have concerns about this choice."

Ron was quick to reply. "I don't know how anyone can help with this S3 interrogation. I requested Detective Taylor because he conducted the initial investigation of the liquor store killing. The detective who took over the case has passed away. Detective Taylor knows all aspects of the shooting, knows the man whose deathbed confession convicted me and, most important, he knows the details of my alibi. He's most knowledgeable."

The Warden continued to step over the line; no doubt Ron was his favorite. "I understand your rationale, but I think you should search for someone else. You know Forensics can allow scenes to play as long as they wish. The scanning technician does not reposition the memory probe until the Watchers signals. With Amendment 33-2, any past crime has to be assessed. A detective will force any suspicious scenes to be played out to ensure you are innocent. There must be someone else."

"Believe me, I've reviewed this many times, and I think Charlie Taylor is my best bet; I don't have many options."

"OK Ron, it's your decision. The Warden at White Rock Prison told me the recent implementation of Amendment 33-2 has made the Historians more aggressive. The mood seems to be any scene, which can implicate you in a major crime, is sufficient to allow the execution to take place.

Their attitude: on the table is a convicted killer, and when a scene appears involving a violent crime, this is often enough justification. They're in a hurry and don't need much to be convinced an execution is justified. If it's been a hectic day and they are running short of time, a short crime segment from memory may be enough….that is sufficient to trigger a final verdict. You should be aware of the fact: this Forensic team has an enormous workload."

They continued the discussion, Ron not receptive, and the Warden, over the line in a useless argument, surrendered and turned away to continue his wandering.

Ron's doubts had been amplified. He felt confident with Father Ed but different about Charlie. Their meetings consisted of three poignant encounters: once when he was a teenager, next early in the robbery investigation when Charlie was still in charge of the case, and yesterday when he came to the prison.

Charlie certainly presented as a hard-nosed cop. He hadn't projected an ounce of sympathy. His position: Monk recommended he serve as Watcher, and he would do it, nothing else, not a word about a drunken teenager stumbling down a country road. Surely Charlie knew it was this first meeting which had to be controlled.

Ron wondered: could he keep the teenage scenario from surfacing? Doubtful. The S3 interrogation started with a couple of random probes, no one in control of the locations, certainly not his neurology. An irritated brain leaked out streams of memory. Since the teenage killing frequently haunted him, one might guess it would surface quickly.

The questions were: will Charlie recognize the scene? Will he allow it to play out? Will the detective get the scanner to move ahead And, even if he does ask the scanner to move, will this happen soon enough to stop details of the night from flashing on the Historian's monitor?

He knew much of what the Warden said was right. The rampant rumors confirmed everything the Warden said. These Forensic teams were not sympathetic to convicts.

His interrogation position, as the last man, didn't appear to be an advantage. It would be late in the day on a Friday afternoon, and staff would be anxious to get out, to head for home or to the bar. A violent teenage scenario dragged from his memory would be sufficient justification. Had he been too naïve in requesting Charlie? He trusted his life to a hard-nosed cop.

Maybe he should call Father Ed.

CHAPTER 29: CHARLIE'S LOG: SAM AND RON

We're in one of the three off-lease areas the city provides for dog lovers.

I occasionally come to the park with my brother, Sam, and his dog. Sometimes I just run the park with Herbie. The heavily treed area hugs the river for a few miles. Since it is mid-week, there are not many people at the park, but there is still a multitude of different dogs, all running loose in doggie heaven. Herbie, a big dog, a lab-shepherd mix, continues to dance around us. Sam is always pushing. "Catch a good woman on the weekend? Emma? Or for that matter any woman?"

He knows damn well that I haven't bothered, but he feels obligated to keep pressuring me. I ignore him and throw another stick for Herbie.

"Charlie I don't know how you survive without any female companions. Not true. I do. You work from early am until as late as possible; then you play basketball twice a week. And to top it off get absolutely hammered two or three times a week. Did I leave anything out?"

"Give it a rest for Christ's sake. I have taken Red off my radar screen, but I think I'm turning a corner......... I have booze under control."

"Some corner. I hear you and Monk are up to something."

"That bloody Monk he is supposed to keep this confidential and already he's out spreading the word......son of a bitch." I'm upset, and my voice and body language reflect my attitude. Herbie immediately moves between Sam and me; the damn dog is smarter than Monk.

"Calm down. The three of us go away back, and Monk knows I'd never betray you. After some further thought, he was getting worried and needed to talk, and I don't blame him. I can't believe what I heard. You're going to beat an S3 interrogation for Ronald Bowen, a convicted murder?"

I didn't reply; I keep throwing stones and small branches. Sam pushes. "Well let's hear it. You've never participated in an S3 event, and you're going to be a Watcher for a murder and get him off the hook. You don't even know the guy. Have I missed something? Is this as crazy as it sounds? Tell me I am wrong!"

I'm trying to cool down. I'm not angry at Monk. More than anything, once I make up my mind, I don't want to go over the ground again and again and try to convince someone else it is the right move.

I'm rather brisk in reply. "You want in? OK, let me set the table for you: first, I think Ronald got one of the worst deals of the decade, but under our current legislation there'll not be a new trail, it's straight to an S3 brain scan. And, I will not interfere with the playback which will show the robbery and killing where he was found guilty. But there is another incident where I may be able to assist. Do you remember when I was in Grade 12 and used to ride in Mark's police cruiser on some slow weekdays?"

Sam nods. "Sure Mom was furious with Mark for setting that up and couldn't sleep until you were safe and back in your bed."

"You probably also remember the night the Parson's girl was raped and murdered…..including the drunken assholes that Mark chased until they crashed."

"I remember. The two young killers ran into the concrete abutment and ended up greasing the highway; that was the last time Mom let you ride the cruiser."

"Before we took chase, Mark stopped a rather drunk and weepy young man staggering around on his way home. Mark got out of the cruiser and talked to him. I remained in the car and watched the action. The young man Mark sent home…. Ronald Bowen……you see I met him a long time ago."

- 253 -

"I gather you're saying Ron and the drunken duo are connected. This doesn't mean you owe him a damn thing. The risk is enormous."

"I'll not try and beat S3 on the liquor store murder. I want to direct it away from that one night and get the focus on the robbery-murder. You know with Amendment 33-2 any felon on death row can be executed for a prior capital offense, even if it's not part of his original sentence. If this drunken teenage episode surfaces from Ron's memory, we don't know how the event will play out. As fragments get displayed, it might be enough for the Legal team to declare an Amendment 33-2 death sentence.

I'll try and ensure these fragments don't get prime airtime. All I have to do is recognize our old neighborhood, the park, anything which will allow me to signal that the probe should jump forward to a more recent time frame."

Sam thought for a few minutes and then came the key question. "This means Ron and the Monk have convinced you he was not responsible for the teenage rape and murder?'

I tried to sound confident. "I can't be 110% sure, but I'm very confident. I think in the worst case scenario he was a bored teenager who made a wrong decision and hung out with a couple of assholes. It seems too high a price to pay for one poor decision, and I think Ron has paid for it most of his life."

Sam throws another stick for Herbie and smiles at me. "Brother I understand and agree with the two of you but how in the hell are you going to pull this off?'

I decide to reveal some of the details of the plan. "There a lot of unknowns about the procedure, but I have been spending time with the John Wojecki, the Historian, who will be part of the Watchers' team at Fort Green. He has been telling me what to expect and the details of the process. Of course, he doesn't know why I am asking the questions.

Monk and I have reviewed all the details of that night and the days leading up to the drunk; Monk gets the information from Ron and then he, in turn, briefs me. I'm trying to develop a frame by frame sequence of the night, really of the entire week. My intent is to recognize the event as soon as possible and get the Scanner to jump ahead to another point in time.

A couple of concerns: first, with no control, any frame might surface, possibly the first scene we may see is Ron waking up, and his two buddies are still arguing over the dead girl. If this happens with all of them in a frame, I can't request a jump ahead. The Historian's presence means it's not likely I will be able to switch to a future event.

Second, Ron was passed out during the rape and killing of the girl, but I had a troubling thought. He wasn't conscious when the brothers started killing the girl.

But the other day I was channel surfing and happened to catch a specialist of some type; he was going on about how the unconscious mind absorbs and possess knowledge that escapes the conscious mind. ….events are absorbed subliminally. Just suppose, in some way, components of Ron's senses were able to capture the rape, and he absorbed and retained full memory of the event. If that happened, will we see a girl getting raped and beaten? I know this thinking is rather far out but so is the entire S3 interrogation. I'll try and be prepared for all combinations, but a scene with a dead body will have to play to completion.

Come on Sam help me out with this black magic. Events absorbed subliminally….below the threshold of the conscious mind. What can you add? Is this all bullshit? What might get captured at a level we are not aware of and are usually not able to access? Should I worry?"

Sam calls Herbie back then turns to me. "I don't know what to tell you. You're getting into an area where people question the impact of the unconscious mind on our instincts and challenge the concept of free will and rational behavior. I don't see it applying to your situation. But I'll search some of the recent research papers; my guess: there isn't anything which will provide the answers you want. I doubt any of the research has had time to relate this work to an S3 memory scan."

"OK ...it doesn't matter; I'm just venting. I'm committed in any case. How the hell could I back away at this time?"

We're at the car and Sam is getting Herbie into the back seat. "Charlie, I get nervous just thinking about this project of yours. You know they record everything that surfaces and the Forensic Team also assess each frame before they move the probe. If any questions get raised in future, they can review the material at any time, as long as the technician decided to retain that memory stream.

And some news, which it appears, has not reached you: a press release early this morning named Emma Collins as the senior technician supervising at Fort Green. This means the woman of your life, Emma will be on top of you and ready to jump on anything unusual. So to quote a famous detective I know..............Jesus H. Christ."

CHAPTER 30: ANOTHER LOOK AT HARRY

Karen's feelings reverberated: first impatience, then frustration and finally anger.

Over a week ago they'd listened to an FBI edited statement from the latest victim. The fragmented dialogue described the victim's wild encounter with a rapist, a self-declared lover. A great break but since then nothing. Within a few minutes, they would tackle a brainstorming session.

The senior detectives couldn't be released from the Five Star Couple case, but Charlie was able to bring in a detective from Sector 13, Joe Kowchuck. While Charlie went over a few details with Joe, she studied the big whiteboard. The organized collection of pictures, maps, and text summaries covered the entire board. She understood Joe reviewed the material last night, but he'd never participated in one of their brainstorming sessions, not an encouraging development. Charlie started.

"Karen why don't you begin. Joe and I'll throw in comments or questions. If we don't interrupt, keep going. You know the routine."

Karen knew all the relevant details without any reference to the board. "First, the damn recording equipment turned out to be rather ordinary or at least not specialized enough to warrant any special attention from the vendors. With the right software package, you can do wonders even with poor quality video.

We've returned to the crime scenes, but other neighborhood surveys haven't uncovered a thing. To be more accurate, I should say: we returned to the location where the girls were found and not where they were assaulted.

I'm convinced the guy used to be a cab driver. He must be disguising his car, even has a cap which looks like an old fashion cabbie hat. And he knows the city, the quiet areas, the action streets, and the locations of the high-end clubs. And last, he's not picking up ladies of the night, avoiding areas where most hookers work the street."

Charlie challenged her. "Maybe the guy is just observant. We've all been in a taxi. If he's a frequent customer and alert, this would be enough to put together a disguise."

"Yes, I'll concede that, but it's the way he cruises and gets away without being noticed. In all the cases, we have no witnesses who saw him coming or going. He blends in and mixes with the regular traffic. He seems to know his way around this city better than some of the patrol people. Moving on, two women are still alive but can't describe his face. The old taxi cap hid his face until it was too late.

His voice? Well, one girl does remember. So, if we get a suspect, this might be useful. But shit, the bugger doesn't care. We have his damn DNA."

Charlie has questions. "Is the bastard lucky? Never been caught? Or has he just started this crap? And if he just started, does this mean he's very young, and his hormones began to overwhelm him? No, I don't think he's young. If he just started, what the hell triggered him to start this rape and beating routine? If not a new game for him, how long has he been at it?"

"Charlie I reviewed our old cases and have searches ongoing in other districts. Nothing surfaces which demonstrate a pattern close enough to warrant chasing. I mean there are numerous unsolved rape cases and battered women but nothing with this pick-up routine."

Young Joe was not bashful. "Let me try some rambling. The guy's start could have been on a rather slow gentle learning curve. What if we've someone who became an occasional date rapist; you know he might force a girl after a night of heavy drinking. Most of these are never reported, our guy gets what he wants without any repercussions.

One night the girl isn't as drunk as he thinks or is just a fighter, and they get into it. He beats her up and after he's finished with her, takes a few pictures, maybe she's a prostitute, and nothing gets reported. Our friend discovers a couple of things: first, he enjoyed the beating so much Harry knows he'll do it again; last, he loves reviewing the pictures. He can now get recharged at his own convenience."

What Charlie failed to reveal was Joe's background: a Master's degree, majoring in abnormal behavior. His plan is to work as a police officer for a couple more years and then return for his psychology Ph.D. Psychologists were not among Karen's favorite people. A few years ago, a couple of cases derailed because of some shoddy analytical reports.

Charlie jumped in. "Once started, he can't get the genie back into the bottle. Harry tasted blood and doesn't want to go back. Maybe he does a couple more, still sticking to prostitutes and not killing them. Even if a beating is reported, it may not get a serious response. He may be brash with his public confessions, but I think the guy is intelligent, and it's easy to see how his photography could morph into elaborate recordings."

Joe jumps back in. "Let me take it. He wanted more excitement and ramped it up when he moved beyond prostitutes. I think he intended to beat the girls to death, the two survivors were lucky; he thought they were dead. He doesn't want witnesses. I can see this development. Our guy has never clashed with the law, maybe something minor with no formal arrest, well below any radar."

"Charlie, if you and Joe are right, I can stop searching the arrest records. He started with the cases in front of us. Next issue his frequency. I looked at the full moon schedule, and there was no tight correlation, but it does appear he strikes about every four weeks."

Joe observed. "Even though he pounded them with a pipe, he also used his fists with no protection, scrapes of his skin embedded in the faces of all the victims. I think his dormant periods are possibly related to the healing time his hands require."

"I can accept parts of the conjecture. Let me branch in a different direction. I've analyzed the locations of each incident and again no geographic pattern. So we have the dump spots and are guessing about the pick-up location. What we don't know is where the crime happened."

No response from the group. Everyone appeared to need a break. Charlie left the room, and Joe refilled his coffee cup. Karen paced the hallway. In a few minutes, Charlie was back.

"Karen, try this, draw a five-mile radius circle around the last three incidents. Center point to be where we found the girls."

Karen worked on the computer for a few minutes and then projected the incident maps onto the far wall. They all studied the maps one episode at a time. Charlie spotted a potential pattern. "If you look, within each circle, you see one our parks: Bolton Park.

At night, there is some lighting in most areas of the park, but this is the largest park in the city. It's not as good as our street lighting, and the large mature trees provide more shadows and create dark regions. This is the main reason many residents avoid the place after dark.

There are numerous entry-exit points, and some are a few minutes driving distance from our better nightclubs and expensive hotels."

Karen needed clarification. "You think he cruises in the bright lights because he wants the women to feel safe, and he wants the particular women who patronize those spots. They feel safe in the bright light. Once in the cab he subdues them, and within minutes he is into a dark region of the park which at that time of night is deserted."

Joe wanted in. "Sure and when finished he moves fast to get out of the park but not too far because he can't afford getting picked up with a body in the car. Harry drives under control and within a few minutes is out of the park, driving just far enough to find a quiet spot, a place with no one on the street and dumps the body. There is no pattern because depending on the direction of his exit from the park and what else is going on in the streets, he will encounter different quiet areas. We have a random selection of dumping areas."

"Gentlemen I won't argue with any of the conclusions, but this does not put me any closer to nailing the bastard."

Everyone was silent, took turns standing, stretching and yawning. Karen started again. "Although I agree he's probably waiting for his hands to heal, I'm sure he's anxious to attack again. We think we know his hunting region and now Bolton Park with the lighting and trees of the size to provide the shadow cover he needs. As well, we may know the color of the cab, dark green. The question is: can we get some extra patrol activity in these vicinities during the evening hours?"

Charlie wasn't sure but didn't want to disappoint her. "Karen, you analyze the park and the various entry spots and associated night-spots; give me your best guess about the most likely locations. Unfortunately, Bolton Park is vast, and there are numerous exit points but remember he'll be coming from the elite hotel-club zone.

I'll go to the Chief and see if he'll release manpower for extra patrols. I know you're hoping for more, but at least we do have a better picture of the guy and his plan of attack. And thanks Joe. Sorry, I have to run."

He made an abrupt exit with Joe hurrying after him. Charlie was right she had hoped for a better result. She knew the extra patrol was a long shot. Harry was smart, and if he spotted a patrol car, he would just keep cruising. Karen didn't understand why she wanted to nail this bastard to the point where it was almost an obsession. Sure his attacks and beatings were mean and ugly, but she had seen worse.

She knew this intense focus was not viewed as a strength. At a previous performance review, her supervisor noted: she was too fast converging on one solution or suspect and not prepared to let go when the time came to move on or change direction.

This evening she would cruise those regions where the affluent young crowd regularly sought some action. Karen reviewed the crime scene circles drawn on the whiteboard. As she stared at the maps, something nagged at her; within minutes another coincidence emerged.

Harry's last victim, circled on the board, laid only a few blocks from the Ritz Hotel where the Five Star Couple last registered. She dismissed the thought. It meant nothing; these two crimes were not related.

CHAPTER 31: DR. MAX'S INTERROGATION

Lust made logic easy to ignore.

That afternoon the bare young flesh had dominated; the string bikini and thong revealed her entire back and buttocks, a soft umber, almost black color. Her dark tan the result of many hours spent on the hot sand.

Dr. Max Armstrong was not worried about the session. The memories of that afternoon often replayed for his enjoyment: Sally lying face down on the lounge and the hot sun warming her back. He understood the danger but was confident he could control the interrogation.

In his saner moments, he thought it was time to seek some professional help because his attraction to teenagers represented a serious threat to his reputation. The man knew the line, but the damn teenager was fantastic: the afternoon had been unbelievable. Again, it had been one of those times when his attraction to young girls crushed his better judgment.

Numerous women willing volunteered to pair up, in whatever terms he dictated; his good looks, media star status, and casual manner overwhelmed many in the female crowd. His hectic research schedule controlled his life, but at recess, the urges prevailed. Months ago, he made a connection with the teenage model group, and this proved an abundant garden for him. His occasional weekends of debauchery were justified as diversions, required to maintain his grueling research workload, a means to release pressure and be reenergized.

Routine bored him. And, when he was in that state, he occasionally did something imprudent and stupid. The birthday party had not been a surprise. Dr. Max, a most respected man of science, made a conscious decision to go to the house, hoping she would be alone. A rash decision. Now it was time to undergo the embarrassment of an interrogation; this would take total concentration and great care to ensure he stayed on course.

His debriefing with Jessie had been short and abrupt. Max was not surprised they had introduced a blood test as part of the interrogation, and soon he was ready for the main session. He opened the door to the room marked 'Interrogation S1' and saw the two waiting ladies.

Janice had been introduced when he first arrived. Dr. Kate he had known for years, her presence not unexpected. The Sector needed their most senior person in charge of the entire process, from initial set up to final analysis; his denial of the charges demanded the best interrogators. He flouted his confidence as he strutted around the interrogation facility

"Dr. Kate, I want to document these sessions, before, during and after. I want to capture my feelings as the medications take control, so I have my recorder. I don't believe my comments will detract from the interrogation. Will this be allowed?"

Janice answered. "Dr. Max I don't think it will be an issue, as long as we have an understanding: I'm in control of the process. This is a criminal investigation, and if there is any confusion, your recordings stop."

Max gave Janice his winning smile. The man wanted to be in charge and couldn't stop. Kate understood Janice's irritation with his behavior, so much for seductive charm.

A well-rehearsed process began. Sally Grovernor's interrogation provided the base for Legal's recommended sequence of questions; however, their investigation scenario was only an option. An experienced technician, like Janice, made the final decision. She controlled the pace, altered the sequence and adjusted as the unanticipated occurred. It was only if the case proceeded to S2 when Legal assumed full control of the interrogation.

The physical preparation began: room temperature lowered, the lights dimmed, and Max lounged on a large couch; after the blood sample, Max swallowed the medication. Last, a warm blanket covered the accused rapist. A short recess followed, waiting for the drug cocktail to take control.

Janice sat near the couch and reviewed Legal's questions. She considered ignoring the prepared set and instead start with open-ended questions: let Max detail the incident and the relationships with Grovernor and his daughter. A structured approach with a question and answer set might give him too many opportunities to manage each response.

While they were waiting, Dr. Max began to speak into his personal recorder.

"The warm blanket is a splendid idea for relaxing, and even though the meds haven't completely taken control, I feel very calm and relaxed but not sleepy. My mouth is becoming dry but not excessive..... eyesight is failing, and I'm very sensitive to the light. I'm glad the room is dimly lit. I'll keep my eyes closed because of the problems in focusing.......result is a touch of nausea. Oh yes .....I can now feel the drugs starting to work. I want to talk.

I feel a need to explain and clarify. I want to please the world and clear up any confusion. I've no concerns about my personal safety and no concern for my reputation, image, and future, just completely relaxed and confident that nothing can touch me. I'll feel better if I tell...... and not try to be devious..... I know I can't lie...... just thinking about a lie is upsetting. I want to be friends with all of you and make you understand. I'm ready."

Janice listened to his monolog, reviewed the monitoring equipment and agreed. She was alone in the main room, Kate and Legal in the adjoining room, the entire session being recorded for analysis.

Janice decided to let Max control the flow of the story. The man was a genius and aware of all the implications and concern. Rather than attacking questions, this soft approach may get a better response; she would start this way and see how he responded, about himself and his reputation. "Dr. Armstrong, why don't you tell me your version of what happened? And why you think this all happened?"

He began: his voice now much deeper and his cadence much slower. At times, there were long delays between words, a typical reaction and not an evasive maneuver. The blunt confession blurted out, fragments, phrases, and sentences with surprising emotion.

"There is no doubt Sally Grovernor is one helluva a woman, not a girl......... she stopped being a girl when she was 13......at times, I would have given away the Nobel Peace Prize to undress her and ......well it would have been a helluva a night....... And God.......... I was close a couple of time to reaching out and stroking that magnificent ass. But Vince and I were close and I, for once, kept my hands to myself. I probably inadvertently signaled my real feelings.

You know I'm not known for self-control when it comes to young females…….. Oh, I certainly wanted that woman and……… I was very…………very close to going over the edge."

"Dr. Armstrong if all this is true, why did Dr. Grovernor and Sally bring these charges?"'

"Yes, I know it's strange. Let me go away back. I started working on my science degree when I was 15 and had my Ph.D. at 20. At University, Vince and I first met at some evening seminars. Vince had already graduated, but these sessions were open to anyone in the industry who wanted to attend.

Vince's company arranged to utilize an extraordinarily expensive and complicated testing device………a recent acquisition by the chemistry department. Even though I was busy with my Ph.D. thesis, the department assigned me to help his staff. His team struggled with the device, and I ended up doing most of the work for them. Vince appreciated my efforts and insisted on a monetary bonus; the results of this testing became part of Allied Scientific efforts to modify their products. And a year later, after my Ph.D. was granted, he asked me to join and help develop products for the company.

He's an excellent businessman and his business really blossomed. My contribution started in the lab, and we patented a number of processes and marketed a few highly profitable pharmaceutical products. The best ones were the birth control meds and the erectile dysfunction meds. I made a lot of money, but I want back to the academic life and freedom with my research ideas……..I wasn't happy. There were always presentations to make……………….. to take me away from the lab………. mind you, the wine and women were excellent.

That's when the press started on me as the wonder child who hadn't learned to zipper up his pants…………..those bastards. One fucking cartoonist published some ugly stuff …. clever and gross enough to get worldwide coverage……….. almost cost my University appointment. Thank God I had already signed up at the University before all the shit started flying."

Max stopped and drank from the supported water container. Janice was patient. "Dr. Max is this when Vince got upset when you quit his company and went back to academic to pursue the academic career?"

"No, Vince was good about my returning to a university life. I think he wanted to end the negative press and my association with his products…………… you know a horny scientist who is developing birth control pills …not a good combination…….besides, he thought he had enough brains in the lab to continue without me.

We remained friends for a long time, during my departure and after……. the Nobel Peace Prize, my appointment as Dean of the Science …….all my accolades not a problem for Vince. Shit…. I was at their home on many weekends. Vince loved to BBQ, and he's an excellent cook; it didn't hurt his company for me to be trotted out as a one-time member of his business…..Nobel Peace Prize winner etc.

Then the competition got lucky and developed competitive products at a substantially lower costs. Vince has tons of money………. but wanted more and was not about to fold his company or sell out.

He insisted I return for an 18 to 24-month stretch to tackle the cost problems. I tried to explain to him I enjoyed my new role as Dean…… and interfacing with many different branches of the academic, scientific community. He didn't believe me……..accused me of being too busy screwing anything available on campus ……..bottom line ….. he became furious and accused me of trying to destroy his company. It never came to blows, but it did get ugly, and I was told to stop coming around…..no more home visits or BBQs."

Max stopped and started to breathe a little faster. "Are you alright Dr.? Your temperature is down, your heart rate has decreased, and your breathing is rapid and rather shallow.'

"Janice just …give me a few minutes. I'm reliving the central scene…it's very stressful."

Janice nodded and adjusted her earphones to hear if Kate or Legal wanted changes. She heard Legal team wondering if Max was trying to establish some meditative state, a yoga trick to control the medication and his responses. Was he attempting to avoid something? Kate told Janice to proceed and not wait. Janice restarted.

"Dr. this is normal. Let's proceed. You have explained why Vince was angry and may have a motive to discredit or hurt you but what about Sally? She was certainly not part of the business standoff."

"You're right and here comes………… some of the nasty parts. As I said I at one time I was a regular house guest…… Sally frequently present………. about ten years old when I first meet her….. I was a recent grad who'd just joined her dad's company. I've to admit even at that young age she was aware of me and ….and yes, an element of lust surfaced in my mind …but didn't take control ….and .."

He stopped; Janice didn't push this confession; she would wait until S2 if it went that far. She continued with her strategy to allow him to tell the story.

"As the years went by, it became more and more evident she was becoming the proverbial 14-year-old going on 35. I won't go into details but you've seen her, and you can't deny she's a package. Something else which you may not uncover….. She's as pigheaded as the old man……. and if she wants something she will do anything to get it…….. a ruthless woman."

Again he stopped and slowed down his breathing, now a more measured cadence.

"Weeks prior to this birthday, Vince had stopped talking to me and had me thrown out of any functions he could influence. A few days before Sally's birthday I received a gift from one of my grad students…… a bottle of champagne. Vince and I used to challenge each other with questions about champagne, its production, its provenance, the works….. I knew this champagne to be one of Vince's favorites…………. and I thought a gift of this bottle might soften him up. I was also aware that Vince and his wife had gone to Europe.

I thought I would run it over at noon…….we just live a few blocks apart. No, no…not true, I really hoped to be alone with Sally. And lucky me.....when I got there, no one was home except Sally, who was spread out on some large piece of lounge furniture …..by the swimming pool. She invited me to sip some orange juice, and I admit I didn't give a damn about the juice…..I couldn't take my eyes off her….. in this low cut bikini. Shit, she was practically falling out of it…….there was not much left uncovered. I was explaining the bottle was for Vince, she said………'Fuck the bottle.'

It was getting too hot for me…….. she knew I'd developed an excited state. I thought it best to sneak out……. make a fast exit.

When I stood up to leave, she came right up to me and said something like……….. 'Max you have wanted to take my pants down for a long time. Why don't I help you?'…All at once her top is off and……. so is the bottom. She reaches up and kisses my like an expert, and I responded…….unfucking unbelievable. What was I thinking?………….. No blood left in my head…. my brain couldn't function. Oh and by the way, I knew it wasn't her real birthday, and she was only 14. As a frequent house guest, I'd been to a few of her real birthday parties."

Max stopped and was silent; his breathing became even again. Janice pushed. "So, Dr. Armstrong is this when you had sex with her out on the pool deck?"

"There're times when I dream I had……… but it didn't happen. Just as we're standing there in full embrace, her completely naked…… and her hand wrapped around my penis, the phone rings. And one of her friends leaves one those teenage messages…. a young girl's voice, her vocabulary, slang, and giggle …….all reminded me of grade ten kids. It was enough to return me to sanity…….. this was a kid.

I tried to back out of the scene in a graceful manner. She became extremely hostile, and it didn't matter what I said Sally told me she would tell her Dad I had raped her. I tried to stay until she cooled off, but it wasn't working. She'd been rejected and humiliated, and this doesn't happen to her. I just gave up and almost ran from the house. For the next couple of hours, I waited for the police........ when no one came, I assumed she'd calmed down, and it was all over."

"Dr. did you ever talk to anyone about what happened? Police? Friend?"

"Oh no...... What the hell could I say? We almost had sex....... she screamed and threatened me. I didn't want more press, and I was sure this would leak if I talked to anyone."

Janice noticed he was tiring, which was not surprising, after about an hour of interrogation, so she summarized. "If I understand you correctly, you think Sally is ruthless and angry over your rejection of her advances. And, this is the reason she wants to damage your reputation. And Vincent either doesn't know the truth or knows but wants revenge for your refusal to help with his production problem. Is this your position?'

Max took a little time before responding. "Yes that's it, and it's more intense than your summary. Vince will probably lose his company or have to sell and lose control, which for him means the same as losing the business. Could I have saved his company? I don't know, and neither does he, but with me as the focal point, he has a convenient excuse.

Sally matured into a female version of Vince, smart, mean and stubborn as the proverbial mule. I knew she developed some fixation on me... flattering for me.....and I did nothing to discourage it. Did I lead her on? Don't think so............ but I have to say our encounter rates as one of the most sexual charged five minutes of my life. And to finish my confession, if Sally were five years older, I would be aggressively pursuing her without let up. She's one of the few women, and I use the term women, I've ever felt would be a lifetime partner for me."

The conclusion left Janice in a quandary; he confessed that in some parallel universe he would marry Sally. The man was unbelievable, an unrepentant womanizer.

In the observation room, for Dr. Kate the confession looked and sounded authentic. He threw in enough to prove he wasn't a saint and then denied the rest. How was the bastard beating the system? He's practiced yoga since high school, also continued to make regular visits to India. Some yoga experts claim they can control the involuntary body functions; had Max reached this level or beyond? What sort of control could he achieve? Was this why he had the courage to challenge the S1 Interrogation?

His blood work will probably be clean. Max was it too good to be discovered in that fashion. His intense attraction to teenagers may or may not be abnormal, but he persisted in taking advantage of his looks and his high profile status.

In a matter hours, Kate would be in Stephen's Chambers where she knew he anxiously awaited some good news. First, she would work with Janice to run both dialogues, Sally's and Max's, in a parallel pattern, a start-stop mode, attempting to uncover anything false. Her instincts told her, she wouldn't find anything, both interrogations appeared stable. Later this afternoon she would have to deliver the news to the Judge's chambers: both parties were telling the truth. Impossible.

Stephen would not be pleased.

###

The female half of the Five Star Couple sat in the lounge with a cup of tea and listened to the pianist playing a classical piece: Beethoven's Fifth Symphony, L'Empereur, composed when Napoleon was conquering Europe.

She was conservatively dressed, a large hat, short white gloves. This was to be the next hotel visit and the last kill. She wanted to assess possible police stakeouts. The hotel certainly rated the five-star classification, and she was pleased with the setting. The interior was stunning, and, best of all, the stairs from the upper floors exited close to the large front entry doors, an easy walk to the street.

The killer could not detect a police presence which in some ways was a concern; was she missing something? Surely they would stake out some of the better target hotels. However, since he ignored prostitutes, maybe Horny Harry was the first priority, it made sense, a better utilization of scarce resources.

As well, the media reported the Prison Decommissioning project demanded more personnel. The Warden had expressed his concerns: if all the convicts were forced into an S1 interrogation, there might be a riot. As a precautionary move, some police resources had been diverted to Fort Green prison.

If resources were stretched, her partner was right; the timing was excellent: one last strike while the police dealt with all the demands.

She finished her tea and exited the hotel. One more chore. A leisurely walk around a three-block radius of the hotel. Would she spot any stakeouts on the street?

CHAPTER 32: THE SCHEMER

The schemer enjoyed the sound of ice cubes rattling against the inside walls of his glass.

A confident smile persisted, and he drained the remaining third of his scotch. A high-speed review of all his Confidential recordings revealed no further insights or opportunities. The recordings were a career-ending risk, but he hoped the appropriate gain would follow the endeavor.

He wondered about the Judge's handling of the possible flaws in the S3 Interrogation. Was Kate's analysis on the duplicates correct? His sources told him that Stephen had not informed the Regional Director about the duplicate problems, an excellent decision for the schemer, because he knew the Region was upset with the omission. Would the revised filtering software allow most convicts to be processed in under 45 minutes?

Dr. Max's situation remained a Board secret. An error in judgment? As it progressed, the issue would become complicated. When would the Judge make this public knowledge? Would his delay cause Stephen more problems with the Region?

Today he heard an error in judgment was being covered up by the Investigative Division, more subterfuge and more turmoil for the Judge. The Investigative blunder occurred when the Chief's staff used a random selection process to solve a long outstanding murder investigation. The Division blocked any announcements because the results of a 'random selection' are deemed inadmissible, regardless of what an S1 interrogation produced. Although the justification for an S1 interrogations was not stringent, the police could not indiscriminately round up suspects and subject them to an interrogation. The schemer's paid informer told him the Chief was furious and looking for a way out of the mess.

When this reaches Stephen's Chambers, he will have an ugly dilemma on his hands. If the Judge decides the results of that S1 Interrogation are not admissible, there will be a public uproar when a brutal killer is released. On the other hand, Regional had always been adamant: any Sector using 'random selection' as means to solve crimes will be severely admonished, demotions to be expected, the entire scenario a no-win for the Judge. His Sector branded as undisciplined.

All the issues would soon be in play. Nothing he could leverage, yet. There were going to be more opportunities; he had to be patient. His recordings may prove invaluable for playing the second guessing game. When the time came, he would project an image of a concerned servant of the justice system and not someone who had allowed ambition to distort his common sense.

Now, the biggest problem was controlling his emotions in the presence of Judge Stephen. He didn't understand all the reasons for his jealousy; but, whenever the Judge came forth with one of those judgments full of wisdom and empathy, he almost lost it. He saw the job as rather straightforward and had no doubt he could handle it with ease.

For now, Stephen was safe, but with so many potentials controversies he was not on a secure perch. It didn't matter if it was Stephen's fault. All the schemer required was enough to start the splattering; typically he would start with small rumors plus regular updates to keep the turmoil going. Innuendo was an excellent tool, and he was the master.

One other thing he was sure of: he knew Stephen. The Judge was such a self-righteous bugger, prepared to accept responsibility for all the world's problems and would do anything to protect the office. Given that scenario, he thought Stephen would resign quickly rather than allow doubt to build about the system or the Judge's position. Stephen didn't have the backbone to get into the trenches and take the heat, didn't understand that he had to protect himself, not everybody played by the rules.

One more explosive revelation should be enough to sink Stephen. Would the Dr. Max's case do it? If Max got through S1 and S2 interrogations, the schemer had an opening. The rumor to start: the Judge allowed the Fort Green clearance of death row to proceed even when he knew there were doubts about the validity of the interrogation techniques.

This wasn't true, but the timing was so close he could get the rumors going, and when the denials started, the opportunity for more confusion would present itself. The objective would be to create a picture of Stephen as someone so enamored with technology he was willing to gamble with lives.

Duplicate memory streams, random selections, and Dr. Max: three situations which could be manipulated into career-ending events. Plus whatever crap the Chief was trying to hide. Best to be prepared with half-truths and distorted timelines. Let the suspicious public come to their own conclusion. There was one journalist who would run with it and keep the source confidential.

He felt like sending Dr. Max a bottle of his favorite champagne. The bugger had to have the biggest libido in the scientific community. A friend told him Max had been pushing the limit for months with many young models. If there was an Olympic medal for sex drive, Max would get all: gold, silver, and bronze.

###

The Chief's anger was evident; the phone almost vibrated as he yelled his demands.

"Charlie review for me what you are doing, not all the details. The couple must be close to another attempt."

"Chief, I've a set up at all the four and five-star hotels. I don't have staff in the lobby, but the hotel staff is ready. They're to send us pictures of any woman who registers and demands the second floor and is wearing a large hat and white gloves. They're also to monitor all calls from that room until we arrive. We'll be manning a 24/7 phone, and I'm thinking about getting the same directive to the three-star hotels."

"Now what about that damn Harry?"

"Since you couldn't release more men for the park surveillance, Karen has rounded up a couple of volunteers from Vice, and they'll start an evening patrol of the area. The next step will be to try and bait him with one of our own.

The problem is, even though we're convinced it's the general area around the best hotels, it's still a large zone to cover; we'll need a few teams to have any hope of trapping him. I'm talking to Vice to see what we can put together.

Now, Karen thinks he possibly worked as a cab driver. We started to look at former employees, but there is a horde of former employees; many only worked a few shifts, maybe students working a short time to make a few bucks. On top of that their recordkeeping is atrocious; I'm surprised the income tax crew hasn't shut them down. So I'm saying this avenue is not likely to yield anything."

The Chief never commented, just hung up, the abrupt ending a sure sign of stress; the man was always polite to everyone, even his own subordinates. The gossip slipping and sliding around the building: one of the Deputy Chiefs pulled a fast one, and now the Chief was trying to recover. Charlie's busy schedule didn't allow him time to chase that rumor.

He didn't care for any of his own action plans. Maybe get some people in the lobby. No, if the killers were ex-cops, they would spot the undercover men. Leave it.

As much as his serial killers pressed him, the Judge's clandestine assignments continued to plague him; he didn't want to disappoint the Judge. First the damn secret recorder: Charlie reviewed each Board member, aided by unfettered access to confidential files. Last, he stepped through his personal assessment of each, based on his interactions and observations.

He concluded it had to be either Doug, the man who wanted to be a judge, or Jacob, the man who didn't fit with the rest of the Board. Charlie didn't have time to speculate on motivation; it was time for action. It would take time to acquire the equipment and staff. He'd have to roll the dice, a gamble the only alternative.

On top of all this, he couldn't stop thinking about Emma. It was hopeless, and he had blown it; nevertheless, she kept coming into his thoughts. Nothing he could do. And once she found out he'd run a clandestine operation on the Dr. Max interrogation, possibly undermining her friend Dr. Kate, she'd probably turn her back on him forever. The two ladies were really close.

The Judge refused to allow to coordination with Dr. Kate; he wanted two entirely different lines of attack, independent thinking. The problem: Charlie's thinking was getting nowhere. No matter how many times he reviewed the Interrogation recordings, he couldn't detect how Dr. Max achieved the impossible, circumventing the S1 Interrogation, lying to Forensic staff.

Of course, the Chief would be furious when he found out the Judge had not informed him. But since the Judge was safe, the Chief's fury would be turned in the other direction, right at Charlie.

All these problems stuck to him, no hand-off possible. Every issue belonged to him until resolved or he was demoted. Best get going and round up the detection equipment to catch the Board recorder. If the equipment worked and he guessed right, one problem was solved. If not, best not to think about that outcome.

CHAPTER 33: THE JUDGE, KATE AND JANICE

Only three people occupied the room, but his Chambers felt crowded.

Even in the late afternoon, the hot sun forced the Judge to keep all the drapes pulled shut. Stephen looked in Kate's direction but avoided direct eye contact and kept his voice neutral, for him she would always be an attractive woman. She'd been divorced for some time, but he knew he would never follow through on his feelings. He thought about their affair and how it fit the classic pattern: an explosion of reckless passion, then more intimate lovemaking, followed by a more sedate period. When a friend warned them their affair could soon become common knowledge, they walked away from each other, a mutual decision. The problem was the feelings did not disappear as quickly.

Now years later, he's selected her for his Board. A wise decision? At times his desire flared and this concerned him. She never gave him any indication she would be interested in resuming an affair. Stephen knew it was over, time to grow up. His wife remained steady as a rock, a political strength and could work a room better than him. No way would he endanger that support.

Kate and Janice settled in his office; the time arrived to assess progress on the Dr. Max interrogation. Both ladies looked haggard as if they had missed numerous hours of sleep. While the Judge reviewed the reports on his screen, Kate's memory took a fast trip, and she remembered the first time she saw him.

She never told him, maybe she never admitted it to herself until now, but there'd been an immediate attraction; he was tall with an athletic frame and had a reputation as someone destined for success. Even today, she found it hard to believe that the one night led to such an explosive and wild affair. She often regretted the mutual decision to end it. A stern Stephen never tried to lure her back; did he regret the decision? Well, at least she had Sonja, a daughter who was a first-class student.

The Judge finished reading the report and looked across his desk at the two women. Janice a tall, handsome woman, in her mid-20s, maintained an active social live on her way to becoming one the best forensic technicians in the country; she would soon be doing S3 interrogations with Emma. Kate explained the results of the S1 examinations of both Sally Grovernor and Dr.Max.

"Judge, according to the results of S1 both stories are true. We've reviewed the recordings and watched both people respond to questions and react to challenges. Everything appears correct. I can't detect any anomalies. Janice, do you want to add anything?"

Janice spoke softly but with the confidence of a well-trained technician. "I can only say what we all know: the next step will be to proceed to an S2. We only move to an S2 when an individual is fighting off the S1. These are usually addicts with a long history of drug abuse; they have higher tolerance levels and need a different concentration.

Also, when an individual is struggling during the interrogation, it is obvious; he fights every answer and responds with abbreviated bursts, short disconnected phrases. Our monitors detect the stress with high blood pressure and extensive sweating; we detect the anomaly and know the results from that S1 may not be accurate. This was not the case with Sally or Dr. Max. They both provided standard responses, and it's all normal."

Kate knew what the Judge wanted to hear. "Stephen, I don't know how Dr. Max manipulated the system. I know he's yoga master, and this may be a factor. We'll start research in this direction. Regulations require 24 hours for the S1 drugs to leave their systems and then we can proceed with an S2 Interrogation. If our research doesn't provide any immediate answers, I wonder: could you proclaim an additional delay is necessary?"

The Judge sensed the frustration but as always lived with the standards. "Unless you can come up with a medical reason to prove it's unsafe to proceed, you have to stick with the 24-hour time limit; we have no alternative and remember Dr. Max knows all the medical implications so we can't run a fast one by him....sorry."

Kate struggled but was still trying. "I do have one avenue which may prove of value. A visitor from Japan who is a yoga expert and has also studied and lived in India for many years. As good as Max? I don't know.

This medical doctor showed up at my door yesterday. I knew he was coming but completely forgot; Japan wants to assess our approach, witness the Death Row clearance and all aspects of Justice Reborn.

He's brilliant and might be able to provide some insight into yoga as a possible answer to fighting off the impact of our S1 drugs. I'll try to talk him into an S1 interrogation and see if his yoga skills will allow him to control the session. If it sounds like I am grasping ...well I am!"

No one spoke; the room remained silent for some time, and finally Stephen summarized. "As you both know, these results are shattering. You have to find an answer. I don't have to explain the implications. Proceed with the S2 and

- 292 -

please feed me information as it unfolds, even preliminary observations. Don't wait for a final report.

I've two contacts at another university and will talk to them about other experts we may be able to solicit for help. I have to remain optimistic. I won't keep you any longer."

It was an abrupt ending. Stephen watched both ladies leave, not a good ending; their body language spelled: defeat.

What he never told them: he'd given the problem to Charlie when it first surfaced, a clandestine mission, assigned late in the evening in his home office. Maybe this was beyond Charlie's abilities. But the Judge desperately needed someone to take an unconventional approach, apart from technology, someone who would go outside the conventional boundaries to abuse rank and privilege in search of the answers.

Charlie numerous contacts reached beyond the academic community. A desperate move. At times, he seconded guessed his decision. Why had he bypassed the Chief? Another questionable move but the secret recordings had erased all organizational lines.

In the end, he knew he would have to pick up all the pieces, and it appeared most of the pieces would belong to Charlie, who was beginning to look like he was ready for two or three days of hard drinking.

CHAPTER 34: CHARLIE'S LOG: THE BLOWUP

I'm in a mood dangerous to myself and my surroundings.

Wes recognizes my disposition and dispenses with any conversation; we're in the elevator heading down to the ground floor and back to my office. Moments ago, we finished 30 bloody minutes with the Chief, and he's not pleased with the two high-profile cases. I tried to explain that we may be on to something, but he merely kept ranting; he sure as hell was not listening. What the hell is wrong with the guy? I think he keeps me around so he can blow off steam at will, knowing I'm vulnerable and not likely to deliver a vigorous protest.

The progress on the Five Star Couple has stalled; the personnel data we requested from the other cities has not arrived. The Chief claims a formal request was delivered to both cities and ensures me, we'll see the results tomorrow.

Next, Horny Harry: the idea of a high-end recording gear proved to be a useless clue; the special cameras and sound equipment is standard stuff and is sold all over the world. Christ, you can hide the damn thing in your shoe and record your boring after dinner walk.

To cap it off, the bloody Chief still refuses to authorize extra patrols for Bolton Park, insufficient evidence the excuse. I haven't had a chance to call Karen; she'll probably patrol the area on her own. Her Vice volunteers were ordered to stand down, against Vice Department regulations.

The irritating complication: I can't talk to the Chief about the Judge's assignments. I understand the Judge's priorities, and I appreciate his security precautions. But by keeping everything to myself, I've accumulated a lot of pressure and also confused my squad who don't understand why I'm delegating significant segments of work on our most important cases.

The Judge wants me to aggressively pursue the Dr. Max case plus the damn secret recording in his Board Meetings. I end up with two challenging and technically oriented cases; technology is not my strength. Oh yes, I can seek technical help, but I can't reveal all the details. Jesus Christ!

The Dr. Max situation will probably end up as a shit storm because the Forensic Division is the project manager, running the case in the prescribed manner, and I'm running a parallel covert investigation. And, the goddamn secret recording case appears hopeless; the only idea I have is the one that surfaced during my first lunch with Ann, the Judge's assistant. I'm gathering the players and equipment to implement that idea. I don't like the choice; the risk's too big.

I need some technical help; but how do I get help without explaining the secret recordings?

All this cloak-and-dagger work means little sleep. I'm tired, and the idea well is dry; my favorite way to generate new ideas and create new channels is brainstorming with the crew, no longer possible. Jesus, I'm getting a headache. I forget to mention I'm not drinking.

The topper is rather mundane: I'm hungry. I haven't eaten a thing since my meager breakfast, and it's well past my evening meal. Add it all up, and it means: I'm ready to kick ass: anyone's.

The damn elevator stops at every floor: one asshole gets off, and another asshole gets on for a ride to the next floor. Asshole on, asshole off, way we go. Just my day. The door opens and in steps Jake the head of the Prisons Division and his female assistant with an armful of files; it doesn't take Jake long to start laying on the sarcasm.

"Look Helen, it's Batman and Robin. They're searching for clues in the Hall of Justice building elevator, not a corner will be missed. How's it going boys?"

Wes and I don't respond. The idiot doesn't know when to stop and continues to talk to his assistant as if we're not present. "It's a shame the so called homicide squad in this city can't catch the Five Star Couple; the city is terrified, and still we have detectives riding around elevators and doing other important stuff. When five-star hotels become killing zones, it's a tragedy. My wife is terrified."

I glare at the asshole. "Your wife is terrified?"

Jake moves right into my face. "That's right Charlie, but you wouldn't understand."

I've had enough today and let him have it. "Jake my friend she has nothing to fear, unless........unless she's gone back into the business and is going up to hotel rooms and wrapping her lips around some stranger's big kahuna."

Wes grabs my sleeve and tries to pull me away. Jake's face is flushed; his assistant is looking at the floor. We hit the ground floor, and when we all enter the main lobby, I let him have the rest.

"Jake just make sure she washes up when she gets home.......you know .... she has to give Miss Pussy a good rinse.......let me show you." I bend over a little, spread my legs, and move my hands under my crotch as if I was waving a hose with a stream of water.

"Just remember, full pressure on the hose and give Miss Pussy lots of water and that hotel stuff will run right off."

He walks two steps closer but is barely able to talk. I know he is very proud of his young wife.

"Taylor you're finished. There are too many witnesses this time. You're finished!" and with that, he turns and walks toward the main entrance.

But I'm not finished and go for a parting shot. "Be sure to give her our love and kisses."

This last comment I punctuate with a few kissing sounds and loud smacks of my lips, a number of times____smack, smack, smack___ loud enough to carry to the front. There is a small crowd in the front entrance, some heads turn.

Wes and I walk down the corridor to my office. "Boss you are the craziest bastard I've ever known, and when the Chief hears about this one, it'll be ugly."

I raise my hand and stop him. "Jake and I have a history, and he won't let it go. I try to give him all sorts of space, but he keeps coming back."

We continue to the office. I know this is a bad one. A mistake. I shouldn't have done the pantomime with the damn hose and the smacking lips a dumb move.

Jesus Christ. What a mess!

CHAPTER 35: RANDOM SELECTION

They had identified a killer and the burial grounds for six young men.

Doug Brewster, head of the Legal Division, was elated. But, Chief Duncan Stirling sat at his desk, staring into space in an angry mood. The news about the killer would be a bonus for him and his Division; his staff solved the crime. So Doug was confused. "Come on Duncan, why the long face? This is great news."

The Chief put down his coffee and walked to the window. He was gaining control. "Let me start at the beginning; it doesn't excuse what happened, but at least you'll understand how it occurred."

"Jesus man, now you have me scared. What the hell is going on?"

"Be patient. If I can tell the story from the beginning, it helps. For the past year, an irritating series of incidents plagued our northeast quadrant, some serious, some just bullshit small stuff: everything from rolling drunks to rape. We thought it was the same two or three guys, but they were fast and shrewd. Eventually, with the help of some new software, we isolated their home base to a four square block section in a northern district. Although we were sure this was their home base, we didn't have a good plan for proceeding, other than an increase in surveillance. "

The Chief stopped and drank his coffee. Doug thought he must be getting to the good part because he was having control problems.

"Last week the Regional Conference tied my up for a few days and kept me away from the office. Christ, it was only four days. My back up, my second in command became upset with the vigorous neighbor complaints and decided we had been procrastinating for too long. My brilliant team member decided to surround the entire area and round up all the males who were in the right age bracket."

Doug couldn't believe the news. "Oh shit, his frustration was his justification? Tell me he's not that dumb. Surely he knows that the 'random selection' clause means the police can't pick someone off the street and start using the S1 Interrogation."

"Sorry, I'm not sure what happened for him to leave his senses. And I don't know why the rest of the crew followed without protesting. In any case, once they had a couple of cells full of candidates and after some verbal interrogation and checking of alibis, he ended up with 15 guys who needed more follow-up. My assistant organized an S1 inquiry for all of them. Your staff was given some bullshit story about the group."

"Son of a bitch. I can't believe where this is going."

"In the group we did uncover the two who had been terrorizing the neighborhood; but, with no substantial justification for subjecting them to S1, I ordered these two released; you concur? Good."

The Chief turned, marched to the big screen on the back wall and loaded a recording. He hesitated before starting the video. "Here is the stunning part of this goddamn mess. I won't play the entire tape for you, just enough for you to get the flavor. I didn't release everyone out of the 15 we grabbed; I'm still holding one in the back cells.

As you see this guy, he has already been administered the drugs for S1. His reaction to the drugs turns him into a happy drunk. Some of his words are slurred, and he looks and acts like he spent all day in the bar; he wants you to be his friend and wants to share with you. Are you ready? Here we go."

The video displayed a mature male, around 40 years old, some hair loss, glasses and carrying a few extra pounds. He certainly sounded like he was drunk; his name was John Ryan, the introduction went quickly, and then it started with a leading question.

"John, it is my understanding that you have been a naughty boy."

"Yes….Yes, I have been …in fact I have been very naughty……oh yes I have been a real bastard…..well not all the time ….only on the anniversary …"

"John, that's a good start. I'm glad we're friends, and we can share some our troubles………….. tell me more about the times when you have been very naughty."

"God it's good to have an understanding friend….Oh God where to start……ok let's go with the first one…. just a kid in my mother's neighborhood. I'd been house sitting the neighbor's place, right next to my mom's home, while the neighbor went on her annual jaunt down to Mexico for a few weeks. The kid snuck around after dark, looking for a free beer and some bullshitting. His parents didn't seem to be worried about his hours.

One night we started sharing some beer and a few joints…..when he got drunk enough, I made my move…………he'd been giving off signs all week ….. but now he resisted ….that really pissed my off …the first thing I know he's on the back porch dead. The bugger should have relaxed and let me ……well now I had a problem …the body.

I was lucky. I'd been building a small patio off my mother's back porch. It was a dark night, and he was easy to carry over to mom's back yard. I dug the base a little deeper and buried him. At 8:00 am next morning the concrete truck arrived, and he was part of the patio."

"John, didn't anyone question you?"

"Oh sure, there was a massive search for the kid. But two things saved me…..one he always came after dark, and no one saw him…….second some noisy woman at the end of the street swore she saw him get into a red SUV earlier in the evening.

Mom came home, and I went back to my neighborhood, out of the area. The cops kept combing the area, but of course Mom was so innocent they just left her alone……..see I told you I was naughty."

"But John, you said very naughty, and you mentioned the anniversary."

"There are five more ……..I just do one annual on the anniversary of the first …I"

Chief stopped the recording. "This asshole goes into great detail how he plans each birthday; how he selects the boys and where he puts the bodies; Mr. Ryan has been expanding his mother's patio for the past five years. She still lives there, but we have not moved on this information."

Doug understood. "We have a killer of boys, and we know where the bodies are; the problem is all this information was acquired using an illegal interrogation. And, the unspoken question is: what the hell do we do next? Let him go? Dig up the bodies and not tell how we knew? Arrest the bastard and proceed to the S3 Interrogation?"

Both men looked at each other. The silence did not last. Doug started.

"You know Chief there are a few politicians who are pushing to have random interrogation passed into law. However, the strong opposition argues this is one more step toward a police state. The issue comes up on a regular basis, and the debates are intense. So far, no resolution or worse for us, at this time, random interrogation is not legal."

"Goddamn it, we can't let this guy walk. Isn't there anything in your bag of legal tricks?"

"If you're prepared to support me and take some of the heat, here is what I propose: first, suspend your supervisor without pay pending a formal review. The suspension will send the message you do not support his decision.

But my primary strategy will be to develop a series of unconfirmed news leaks which raise hope that the murders have been solved. The stories can escalate but always will be unconfirmed and denied. My delicate task will be to manage two reporters.......I trust them and have utilized them for other breaking news stories.

The problem will be: how to frame the story to ensure the random interrogation doesn't surface immediately. First, a rumor will suggest a suspect is in custody, and the victims' families have to be out front and pressing for more information. We'll have to stonewall any questions as long as we can.

The rumors will create a lot of pressure on the both of us; we must take the heat. When it appears that the street is prepared to lynch the guy, I will leak the difficulties in prosecuting because a random selection occurred. I predict at this point the public outcry will be massive, and the implications of an illegal interrogation will be considered very minor. This guy has no redeeming qualities which will cause someone to take up his cause.

Last, I'll bring it all to the Judge. My position will be: we held back because we were hoping we could come up with some way to legally arrest the guy. We were playing for time and hoping. I don't know if the Judge will buy it; he will be furious for being kept out of the loop for so long. But given the political climate and public outrage, I'm not sure he can't do anything except use his annual discretion."

The Chief wasn't sure. "Review this with me……. this annual discretion. How far can the Judge go with this authority?"

"Ok, it's a misnomer and not an annual event. It means the new legislation allows a Judge to use his discretion to allow an S1 Interrogation, even if there is insufficient evidence of guilt. There are no restrictions. But the understanding is: it would only be used in exceptional circumstances, and if used too often, the Judge has to answer to Regional.

But the bottom line: he overrides the need for a formal justification before an S1 interrogation. Every Judge is extremely reluctant to use this option and insists he is informed before an individual is targeted for this type of Interrogation."

"Goddamn it. I'm with you, but you're going to have to script this all the way. One wrong press release and I see trouble. I have to run. First, I've a supervisor who needs his ass rearranged. The rest I leave to you…...shit …. what a goddamn mess. ….I'm sorry… I've to run. They're screaming for me to get upstairs." And with that the Chief was gone.

Doug smiled, pleased with his performance, his feigned surprise, his acute indignation. What he hadn't told the Chief was: this random selection screw up was already common knowledge for those with the right connections. He had been well prepared before the Chief even requested a meeting.

He knew it wasn't going to be as easy as he described. His ability to manage the press leakage would be most difficult. The Judge would be furious: first with the Chief for the random selection, and he would guess Doug set him up, so there was no choice. Stephen would see Doug as someone who could have come to him at the beginning.

By withholding the information and allowing the public frenzy to build, it would appear the Judge was a reluctant participant and only used his discretionary powers because his hand was forced. Not because he wanted justice served.

Doug understood all this; the Chief had not have picked up on the undercurrent; he was just anxious to get the case off his back. For Doug, this became a golden opportunity to demonstrate his prowess as an aggressive legal mind, attuned to the public's needs and able to deal with the tough cases.

He knew that some of his distracters thought he was an artificer, too ready to bend and twist for personal gain. This, he was sure, was Stephen's opinion as he seemed to force Legal into lengthy debates over many of its recommendations.

###

Harry had enough for one day. When he thought back to the last one, he began to grin. Yes, the result had meant a vigorous cleanup of the cab's interior, but her aggressive fighting was turn on Harry enjoyed. God, she was a prize; boy he was almost ready for another one.

He needed a diversion; he had the answer, walked down the hall and into the bedroom, to the five-drawer chest and the third drawer from the top. Under his folded sweaters the recordings. Soon this drawer would not be able to store his entire planned collection He selected the most recent and on the way to the living room stopped to grab a couple of beers.

He started a ritual which ranked as his best diversion: all the lights out, drapes pulled, beers at his elbow, in his big lounge chair, and his pants off. He always hesitated to allow the tension to build. When his imagination triggered a stirring in his groin, he pressed: play.

CHAPTER 36: ANOTHER SPECIAL BOARD MEETING

The Dr. Max case annoyed and troubled Emma.

She'd arrived early and paced the halls. This new science had commanded extensive amounts of her time. She relished the challenge, developed new procedures and completed numerous brain scans to a point where within a few minutes she could, in most cases, determine the underlying memory storage patterns. Now it all appeared to be based on a faulty foundation.

First the damn duplicates and now Dr. Max challenging his own system. If he could beat S1 and S2 interrogations, what other deficiencies existed? It appears Dr. Armstrong was rather selective in what he chose to publish. With the damn duplicates, he made sure the early detection was well buried so no doubts would surface to challenge his brilliance.

This unresolved rape could destroy the entire system, S1 and S2 interrogations deemed inadmissible. These doubts would migrate to S3 memory probes; the result would be chaos, the impact unimaginable. All her efforts for nothing. She avoided thinking about the prisons because those interrogation scenes swamped her in a turmoil of doubt and guilt. Did innocent men get executed?

She was alone in the hallway, but soon the front door would be a busy passage as the other attendees arrived. Emma's mood didn't match the desired camaraderie for a meeting of senior personnel, but there was no option. For this emergency meeting, the Judge's assistant had been adamant: attendance mandatory.

Staff arrived as singles or pairs, and as it would happen, Charlie and Jake met at the entrance. Charlie tried to avoid him. He never had a chance. Jake walked up to him, physically bumped him and declared: "You idiot. It's only a matter of time. Your career is destroyed. This is a promise."

Charlie hustled to his chair next to the Chief, who had witnessed the interchange.

"Charlie, what was that all about? If you insulted Jacob again, you could be running out of support. Everyone knows what he is, but his political support is strong: he can't be budged. Best to suck it up and let him win the exchanges or he'll bury you. Are you listening?"

Charlie unsure about the Chief, still couldn't believe the Chief had bailed him out of the basketball game incident and then promoted him. Before he could reply, the Judge entered and immediately went to the front of the room, and his demeanor told everyone: let's go, no preliminaries, no warm up topics.

The Judge's assistant, Ann, occupied her spot at the front table; she saw Charlie waving a negative, she understood not to use the 'emergency door' as departure portal. All support staff in attendance.

"I'll start by declaring this a Condition Confidential and note all recording has been suspended for the entire meeting. We have a situation which threatens to destroy Justice Reborn and all the advances we have made. I'm, of course, referring to the Dr. Max Armstrong case.

What happened is theoretically not possible. Dr. Max and his accuser young Sally Grovernor have been processed through both an S1 and an S2 interrogation; we used our best technical staff with Dr. Kate observing the sessions and reviewing the results after each interrogation. The results are extraordinary. Both people tell different stories: one describing an underage seduction and the other a story of unfilled lust but no wrong action, the result a young woman spurned and angry.

The point: both stories told under the influence of our drugs in a controlled setting appear to be true. The fundamental question: how is Dr. Max controlling the results? We know if he finds it interesting or a challenge, this genius is capable of almost anything."

Around the table people shifted in their chairs, shared disapproving looks with colleagues, shaking their heads in disbelief, and muttered curses. All understood the implications of what they were hearing, an absolute disaster.

Doug Brewster commented. "Judge, I think Max set this up to flash the entire the world: see the genius. Once safe under a not guilty verdict or plea bargain, he will confess and tell us how to fix the system and get back on track. The bastard is all ego and needs constant attention. The more outlandish the press coverage, the more he glows. This is a setup."

"Doug, I don't dispute your character analysis, but this seems too high a risk and too wild even for him. Are you saying he had sex with an underage girl to prove a point? That doesn't make sense. He can't be that irresponsible. Chief you want to add something?'

The angry Chief blurted. "Judge, I know Doug's comments appear to be at the far end of the solutions but consider some facts. We are aware Max lusted for this girl for some time. I think he did know her date of birth. My point is all he had to do was keep his pants on for a week and then go after her, his relationship with Dr. Grovernor no longer an issue.

I think the girl wanted him. Why the hell doesn't he wait a few days? This makes me support Doug's theory. I think Max planned this, but am not sure what the hell his motive is or what his overall plan is but I'm sure the glorification of Max is part of it."

The Judge sympathized with their frustration. "I'm going to have to cut this off and give you the rest of the news. I told Dr. Grovernor if he wishes to prove the charges, his only choice is to proceed to an S3 brain scan. Instead, he and his daughter have withdrawn the charges and are prepared to drop the incident.

This leaves us with a question as to the efficacy of S1 and S2 Interrogations. If these Interrogations are not absolute or are capable of being manipulated, then Justice Reborn is finished, and previous guilty cases are in question. At this point, I thought the situation couldn't get any worse. But I was wrong."

The Judge stopped, dropped his head, not utterly defeated but close to the edge. He looked up, in Kate's direction. "Dr. Kate will you please inform the Board about the most recent development."

Emma was shocked at Kate's appearance. Her hair was unwashed, her clothes were the same ones she was wearing for the last two days, and the circles under her eyes were almost black. She spoke softly with a hoarse voice; the room strained to hear her. This woman struggled through each escalation of the case. She clenched her hands together to control the trembling.

"When I told Dr. Max all charges had been dropped, he wanted to know why. I told him about the results and that Sally would not go through an S3 Interrogation. He was furious. Although speechless for a few minutes, he soon started ranting; I won't play the recordings for you…… it boils down to his one decision.

Dr. Max demands he be put under the S3 brain scan to clear his name. He knows the risks but insists we can use a 30-minute clock to stop the interrogation, to ensure it doesn't become a prolonged session."

Kate continued to stumble with the explanation, and the Judge intervened. "Allow me to continue. Our problem is we can't refuse Dr. Max. He's been accused, and it's his right. The decision to proceed to an S3 causes our Sector a couple of fundamental challenges: first, can he beat an S3 interrogation and utterly dismantle the remainder our system?"

"Second, even if we keep the interrogation under 45 minutes, there is no guarantee he will not suffer brain damage. We, then, become known as the Sector, who destroyed a Nobel Peace Prize winner, a man the President considers a national treasure."

The Judge stopped and gave everyone a chance to catch up; Charlie had a hard time suppressing a groan but only mumbled a few silent profanities.

"We can't stop him. I've been able to delay his S3 interrogation with excuses about our work on Death Row and the associated constraints on staff and equipment. Dr. Max has to wait. The delay provides a small window to try and find out how he beat the S1 and S2 interrogations.

Dr. Kate is working with a scientist from Japan. All other resources have been contacted, but many of the experts are friends of Dr. Max and reluctant to come forward.

The expert from Japan, a yoga guru, has agreed to submit to an S1 interrogation. The intent is to determine if he can control the questioning. Published research confirms his ability to regulate his heartbeat and some other involuntary body functions. Will he be able to establish a mindset which will allow him to lie and tell stories or will the S1 drugs control him?

I could go on, but you see the situation and understand why I ask you to ensure your staff gets this message: if Dr. Kate has a request it must be treated as top priority. There are no clocks. You must manage our operation as a 24 hour day, and the cost is not a barrier.

You're too smart for me to repeat any of this, just make sure your staff understands. But the reasons remain top secret and can't be revealed at this time. Are there any questions?'

It was an abrupt ending; no one asked a question. Everyone too stunned? Frightened? Confused? The Judge didn't wait long.

"Alright, this meeting is over and let's hope our next meeting has some answers." And with that comment he left, and the rest of the team filtered out; no one went over to speak to Kate.

Charlie, a subdued detective, waited until they all cleared the room. Ann, the Judge's assistant, had set up another secret meeting early in the day, Charlie's instructions were to wait until the others left before proceeding down the hall.

Ann ushered him into the Judge's chambers thru a side door; Stephen sat, waiting, sipping coffee. "Charlie, help yourself. The coffee and tea are on the table. Ann that'll be all right; I can take it from here. Thanks." Ann closed the door, and Charlie was alone, again, with one of the most powerful men in Sector 14.

"I assume you've not made any progress on Dr. Max."

"No I haven't, and I can't say I feel comfortable about this assignment, Judge. My science education stopped with Grade 12 chemistry, and you've put me up against a whiz kid."

"I understand. I want you to go at this problem from an entirely different angle than Kate and her team. Your technical limits will force you to search in different directions. You know we don't even have a proper understanding of why this all took place. Yes, I know about Max's past, but the timing of this last incident bothers me. I'm convinced logic and science will not be enough.

What about our other problem? Ann tells me that you will be requisitioning some specialized equipment and resources. She doesn't understand and is concerned. Can you share with me just what you have planned to catch our recording pirate?"

This was the conversation Charlie hoped to avoid; his philosophy being: it is easier to beg forgiveness after the fact than to try and get clearance ahead of time. How would the Judge react? He could stop the entire process. "Judge, I wonder if it would be better if you let me proceed and if it doesn't work, take the lumps?"

The Judge thought it was time to press. "No, I have to know what you have planned, and how I fit into this operation. I need to hear, and I mean all the details."

For a few minutes Charlie stumbled, but once warmed up, he explained his approach and the rationale behind it. It didn't take too long. The Judge always a good listener, meant there was no need to repeat either the explanation or the details. The Judge looked at the detective for a long time.

"Charlie, remind me never to play poker with you."

CHAPTER 37: AN ULTIMATUM

A sliver of sun flickered on the horizon, an unusual time for a meeting.

Jake insisted it could not wait, and Stephen accommodated him with this dawn meeting. The Judge waited for his visitor to begin. Jake appeared nervous, an unusual state, because with so many well-placed friends he rarely worried about the Judge's opinion or assessment of his performance. Nevertheless, Jake started on a shaky tone. "Judge, I promised to inform you of modifications being discussed for the Citizen Team. If there continued to be disagreement, I believe you wanted a chance to address my working group."

"Jacob, I hope your group is still open to alternatives. I want to be sure your team is aware of all the legal implications and Sector limitations."

"Judge, you know most of this, but there have been some changes; so let me summarize our current situation. Since juries have been dropped from our legal system and the death penalty demanded by society, the Region decided citizens should participate in executions, in other words, become the Execution Team.

On each Citizen Team, we have three members of the public; they all push their button on Legal's command, but only one button releases the fatal dose, and no one knows which button is deadly. We've not had a problem, as some pundits thought, filling individual teams; in fact, we have lists of volunteers, some prepared to pay to get named on to a Citizen Team."

While Jake searched his material, the Judge was getting impatient. "Then I don't understand the problem. I know you have been allowing some to be exempt on various grounds. It looks like a smooth operation."

"On the surface, the process looks solid, but it's after an execution when problems surface. Some people began suffering from a type of guilt complex. After an execution, some participants complained about depression, problems sleeping and doubts about the role they played. We've stopped the news media from playing it up, but with another set of mass executions, the complaints may become more strident.

Our new proposal is: the Citizen Team be provided a large wall mounted monitor. Once the crime scene has been isolated, and Legal has certified the situation, the crime scene is to be played out for the Citizen Team, on the big screen, in full color.

Before the execute command, the Team will witness the crime unfold, watch from start to end. Many of these scenes are extremely gruesome. They'll see it all and hear it all. Our belief is once they see the victim and all the suffering, it'll be difficult to feel any sorrow or empathy with a killer, no matter how handsome he is or repentant he appears. I've run it past a couple of psychologists, and they aren't 100% convinced but are prepared to support the change during our death row sessions."

Jake stopped; he knew the Judge needed time to consider all the implications, "Jacob, I will need some time to think about this change, but I agree. Let's use this approach at Fort Green but be sure there is a solid follow up. Now there must be something else for you to demand this early meeting."

Jake stood up and handed the Judge a video package. "A few days I was insulted in a public place by Charlie Taylor. This is a copy of the event as captured by the security camera in the lobby. You'll be able to see and hear most of the incident. Also, my package includes the sworn statements of my assistant and two security guards who were in the vicinity when this all took place. I know the Chief thinks he needs this character, but his behavior doesn't warrant the promotion. In fact, I don't see how you can avoid demoting him down to the lowest rank. I recommend you demand his resignation."

Although surprised, the Judge maintained his composure, but his terse reply sounded inadequate. "Leave it to me, and I'll give it my immediate attention."

"Stephen, I know where I stand in your assessment, and I also know you're one of Charlie's supporters, but I want to make this very clear. I came to you first, because I want to ensure that this complaint didn't get side tracked by some legal process. If you aren't prepared to bury Charlie, I will take this matter all the way up the chain. This isn't a threat; it's a fact.

I want you to understand if you're going to stand by this guy, you'd better be prepared to go all the way because his behavior will bury you as well. I look forward to our next conversation."

The Judge watched Jake leave. The video package and witness statements remained on his desk. He could not begin to guess the contents, but apparently it contained an ugly scene, a bizarre insult with three independent witnesses and a public confrontation. Jake would not relent. Would a demotion off the Board be enough to satisfy him? Probably not. Would he press for a complete resignation off the force?

There may not be anything he could do to save Charlie.

CHAPTER 38: CHARLIE'S LOG: ANALYSIS

There is some pink in the sky but no sun, too damn early. I've been up most of the night with this cloak-and-dagger assignment from the Judge.

Max says he held a naked teenager but then refused to have sex with her; the teen says he ravaged her. Both underwent the S1 and an S2 interrogation, and both passed the examinations. Impossible. Now I have to find out how Dr. Max beat the system; the one he created. And I have to do this without any outside help, not even inform Dr. Kate, who is also desperately trying to solve the mystery.

I'm not sure I understand the need for all the secrecy, but I think the secret recording of the Board meetings has the Judge spooked. The net result: even if I find an answer, in the end the Chief will be furious because of the bypass, and Emma will be upset because her favorite, Dr. Kate, was undermined by a homicide detective. An apparent no-win.

I have every document associated with the case, paper, and electronic files. I printed a lot of the material; for some reason, it reads differently in the written format; also it gives me a chance to spreadsheets on the floor and rearrange the sequence of events. The place is a mess, and I have achieved nothing. No further ahead than when I started.

Jesus, I don't understand why the Judge gave me this assignment. Christ, I'm not a technical guru, and Max a genius plus. How the hell did he manage it without Kate and her assistant noticing any irregularities? Dr. Kate, at times, looks like she's lost her focus. Is she trying too hard to please Stephen?

She had some guy from Japan, another yoga expert, participate in a test of the S1 interrogation. He attempted to beat the S1 inquiry, using his yoga meditation skills, and failed; the drug cocktail overwhelmed the concentration trance he was trying to maintain.

Wes called last night and told me the two west coast cities finally released their list and personal details concerning former employees. We'd asked for any police personnel who'd been fired or resigned in the last 24 months, after working with a leading edge forensic team, a violent Hybrid. The list is rather short, and Wes is ready to establish his top three candidates, for once we may have a substantial lead. I wish I could treat the homicide cases as my priority, either one.

I return to my documents and use a highlighter to assist in keying in on the critical segments. I walk around the mess, picking up papers at random; after a quick read I put one down and pick up another; in short order, the confusion has compounded. As I walk around the house, I go over the original complaint and try to see if I can read anything into

Dr. Grovenor's comments. Next stop, I watch his daughter go through her interrogations, last observe Dr. Max as he goes through his S1 and S2 examinations.

Sally is a beautiful woman; I understand why Max refuses to call her a girl and also understand why he broke the rules. But Jesus, he's a good liar, his performance solid.

I'm sick of the coffee, but I don't want to stop. I've been up most of the night because the Judge tells me Kate is not succeeding– meaning he needs answers from me.

I'm exhausted. Time to rest my head on the kitchen table. I just need a few minutes of rest before the sun rises.

***

My awareness comes back in stages; I'm now on the floor and smell bacon frying; I'm sure I started with my head on the kitchen table. I'm very stiff and sore; then I hear a laugh which I recognize.

"Come on; it is time to get up. It's a good thing I know how you like your eggs. I'll do breakfast, but you'll have to clean up the papers."

I smile and am happy to see my brother. "Hi Sam, I see you still think you know how to cook." Although I smile at him, I'm in an extreme state. The Judge depends on me, and

I want to repay his confidence; I hear he has been my steadfast supporter, but this project appears beyond me.

Sam dishes out the eggs, bacon, and toast, and we tear into the food. I didn't realize how hungry I was. Damn, it's 7:00 am.

"Christ, another day and no damn progress."

At this point, I break the rules and talk to Sam about the Dr. Max case and my assignment. Sam is a good sounding board, as he always says: psychologists get paid to listen. As I wander around the house, he lets my talk until I run dry.

"Charlie, let's try this from another angle: motive. Whatever happened, someone had a strong motive. Why would someone get into this? There must be a compelling reason for someone lie or try and beat the Interrogations. You haven't given me much along that line."

He's right I just kept thinking Max was after a young girl and knew he could rig results. But, why would he suddenly go after young Sally? He'd been lusting after her for some time. Why not wait until she becomes of age? I tell him the latest comments from the Board.

"There a few on the Board, who believe Max has developed this grandstand scheme to flout his intelligence. I think it's more basic; the son of a bitch has screwed his way across the world, let alone across the campus."

Sam ignores my comments and starts from a different direction. "I'll share this with you. All of us have this profound desire for order, and we want to categorize objects. Look at our sciences, like biology. We want boundaries; we want to put things in boxes. It's intrinsic......it's human nature.

The Judge gave you this assignment for a reason; he does not want you chasing the technical aspects, he already has that direction covered with Dr. Kate. She is doing the linear analysis. He wants you to break out of the boxes........look with fresh eyes....assume the inconceivable, the unthinkable....nothing is sacred."

And with those comments, he says an abrupt goodbye and is out the door. He left me all the dishes, the kitchen to clean up, and a bag of home-made cookies.

I know he's right, I've wandered off the track. Is there a better way to review all the material? Am I studying in the wrong sequence? Am I dealing with an anachronism? I tackle the dishes and the mess on the floor; this cleanup is good for the mind; it's like a fresh start.

I'm going back to the beginning and looking for motives and reasons. Sam is right: something extraordinary happened, and someone had to have a strong reason to tackle the Interrogations. I can't solve this via technology. I have to tackle it like a standard homicide investigation.

I put every player, even those on the periphery, on my list and start walking through everything education, finances, family issues, traffic tickets, awards, and whatever surfaces. Brewster's team has done an excellent job: all the details are present, topped off with summaries, and analysis. I crawl through each page, make notes and get frustrated. Then I notice a few gaps in the detail. Well, maybe not gaps but there is something wrong in this detail.

I get on the network and try to fill in the gaps. My position allows access to all the files I'm after, confidentiality not a factor. More coffee and Sam's cookies keep my going. Can you believe this? I just finished breakfast, and I'm starting into the cookies. I guess it is better than booze.

I'm still playing shuffle the deck with all my hard copy, so I have paper spread all over the living room (and dining room) floor. Something isn't right, but I can't get any further.

I phone Monk. We talk about Ron and the upcoming role I have as a Watcher. Still procrastinating, I call Sam and thank him for the cookies. Finally, I grab my gym bag and drive over to the club.

At the club, I start on a new treadmill which allows a wide-ranging of programming, and I set up a long run, with hills, changing speeds, and the works. I'm winded and covered with a fine layer of sweat, well really not that fine.

After this, I get into the free weights. It's early in the morning, but some people are already winding down, in a hurry to finish and join the workforce. I do a multitude of reps with various weights. Last stop is the shower and hot tub. For a change, the hot tub is empty. There are two jets which are exceptionally vigorous and almost push me across the tub. But I find my spot and relax, enjoying the action of the hot streams of water on my back and legs.

The relaxation in a hot tub regularly works for me. I don't understand what happens; my theory is a deep relaxation allows the solution to surface. The oddities in the material I've reviewing become clear, and I know what's been bothering me.

I'm grinning and feel like that ancient Greek, but I'm not stupid enough to go running naked down the street. The damn word 'eureka' bounces in my mind, I can't help it. Did I say I was grinning? Son of a bitch.

The Judge was right the problem needed a different perspective. It's not what I thought. It's old fashion police work which may have solved the puzzle. I'm in and out of the showers in a matter of minutes, the drive home a blur.

A few more screens of data are retrieved to complete the detail I need; now I almost 100% sure about what happened and why. I summarize my finds and conclusions in four paragraphs on one page. You really don't have to be a genius to beat the system but then again to takes a genius to provide the simple or elegant answer.

I phone Manuel and ask him to follow up on two points which have to be rock solid; I need further confirmation, should only take him a couple of hours. Research like this is his strength. It seems almost too simple, but it would work. All you need is the balls to see it through and play your hand.

I think I have the solution to the Dr. Max case, but it will be an awkward takedown. The evidence has to be solid, Manuel's research will be the final step. In the end, I will still need help— I will need to convince the Judge to play his part. This is a case of having the answer right in front of you, and you insist on ignoring the obvious. The end will not be pleasant.

It is well past midafternoon when I leave the house. I have to change gears and deal with the secret recorder. It's time to roundup the technical assistants I need and the equipment for the Conference room exit. I need these men and detection equipment for the next Board meeting. I have about 24 hours. If this doesn't work, I will be unemployed.

But first one other stop at Homicide; Karen guarantees my satisfaction; her message rather blunt. "Get here Charlie; everyone is waiting. We have some answers."

I can't ignore the command but know my biggest challenge will come after Karen's meeting. I will be up against Judge Stephen. Jesus Christ ......what a mess this will be when it's finished.

CHAPTER 39: AN AMAZING VIDEO

Wes, in the far corner, was excited about the personnel files finally released by the west coast cities, details about cops who worked as Hybrids and matched the other parameters of the brainstorm profile. He was anxious to get going; he had isolated three excellent candidates, all resignations in the right time frame, with suspicious circumstances. He would, eventually, have to talk to the west coast supervisors and hope they would be frank and open. But now he had names and photos; he did not have time for this meeting.

At the back, Terry sprawled on a chair and yelled at his partner. "Manuel, where the hell you been? Get back here; I've saved a seat."

Manuel hustled out of the doorway, into the room and to the chair. He'd finished the Dr. Max assignment for Charlie and was still startled by the case Charlie was weaving together. For creating chaos: no one could match this senior detective. No wonder his nickname persisted.

And, Charlie was last to arrive, not pleased with this delay to his meeting with Stephen. He fell into a chair at the head of the table; even Terry was not brave enough to occupy the private spot. "Karen, let's go. This is your show. We're all here and ready." He didn't mention: it had better be good.

She smiled, pleased and confident. "I promise this is the most exceptional video you'll ever see. A couple of days ago a taxi driver was killed on the north side. The press reported a naked cabbie, but he wasn't completely naked; his pants were down to his ankles, and he had no underwear. The scene becomes a little more bizarre: he used a Velcro type of belt, and his fly was also a Velcro construction. Everything a man needs if he wants to get his pants off in a hurry."

Terry couldn't resist. "Jesus, I have to find his tailor."

Charlie wasn't in the mood. "Terry, first we'll get a tailor to do your mouth. Damn it. Zip it. We don't have time for any more bullshit comments. Let's go."

Karen restarted. "Next, Forensics revealed a unique car: a multitude of miniature recording devices throughout the interior of the cab. But it was not a taxi. Everything about the cab was fake. They estimated it would take less than 25 minutes to set up. You could go from a regular car to a taxi in about 25 bloody minutes.

This included removable logos on the doors, the lights on the top, the fare box, the works. With the cab as the front, he roamed whatever streets he wanted, not looking out of place and could be selective with his pickups."

Charlie stopped slouching; he became the first to anticipate where this was going. He blurted. "I can't believe this….son of a bitch. It's too good to be true."

Karen nodded, smiled and continued. "We now have Horny Harry's last recording, and this isn't even the incredible part. As you watch you'll see our theory was correct; we have recovered the other records from his home. Yes, this is Horny Harry, and he did record and replay all his conquests.

He stored a complete library at home, but his latest victim will be the biggest shock. This final recording is what the forensic team recovered from his cab. There's been some editing to make it easier to follow, and it's not up to the standards of a high-quality porn production but still good. If you're ready, I'll start the show. Terry hit the lights…….thanks."

At first, the only sound was the street noise. The quality of the recording was good; as the technicians had told Karen: if you were prepared to spend the money, the software would get the results you want.

Harry intermittently hummed, whistled and talked to himself. Sometimes there would be a good view of him and all his features, but most often, it was the street or the inside of the cab. Karen explained. "We've been editing the material to try and present the best overall documentary. There is a multitude of different recording devices, and you can select which views you want to show or merge; the sound is the same regardless of which camera's view we are using. OK, I'll turn the sound up."

The insane voice of a dangerous man rambled on and on, intermingled with of his laughter and rants. There was no doubt he was their man.

"God do I feel good …this'll be number seven………..lucky seven………I'll give her my special" Laughter and whistling followed. **"I've never been so ready… it took too damn long for my hand to heal……have to be more careful……..time to start my documentary."**

It was early evening, and he was cruising an area filled with hotels and expensive apartments. Some people were bustling around, but the streets were not crowded; his voice sounded more official as he began his pitch.

"This is Horny Harry on the cruise for lover number seven…it's April 18, 2021, and it's a warm evening ……………….I'm well into a hotel district ………well at least there are a few top hotels in this area ……………..am looking for a mature lover tonight……"

The cab turned at the lights; the one camera aimed at the street provided a view of the sidewalk, buildings, and any pedestrians; he passed a few working girls on the corner.

"Oh…. oh …look what's up ahead?........ and it appears she wants to hire a cab…………I knew this was my lucky day ………….God look at that hat ……it's huge …...the dress is tacky but what the hell ……it won't matter."

He pulled up and unlocked the back door to let her in; as soon as she closed the door, Harry's car moved away from the curb. He had a separation barrier between the front and back seat, a sliding window used to communicate with a passenger. Harry opened his jacket and retrieved the dart gun; he pulled over in an isolated spot, opened the separation barrier window and while the woman searched her purse, he shot her.

"What're you doing? You don't need a gun I'm not a threat to you. What the hell is the matter with you?"

"Don't worry love it's only a tranquilizer dart, and when you wake up, you will be in for the ride of your life."

He closed the partition window and kept driving and humming, very pleased with the events. The woman tried the doors, a useless exercise, and it only took a short time for the tranquilizer to work.

"In a few more minutes and we'll be in the park …………………God, I'm so smart …..…this one is going to be special."

He drove on and then they were at the far end of Bolton Park, an isolated spot, not a person in sight. Harry parked the cab; he turned off the outside lights, but the cameras were still recording and getting good results.

Harry reloaded his gun with what was assumed to be an antidote (confirmed later). He walked around to the back and opened the door; he lifted the woman off the floor and onto the back seat, flipped her onto her stomach, all the time whistling and humming. He lifted her dress and cut off her pants and then dropped his Velcro controlled trousers; with his knife in one hand, he slapped the woman on the side of the head a few times.

"Come on my beauty it's time for Horny Harry to introduce you to the finer things in life......good you're awake....... what I have against your neck is rather large knife which I will use to kill you if you don't do exactly what I tell you ....just nod your head if you understand ....that's good ....we are going to have fun............... let's see what you have to offer."

Harry was on top on her and forced her legs apart and reached in.

"My God, what do we have here? ....a pair of hairy fucking balls! .... My God, Horny Harry has got himself a transvestite ....God, I knew I was in luck tonight........oh God

…………unbelievable………Goddamn, this is lucky seven……………what a treat you're going to have."

Harry bent over to whisper in his victim's ear, just like the last victim had reported. The routine demanded the victim sing his praises as a lover; he finished his whispering but in his happiness became careless: he released the knife pressure from the victim's neck, and his weight shifted to the rear for a better view of his prize.

His victim well versed in hand to hand combat had enough room to launch a vicious elbow. The blow was so powerful it shattered Harry's nose. Harry's screaming and the victim's yelling filled the room. It was chaos with Harry losing all the initiative and almost choking as his blood filled his throat and mouth.

The victim took advantage: Harry had fallen back, and the victim was able to kick him out of the cab. Then he'd been able to recover the knife Harry had dropped, and it soon became apparent that the stranger knew how to fight. They both stood outside the cab; Harry with his trousers around his ankles and almost blind from the blood was at a disadvantage.

"Horny Harry nice to meet you … still think this is your lucky day? …now you die, you bastard, die you bastard …die ….you bastard."

The man alternated kicking Harry, hitting him with his fist and using the knife, all the time screaming as he finished Harry. Finally sated he spoke to Harry for the last time.

"Harry, you screwed up my appointment at the Marriott, but this was a good diversion ....I enjoyed this ....maybe I should start going for some variety ....what do you think?.....no comment ?.....I didn't think so .....well there is another great hotel a few blocks away from the Marriott ....super rooms and service ....I'll do it in midweek......what do you think Harry?.....do you approve?"

He wiped the knife, dropped it, kicked Harry one more time and walked away, no running just a casual walk.

Karen stopped the recording. "The rest shows the police patrol discovery and our investigating team. As I said unbelievable. Does everyone agree? We have the late Horny Harry, and it appears the Five Star Couple is a few steps closer to being resolved. Did you see the hat on the victim and hear the comments about the hotels?

Wes this has to be your guy, and it's not a couple. It's a man dressed up as a woman; no wonder the clerk said she had ugly hands."

Charlie agreed. "This is the best news I've had in days. Our Horny Harry cruised the hotel district and picked up our Five Star Couple. It sounds like the Couple was doing some homework and checking out hotels for the next strike."

Wes waved a photo from the West coast personnel material. "Look at this guy. When he twisted and elbowed Harry, the camera gave us a great close up; here he is Jason Reardon. Goddamn it. This is the guy. He was one of three I was preparing to chase this morning."

"Wes, it looks like your brainstorming assessment was correct: a category four killer; the Anger-Excitation killer. And AE classification system also was accurate; this type is a solo killer.

And, Karen you are also right, this one goes down in the history books. No doubt, our Five Star Couple is only one: Mr. Jason Reardon, who uses a female disguise. This is a clever bastard with false clues and red herrings throughout. I don't expect he used his real name to license a car or rent an apartment. Wes, I don't think you will be that lucky. Your best bet will be to catch him at the hotel."

Wes was anxious. "There're only two elite hotels within a few blocks of the Marriott and Jason said he would move midweek. We have about 12 to 15 hours to set up and be prepared. With Horny Harry out of the way we have enough manpower to set up 24-hour coverage in both hotels."

Charlie was ready to leave. "Remember this guy is an ex-cop, very smart and will be able to spot a stake out. I suggest the less the hotel staff knows, the better; we don't want them to spook this guy. We have enough technology to allow long distance monitoring in each hotel. Just make sure you can move in a hurry. I'm sorry I have to run. Wes, the operation is all yours."

And with that, he left. His abrupt departure momentarily stunned the room. What the hell was going on? Charlie was walking away from the takedown of one of the most important cases of the year. What was wrong with the guy?

Manuel thought about the Dr. Max report he had left on Charlie's desk and guessed where he was rushing to: another crisis with some high profile men and women.

CHAPTER 40: THE JUDGE'S CHAMBERS

Kate and Stephen sat facing each other.

One sat on the new couch, the other on a large chair. Normally she was pleased to be meeting with Stephen, but yesterday the call from his assistant sounded more like a summons: 9:00 am Judge's chambers. It did not take long for Stephen to get past the preliminaries.

"Charlie Taylor, on a special assignment for me, has been trying to uncover how Dr. Max manipulated the system to his advantage. Many hours analyzing the interrogation videos proved a useless exercise, didn't even provide a hint, not one clue. So as he told me, he went back to what he knows best, the basics. This detective can be difficult to contain; however, this is what made him perfect for this case. I needed his irreverence."

Tension started to creep through her body, but she tried to remain calm with the hope she would be able to walk away from this discussion.

"His old fashion police work uncovered a series of miscellaneous facts which lead to a few questions. I thought, given our history, I would ask you in private and give you an opportunity to explain. You should know, at this time, Charlie is questioning your technician, Janice. There are a few questions which she will have to answer. For you Kate, the first anomaly we have to clear up is your daughter's acceptance into the University's medical program."

"Stephen, no mystery exists; the basics are obvious: a set of good marks and active participation on athletic teams. And I understand, she impressed the Admission Committee with her written submission and her interview."

"Obvious? No, I disagree. I don't think it's that simple. Your daughter had good marks but not in the top 10 % of the applicants, and her athlete participation proved to be a hit and miss activity, not a stellar performance. As well, the Admission Committee awarded her the Mackenzie scholarship which means free tuition plus a generous living allowance throughout her years in medical school. This was the first anomaly which bothered Charlie.

When he dug deeper, he discovered three members of the Admission Committee had close links with Dr. Grovernor. One is the CFO for Allied Scientific and works on a daily basis with Grovernor; the second sits on the Board of Directors for the company, and the third is the CEO for a major supplier of a variety of chemicals used by Allied; the three might work extra hard to ensure Grovernor stayed a happy man. A ruthless man, like Grovernor, could control the admission process."

The room turned silent. Both wrestled with their emotions; years of suppressed feelings seemed ready to flare. Stephen's scrutiny of Kate was intense, unyielding; she became rigid and shook her head in denial, but the Judge wouldn't stop.

"Kate, I'm going to play hardball. To repeat, Charlie is already putting Janice through the same type of interrogation. Janice's finances improved significantly in the last months, and we need an explanation because, surprisingly, she attempted to keep her good fortune a secret. Charlie kept coming back to this fact: two people involved in the Sally Grovernor – Dr. Max Armstrong interrogation reaped significant benefits. Too much of a coincidence and for Justice Reborn too critical to leave unresolved."

Kate did not know Charlie, as the sole occupant of the adjacent room, was watching the entire discussion. A distraught Janice lingered in an isolation cell; Charlie had deferred her interrogation. He'd been able to identify substantial purchases made by Janice and felt sure there had been a massive influx of cash but tracing the source proved difficult. Numerous complex financial transactions were too much for Manuel in the few hours Charlie had given him. And, since time was running out for Dr. Max, Charlie guessed Kate would be the key, and Stephen should be the one to confront her.

Kate prevailed, determined to stonewall the interview. "You and I both know trying to understand the why and what of an admission committee is impossible. The fact that I'm doctor and an alumnus undoubtedly a factor, and my position on your Justice Board, again, would certainly be taken into account. I can't explain their reasons and don't know why you expect me to be able to justify their actions."

Stephen sat motionless for minutes, but then he voice was hard.

"Kate, let me repeat. I said hardball is the game and I mean it. This evidence allows me to have both you and Janice put through an S1, and if necessary an S2 Interrogation. This is not a bluff. You know the ramifications of forcing us to use an Interrogation when you could have told us the full story. Therefore, it is time for you to tell me what happened and why."

No response. Stephen stared at Kate and waited. Finally, he spoke again. "When Charlie came to me with his conclusions, I almost threw him out of the office; it was only because we're so desperate that I even agreed to listen to him. All my feelings for you continue to fight his logic and his evidence."

His voice broke, wrestling with his emotions, he restarted. "I…I….could not believe you would be part of a conspiracy which would introduce doubt and undermine the system you worked so hard to make a success. I understand your love for Sonja, but what you were willing to destroy for her that I'll never understand."

"Steve, listen I .."

"No...no...... I'll only listen to a complete confession. This was unconscionable and a perfidious act. You can't believe what you have done to my feelings for you and the memories of our time together will become a nightmare."

Dr. Kate looked at her lap, tried to control her breathing but couldn't control the tears; she knew she couldn't beat an S1. She stared at her lap, and soon her sobbing spread into the room. She tried to speak, but it was physically impossible, emotions overriding each word. Stephen never moved, a patient statue.

Charlie continued to monitor in the next room. As the dialogue evolved and the Judge revealed more and more, Charlie began to understand the undercurrents. At last Kate gained enough control to speak.

"Stephen, I'm so sorry. After my divorce, I end up saddled with a huge alimony and money did become an issue. On top of that, Sonja's unwavering goal, almost an obsession, was a medical school; her marks were good but not excellent, and I knew it would be a long shot if she got accepted. I understood how much my daughter wanted to become a doctor but couldn't think of a way to help, just worry.

When Sonja's name appeared on the Admission Committee's interview list, Grovernor's flunkeys let him know about her and how difficult the selection process was going to be. The situation gave him the idea; some old boy's gossip launched this outlandish event; he approached me with a proposition.

If I could get his daughter through an S1 and possibly an S2 Interrogation, he would drop the charge against Dr. Max, after the S2.... use the excuse that further interrogation was too dangerous for his young daughter. No one ever thought that Max would push it and demand S3 for himself.

I wasn't aware of Dr. Max's record and the potential death sentence.....none of that ever became public.....Grovernor just........ Grovernor wanted to embarrass Max, demonstrate his brilliant reputation was based on faulty science, and demand the Nobel Peace Prize be revoked.

He hated him because Max never came back to assist the company when they needed his technical brilliance and prestige. Governor's company is on the brink, well beyond a minor cash flow problem."

She started sobbing and tried to regain her composure. It became difficult to understand her, but Charlie needed more before he tackled Janice, who would be a lot harder case. After a few minutes, Kate started again.

"As you know I'm in charge of assigning the technical interrogators. I knew in a case like this, I would have to assign one of the best. Otherwise, there would be questions. As it happened Janice is one of the best, and I knew about her financial troubles; she's a poor money manager, and prior to the recent downturn, compounded her problems with some real estate investments.

I didn't approach her but told Grovernor about her problems. I don't know how much he gave her or how the funds transferred. I just got a call that Janice I should have lunch. The plan: Grovernor's daughter was never to be given the real medication for S1 or S2.

Janice explained how to behave when under the influence and gave her some recordings of different people undergoing an interrogation. What we didn't know was the girl was a serious drama student, already accepted at the Academy of Arts. She gave a brilliant performance."

After a long pause, Kate gathered her thoughts and finished her confession.

"When Grovernor first approached me, I knew this was Sonja's only hope, and I foolishly agreed. Within the week, I knew it was unethical…. wrong…..... too much for me; I told Grovernor we had to stop.

He laughed and said Sonja would receive her acceptance that morning. Did I want to tell her: no med school? He is a fanatic and warned me; he would ruin Sonja's career as well as mine; his hate for Dr. Armstrong blinds him to all consequences, and Max is right: the daughter has a similar personality.

He recognized I was still not on side, and he promised to stop after the S1 Interrogation and give his daughter's health as an excuse. I knew it wasn't good enough, but somehow I convinced myself that we would muddle through, if we stopped after S1.

I knew there would be confusion and concern, but I conceived an argument........the dosage associated with S1 was not sufficient for certain personality types. Further, we should develop a checklist to identify those individuals who should be automatically be moved forward to an S2. That is, skip S1 for these exceptions.

As long as this subterfuge stopped at S1...... S2 not challenged.....I would be able to argue Dr. Armstrong and similar personalities are such a small minority in our total population base.......we only need a minor change in our procedures to reestablish confidence levels.

The double cross occurred when his obstinate daughter insisted on an S2 Interrogation, and all my planning flew apart. She found the entire experience exciting..... an excellent acting debut with many influential people observing....... as she fooled the world.

I'm so sorry. I caught up trying to help Sonja. She'd worked so hard and wanted the admission more than anything. I knew she wouldn't get in without outside help and allowed myself to get desperate. Steve, she really is very much like you and as she matures even more so….. sometimes the appearance startles me and I worry someone else will see the resemblance and guess.

She doesn't know …….no one knows……I was afraid to tell you…..if you can do anything to help her through this mess…..please …..please. This will be so hard on her. She's so straight…… if this becomes public she will give up her medical dream……walk away from university………..and I don't think she'll ever speak to me again."

The tears and sobbing started again, the depth of her sorrow overwhelming. Stephen left his chair and went to the couch. He held her and soon tears were rolling down his cheeks. The Judge knew had she told him about the pregnancy both of their futures would have been different. He continued to hold her and to stroke her hair; he kissed her forehead and whispered something in her ear. She lifted her face and then their kiss was completed without reservation.

Charlie, still unaware of Jake's ultimatum, was in the next room, shocked and subdued; he knew he had seen and heard too much.

"Jesus H Christ, I can't believe this!"

CHAPTER 41: THE LAST MEETING

The meeting room was silent, the atmosphere tense.

Emma Collins sat, slumped, alone at the Forensic table; her head hung down, eyes focused on some notes. By the time the meeting concluded, the Chief's mood would be radically altered.

The Judge started by establishing a Condition Confidential and went straight to the point.

"I've some good news. We have solved the puzzle of Dr. Armstrong; our systems and Interrogation protocols are valid. Dr. Max told the truth; the lies came from young Sally and her father."

His delivery was rapid, as if he wanted to get past this as quickly as possible. The Judge went on to explain how Dr. Grovernor bribed both Kate and Janice; and, how Sally was coached to perform, as if she was under the influence of S1 and S2 medication.

"Grovernor wanted to embarrass Max and destroy his reputation. His anger stems from the fact Max would not take a sabbatical and solve Allied's production problem. Grovernor talked about this issue as being minor, but the truth is: the production problem is fundamental, and his company is unlikely to survive.

The girl, Sally, is emotional immature with a fierce temper. She has rarely been refused anything, and Dr. Max rejected her advances, after, what even he acknowledges was a torrid kiss and embrace. After Sally had pressed him, he left in a hurry. When Max left the house, she went into a rage, breaking furniture and tearing the place apart. Dr. Grovernor, back from Europe due to an emergency on his production floor, arrived in time to witness her tantrum. He got her to tell him the story. This is when he saw an opportunity for revenge.

The original plan included a complete S1, followed by a retreat due to Sally's mental stress; all charges were to be dropped. Grovernor thought this would be enough to hurt, if not destroy, Max's reputation, possibly get the Nobel Peace Prize revoked.

The Dr. didn't count on his daughter's demands. Sally is a natural actor and enjoyed the part. She insisted on a second performance using the S2 Interrogation. Again, to fool experts who were reviewing the examination, a hubristic ego jaunt for Sally. Her Interrogation cocktail mix consisted of water and a food dye.

The surprise to all these players was Max's record with minors and the possible death sentence. Grovernor knew about Max's tendency and probably his earlier sealed record.

But he didn't understand these cases, all having occurred before Justice Reborn, would still count as part of a series for repeat offenders."

Stephen stopped and surveyed the room; no one spoke. Emma's focus remained on the papers in front of her. Ann gave Charlie the nod, and he knew she'd picked up an interference signal, the secret recorder active. The Judge's technician, not authorized to attend the meetings, had provided Ann with a device sensitive to the frequencies emanating from the secret recording equipment.

"After S2, Dr. Grovernor presented a robust and legitimate case to drop the charge, the risk for Sally too high. They didn't count on Max volunteering, but Grovernor didn't care because he was confident we'd think Max beat the brain scan, manipulated the system again. Questions?"

The silence didn't last long. Legal first off the mark. "Judge, how the devil did they get caught, and second what is going to happen to Dr. Kate and Janice?"

"They were caught because Detective Charlie Taylor did some old fashion police work; I'll ask him to explain."

Chief was glaring before Charlie uttered his first sentence.

"The Judge asked me to look at this case from an entirely different angle. He already had a scientific team in motion with a large resource pool. I was at the classic dead end when I decide to branch in a different direction and make an assumption: suppose Dr. Max is innocent. If true, it meant Sally was beating the system; the next question became: how can a young teenager beat the system?

Only one way: she had help. From there I dug through all Janice's and Kate's records: histories, bank accounts, spending patterns, etc. The big break came when I reviewed the grades Kate's daughter submitted as part of her application for entry into the faculty of medicine. They were not good enough to warrant what happened; her admission to med school was suspicious, and when she was awarded a full scholarship, all the alarm bells went off. This did not appear to be a legitimate award."

The Judge interrupted. "I'm going to stop Charlie, if you want the details you can buy him lunch. I just wanted you to understand the basics. As far as all the players in this incident: Grovernor, his daughter, Kate, Janice, and the three members of the Medical school Admission Board, I can't tell you how this will play out. As of this moment, I'm assigning the entire case over to Doug. My preliminary assessment is that they should all be turned over to Sector 13 and out of our Sector. Any comments?"

Doug spoke. "We pay very high salaries and monitor all staff to try and prevent bribes; once this breaks in the press we must be ready to manage the fallout; do you have anything in mind?"

"You are correct. In Kate's case, even a higher salary wouldn't have prevented the incident with medical school as a goal her daughter. Janice's very ambitious and, yes, money was a factor, Grovernor knew that enough money would turn her. I'm at a loss to think of any practical way we can prevent this in the future.

Maybe random periodic S1 Interrogations for our staff, like the old drug testing program they used to have for athletes. We'll come back to this at the next meeting. Thanks… I'm going to adjourn the meeting. Thank you." Most noticed he appeared subdued and at times rather abrupt; a strange demeanor for a man who had just resolved an explosive issue.

As people stood and gathered their papers, Ann spoke. "We're having some maintenance problems with the main door, so I would ask you all to exit via the small side door at the back of the room. The one Charlie is using right now. Thanks."

People departed as requested and on leaving found, they were going through an archway type of device, similar to the ones employed in the airports years ago. As well, there was armed security staff gathered around the device and in the hallway.

Jacob Konahouse, head man for the Prisons Section, hesitated for a moment before he walked under the arch device. Before he cleared the detection unit, the alarm buzzers sounded, and two security guards took Jake by the elbow and led him into a room off the hallway. The remainder of the people exited the meeting room and continued down the hall. Only a few people noticed the incident with Jake; one being the Chief and he went right for Charlie.

"Smart ass. Where do we begin? First, where do you get off carrying out an independent investigation without informing me? Second, who the hell are these security people? And what the hell is that the piece of junk with the fucking buzzer? And, last where the hell have you taken Jake? Are those enough questions or would like more? What the hell is the matter? You can't talk, for once? Bullshit!!"

As the Chief yelled the questions, Charlie tried to think of the best starting point for his explanation. None of the alternatives were likely to satisfy Chief Stirling.

# # #

In the room off the hallway, another drama began. Jake perched on a hard back chair and standing in front of him the largest security guard, and possibly one of the ugliest, he had ever seen. This guard and the other two members of his squad filled the room. The big guy finally spoke.

"Mr. Konahouse, our scanning equipment detected a recorder either on you or in your briefcase. You can either hand it over, or we will strip search you and find it. As you are a senior member of the Judge's Board, you know what the advantages, at a time of sentencing, are for cooperating. Let's make this easy for all of us."

Jake prepared to push it. "You've no rights to search me, and I will protest to the Judge."

The big guard leaned down and grabbed Jake by the neck. "Look stupid, who do you think authorized bringing in the equipment and my team? First clue: it wasn't the Easter Bunny. I will ask once more, after that we will strip you and march you, naked, down to the Judge's chambers and request an S1 Interrogation. Are we ready or do I turn the boys lose?"

The other two guards struggled with elbow length latex gloves, a hard fit for large hands. One must have whispered a crude remark to other, and they both smirked.

The threat of an S1 overwhelmed him. Jake crumbled. "The device is built in as part of the combination lock for the briefcase. Enter 2233 as the code and the rest of the controls will be displayed, and you can see it's all touch screen controlled."

# # #

In the hallway, Charlie explained. "Chief I never had a choice the Judge called me in and asked me to treat Dr. Max as a priority case but not to discuss it with anyone, including you. I couldn't even use any staff. Stephen insisted all top secret. Christ, I don't know why. Ask him.

My guess is he was so concerned about the integrity of the Board sessions, the fewer people in the know, the better."

" Alright. I get the picture and the Judge, and I are going to have a talk…..now, explain the rest of this shit."

# # #

Inside the room, the guards had the recording device and a sorry looking Jake. They used the inside passage to get him into the Judge's chambers. The big guard handed the device and briefcase over to Ann, who was in the room with the Judge.

"Thank you gentleman, please dismantle your scanners and return to your regular duties. Ann and I will take it from here. Thanks very much."

Jake, alone with the Judge and Ann, stood in the middle of the room rather stunned by the speed of events in the last 20 minutes.

"Jake how many meetings have you recorded and where are the copies? Before you answer, I remind you because of the severity of the offence, you will have to undergo an S1 Interrogation to confirm all your replies, and lies are not something you want to add to the agenda."

"My third recording. I have the other copies at my house."

"Can you explain your reasons for recording Confidential sessions? Why take such a risk?"

Jake recovered a little, and some of his hostility returned. "First, I was guaranteed the recording would not be detected, and I deemed the risk as a minimum. During Condition Confidential sessions, decisions are made which might prove embarrassing, if handled by a good Monday morning quarterback. You do have enemies."

"You were hoping something might come forward to demonstrate my incompetence, and you could use it to ensure your tenure or reduce mine."

Jake never bothered answering.

# # #

Outside the Chief tried to control his temper. Charlie knew the next explanation could put him over the top.

"Ann ask me to find the individual who secretly recorded the Confidential Sessions. And because the first occurrence happened at a regular Board meeting, the list of suspects was short, just you, the Division Heads. I could not discuss it with anyone."

"Where did you get the high-tech equipment to detect the device? And where did you get the security staff?"

" It isn't high tech equipment. All the stuff came from a recent stage play, all props, all fakes, and the guards are all amateur actors and friends of my brother Sam. The equipment didn't detect anything; I told them to ring the buzzer when Jake went through, and we developed the dialogue to use once he was in the isolation room."

The Chief temporarily speechless, his face flushed, blood pressure peaked, and then he almost spits out the words. "You ran a fucking sting on one of the most well-connected guys in the Sector? You're fucking crazy, just fucking crazy. How did you know it was him?"

"There were only four possible suspects: First in Legal, we have Doug: too risky for him and not his style. Second, there is Dr. Kate, who spends so much time in the lab, has no social life, is interested in pure science. No, she has no interest in attacking the Judge. Third, we have you the Chief; I wondered if you were devious enough to try this? But why would you bother? You are only a few years from a full pension. It would be a significant risk for what? Not a good fit.

This left Jake, a political appointee who deals in secrets, cross currents, loves intrigue, likes to have the upper hand, and loves to make a deal. A good fit. What's he after? Anything that might show that the Judge is soft or making poor decisions; he knows the Judge will get rid of him if an opportunity presents itself. It had to be him, a real bastard, and I decided to run the bluff. I did speak to some techies and was told it was not likely we would be able to detect the device once he turned it off. There was only one choice; run a sting."

"Did the Judge know ahead of time you were planning a sting?"

This was not the question Charlie wanted to hear.

# # #

Back in the Judge's chambers, it was silent except for the keyboard, as Ann created a legal document. The Judge kept Jake standing in the middle of the room.

"Assuming everything you said is confirmed via an S1 Interrogation, I'm prepared to make you this offer as a sentence. I think it is generous when you consider how severe the penalty can be for your violation of the Secrecy Act; listen carefully and decide:

First, I need your written resignation, with the reason, you have chosen to devote more time to your volunteer work.

Second, you are to make a donation of 20% of your net worth to a medical research foundation.

Third, you make a commitment to complete four years of active community service work.

Last, you provide a formal withdrawal of your charge against Charlie Taylor and hand over all the incriminating evidence."

Jake was abject but did not want this to go any further; he thought, with a little luck, he could be rolling again before the four years were over. "I agree. I assume Ann is completing the document for me to sign; and then, after signing, I will be lead down to the interrogation room?"

The papers got signed, and Ann walked out the door and down the hall, with Jake trailing, to the interrogation room.

# # #

Charlie didn't have to answer the Chief, the Judge's door opened, and Ann walked out with Jake. The Chief did not allow the door to close, and he burst into the room. Charlie heard part of a sentence before the door closed shut. "Steve, what the hell are you …"

Once the door closed, all Charlie heard were muffled voices. He moved down the hall and collapsed on a hallway bench; tension drained from his body. He could feel the relief and realized how taut he had been. The release of tension was like someone pulled the plug in a sink and the water drained.

He knew his comparison wasn't original, but it felt like a drain starting from the top of his head. Momentary relief.

After about 25 minutes, the Chief came out of chambers, in a better frame of mind. What the Chief didn't share with Charlie: the Judge had been well prepared.

Stephen already knew about the random selection incident and the power play the ambitious Doug was putting in motion; both men had underestimated the range of Stephen's network of contacts. Stephen was waiting for the first unconfirmed news release, about the boy killer, before lowering the boom on Doug.

The Judge apologized for the end runs with Charlie but then pushed back. First he reminded the Chief his Sector position was an appointment made the Judge; and, second, his use of a homicide detective didn't compare to the conspiracy between the Chief and Doug.

Stephen promised to use his annual discretion to solve the random selection mistake but advised the Chief it would be best for him to remain silent about Charlie's unorthodox assignments and solutions. Duncan Stirling, a subdued police chief, thought Brewster would soon discover there were numerous reasons Stephen had been appointed. The Chief knew it was the last time he played politics with Doug Brewster.

Before leaving Duncan had one last conversation with his detective.

"Charlie, I'm not sure I can live with you in my command, but I understand what happened. You best go in; he wants to see you, probably for a pat on the back." The Chief started down the hall and then stopped and looked back at him.

"You know they're right Charlie; you're a crazy son of a bitch. Lucky …..but still a crazy bastard." And with that, he was gone, glad to be away from the chaos.

Charlie went into the Judge's office.

"Congratulations, good job. You know where the coffee is; pour one and come over here by the window; the chairs and the view are both better. I hope I have the Chief off your back. He's an excellent administrator, and the two of you are at different ends of the spectrum, but he is smart, and I think he understands he needs you. If you can wrap up the Five Star Couple, it would help."

"It's close. It might break within the next 24 hours."

"Good, Now, a frank discussion: Sonja, Kate, and I. This has to remain between us. By now it's obvious Kate, and I have a history. God, isn't that a cold euphemism for a relationship that you know was an intense affair.

My wife doesn't know about Kate and certainly not about the child. Only two friends are aware of our affair but not about the child. Yes, I know there have been some rumors, but they are all very low key and mostly treated as low-level gossip. So this has to remain our secret. You agree?"

"Judge, I understand, and there is no need to worry. Gossip is not one of my many shortcomings. Your affair and daughter stay with me."

"Thanks….I know I can trust you. Now since we are sharing, I do have something for you."

Charlie braced himself for some bad news but then saw the small smile on Stephen's face and relaxed.

The Judge only hesitated for a second. "I was the one who forced the Chief to have you promoted, get you out from under the basketball game fiasco, and then keep you after the Spring Dance. I knew the Chief needs your kind of thinking and attitude.

Sometimes the Chief doesn't understand that an organization, just like an athletic team, needs a variety of players and not all clones. Of course, the variety often leads to inner conflict and an element of chaos, all of which gives the Chief grief.

I can see you're surprised; it feels good to get one past you."

The Judge never mentioned Jake's ultimatum and the subsequent forced withdrawal; months later Ann would tell Charlie about his good fortune. They shook hands again, and Charlie left the chambers.

The Judge was on his side. He almost danced down the hall.

CHAPTER 42: AT THE HOTEL

At the hotel, with the surveillance systems established and a few moment to relax, Wes thought about Charlie.

He couldn't shake elevator incident. It had been an unbelievable scene, and given Jake's connections, Wes couldn't understand how Charlie retained his position. Earlier this morning he confronted Charlie, who was in a good mood, relaxed, joking with staff, almost dancing in the halls.

"Charlie, this thing with you and Jake. What the hell is behind it? You've never worked together and don't move in the same social circles. So what goes? Did you do his wife or what?"

Charlie thought for some time; he trusted Wes. Still, this feud with Jake embarrassed him.

"Oh shit, it goes away back to high school."

"Jesus, don't leave it there. Come on what happened?" Wes was not going to leave it alone. Charlie came to one his screw-it decisions and started talking.

"You know this bullshit is for your ears only. Jake was a couple of years ahead of me in high school. I make the basketball team ….he doesn't. He's in love with Brenda, and she hooks up with me. One massive back alley fight, and we're adversaries for life. How damn stupid is that?"

"This is all about a teenage girl. Unbelievable…un…fucking believable."

"Look. I've tried talking to Jake, but he keeps trying to put me down, and I'm stupid enough to react. The Judge told me the situation is now under control."

Charlie sipped his coffee, grinned and started again. "Can I tell you the final chapter? You're nodding, so that means yes. If you go to Walmart grocery section … probably midweek, you will encounter a medium size blond."

"I thought you weren't dating. Don't tell me you started with the blond?"

"Here is all I have to say: I was leaning into the frozen food bin digging for a package when I felt someone at my side. I didn't look up. Next, I hear ….'well do you still have raging hormones?'

Comments like that get my attention. I looked up, and there she was in her uniform, and I see the name tag. All I could think of was …… 'Goddamn it Brenda that's a helluva way to say hello'…….. She was a little heavier but still a good looking blond."

"Come on Charlie you never answered my question…..yes or no?'

Charlie grinned and walked away. Wes didn't know how much to believe. Charlie was good at making up stories; but, Wes knew somewhere in there was a kernel of truth, a teenage feud that never stopped.

Charlie's revelation had diverted him, and he failed to do was pass on the latest grapevine rumor. Everyone knew Charlie agreed to be a Watcher; but the Forensic Division was chuckling as it spread the gossip: Emma Collins had decided it was payback time for the spring dance embarrassment. Since she controlled the S3 brain scan, she would, in essence, be Charlie's supervisor. If he tried to deviate from any standards or attempted any inappropriate moves, she would blast him right out of the room and have him walked out of the prison or into prison.

The homicide detective would have to be on guard from the moment he entered Fort Green prison. Wes decided to call Charlie once he finished his last check of the hotel surveillance. The two elite hotels within a few blocks of the Marriott were fully wired with security cameras and direct feeds to various members of his team. Wes established a 24-hour watch rotation, but everyone wanted to be there for the final stages of the Five Star Couple and were reluctant to go home after their shift.

Their current problem: the Interrogation could not be used until there was enough evidence to warrant the invasion of privacy with an S1. The Horny Harry video was good enough for that one killing, but they wanted to convict the guy for all the hotel murders. To do this, they had to collect evidence to show he followed the killer's pattern before they could move to an S1 Interrogation.

Once Jason, the ex-policeman, made the call to an agency for a girl, they would use policewoman and employ a support team to crash the room when the time was right. This would be enough for the Legal Division. It did not matter which room he was allocated. They could intercept all calls, and a listening device would be worn by the policewoman. For five killings his routine never varied, within a few hours after registration, he made his call requesting a girl.

Terry, at the first hotel, tried to get Manuel to go home——instead, he crashed on a nearby couch. Karen was on the visual for the second hotel, Wes the overall supervisor. Karen was not in total agreement with the plan. "Wes, I don't think we have to send a woman into that room; once he makes the call we should have enough to warrant an interrogation.......Legal will accept the evidence. Let's not risk more injuries."

Wes would not relented——the girl was going into the room, as more prove of the killer's intentions. When they crashed the place, Wes wanted a preponderance of evidence, the killer and his full bag of tricks.

They thought it would only be a matter of hours. The plan was to get the entire team to whatever hotel he registered. Their electronic technicians had prepared for all contingencies, and a policewoman disguised as a hooker was ready to go to his room; concern mounted with each hour.

Where the hell was he? A different hotel? Terry paced the floor; Wes continued with irritating finger drum rolls on the desktop; Manuel stopped tossing and turning and gave up on the sleep idea. Only Karen appeared content, and soon she made the announcement.

"I think our guest has arrived. Look at the feed from the Westin, big floppy hat and the clincher look at those ugly hands in the white cotton gloves. His registration is for the second floor across from the elevators......he's in 202. This is our guy. Go ahead and get the team to move to the Westin, and Wes you best call Charlie?"

Everyone moved to a monitor, trying to get a better view of the guy, impossible with the hat. It took some time to get the entire team over to the Westin, organized, and Charlie informed. Wes worried about the delay, but as long as the call for the hooker was intercepted, they were in control and could manage the situation.

# # #

Shortly after checking into room 202, Jason had his woman and the situation in control. Jason Reardon, ex-cop, ex-Five Star Couple could not help smiling. He knew, in the past, this self-satisfied and superior smile irritated many of his colleagues. Nevertheless, here he was in a great hotel room with an attractive woman, a working girl, but that was immaterial, she was a knockout and certainly a step up from Horny Harry.

Jason was confident and charming. He poured drinks and kept up a natural dialogue: negotiated a price for a few nights of company and gave the girl the money, at which time she appeared to relax and accepted the drink.

# # #

Wes complained. "How come he hasn't phoned up an escort agency? He typically doesn't wait this long. What's wrong? I don't like this. Is he still in the hotel?

Terry started going through the current Westin security tapes, all the footage, the hallways, elevators, the bars, the works. See if you can find him, either with the dress or as a man. Shit, I think he changed this agenda."

# # #

The girl in room 202 began to have some doubts. She had been in the business for a few years and prided herself on being able to spot the crazies. This guy had been excellent all evening, but as they started drinking his front appeared to be slowing dissolving. She couldn't even figure out what it was. Was it body language? The damn smug smile? The perfect teeth? She didn't want to gulp the drink, but she did.

# # #

Terry found him on the hotel tapes. "Sure as hell that's our man. He made a pickup in the bar, almost an hour ago. They're in the elevator cameras and the hallway to his room. The son of a bitch changed his pattern. We're going to have to go in; we can't wait. Another interesting development, he doesn't give a shit if he is captured on camera.

Wes knew he had to act fast. "Ok guys, he's changed his routine: no agency and no dummy room set up. Doesn't care if he is recognized? Maybe he has a new routine in mind and a method for getting the body out of the hotel. God damn it, we have to go to plan B, right now. Let's move it. Plan B. Plan B."

#

All the girl, Lisa, could think of was: mistake, big mistake. Jason stroked her, laughing and talking nonsense about how fate arranged for them to be together before he moved out of the city for good. The smile chilled her and scared her to the point where it felt like some paralysis had taken over her limbs. She could barely talk, and Lisa wasn't sure she would be able to walk to the door, let alone run down the hall.

What happened? He changed from charming to creepy in minutes. Was it the alcohol? Or was he just nervous? She wanted out but couldn't think of how to manage it.

He sat between her and the door; besides he had secured the door, the chain on and the deadbolt thrown. If she tried to rush to the door, it would take too long to get the door open that is assuming her legs would work. Shit, here he goes again, ranting; she missed the first part; she was too busy being scared.

"Lisa, it's time you started taking some of your clothes off, not all of them, just some, come on now." He gave her a big smile. God, did she wet herself? She was too afraid to look and couldn't feel anything. She tried a small stall.

"I have to go to the bathroom first. I think it's the drinks you have been feeding me." She got up on a shaky set of legs, and shaky wasn't because of the alcohol. Then she remembered they were a couple; she should be OK, the killers were a pair.

Once in the bathroom she used a cold, wet face cloth to try and shock herself into a plan but nothing registered; in fact, her mind seemed to be in parallel with her body, in some blank stupor. Shit, shits, shit…….. she knew this bastard was a bad one but how to get out. Maybe a quickie might get him onto another track. More booze? Nothing was registering as a good solution.

He started with gentle taps on the bathroom door, "Come on Lisa let's launch the party. You can't stay in there all night. Come on." Lisa came out and stayed next to the hotel room door; she didn't want to stray from the door. He pulled her to him, and they were pressed together in the short, narrow hallway that led from the exit door to the main part of the room.

# # #

A knock and a voice from outside in the hall interrupted him.

"Room service for 202, dinner for two."   Jason, still holding Lisa, looked through the door's spy-hole and saw a hotel waiter with a full cart. "There must be a mistake I never ordered any room service....go away."

At that moment Lisa's brain flashed. "Oh Jason, I'm hungry, and we're in for a big night; why not grab the tray? It'll be like a surprise package; we'll get a surprise dinner, menu selections unknown; come on be a sport."

The waiter called out again. Jason decided she's right it would be a good way to end the evening, dinner for one. He opened the door to allow the waiter to wheel in the cart. The waiter got the cart in and turned to get Jason to sign for the meal; at this moment Lisa bolted for the door. Jason almost knocked the waiter over as he jumped forward and grabbed Lisa.

When he turned, Manuel, the waiter, pointed the gun at his head. "Jason, give it up."

Even at the postmortem review of the arrest, it was difficult to figure out the sequence of event. But the three people in the small entry way of the room ended up twisted together like some puzzle. It appears: first, the girl pulled hard to get out of Jason's grip; this action spun Jason into the cart, which Manuel tried to keep from spilling on top of him.

The girl got away and ran out the door and right into Karen, who moved her down the hall. Jason, now on top of

Manuel, used the steak knife from the cart to stab Manuel numerous times; he hurried off the floor with the bleeding knife in his hand. His turn to get out of the room. There was an obstacle in the doorway. Terry glared at him and started to provide the official warning. " Police…"

He didn't finish his warning and Jason charged; Terry's shot dropped him in mid-stride, and the sound roared through the room and the hallway. The blood from two sources drenched the carpet in the restricted space. Jason died before he hit the carpet.

Manuel bled profusely but had been lucky. Most of the knife blows hit the far side of his shoulder and upper arm, and only a few strikes hit his neck. Wes's preparation included a standby medical emergency team who were working on the bleeding detective within minutes.

Manuel was going to be okay, but he would never hear the end of his sojourn as a waiter where instead of a tip, the customer stabbed him with a steak knife.

# # #

At the hospital, Wes waited for assurances from the medical team. Heavy footsteps in corridor alerted him; Charlie arrived with a smile, handshake, and more news.

"When you get back to your desk, you'll find the rest of Jason's history. Judge Stephen was able to force some sealed records to be opened.

The son of a bitch's problems started in his late teens, prior to that he was an honor student and star of the high school track team and baseball team. The psychiatrists and his mother think the origin may have been the accident at a baseball game, a freak occurrence. His helmet fell off as he tried to steal third, and a major collision occurred, resulting in a severe head injury. At first, everything seemed all right, but soon his mother noticed voices coming from his bedroom, and she knew no one else was in the room.

Some of the police reports hint there may be other factors at play, both his father and older brother had reputations as neighborhood bullies, fast with fists and boots. The question often asked: where did the head injury occur, on the playing field or at home?

In any case, young Jason had a visitor, a friend.......a partner....... no one else could see or hear her. The friend was not someone he shared with anyone. Jason developed an attachment to his female partner, discussed his problems with her, did his homework with her and wouldn't make decisions without a consultation. His mother insisted on further medical intervention.

It's about this time his father fell down the basement stairs and almost didn't survive the fall. His older brother witnessed the accident, and it traumatized him; it became a life-changing event for him......... he stopped being a bully and moved out of the city. The analysis goes on for pages, but I think young Jason realized the only way to be released from treatment was to cooperate and give all the right answers.

Only one of the psychiatrists disagreed and refused to stop sessions, but the treatment team overrode him, and Jason was declared cured. The minority opinion: Jason's problems were more severe. You can read it all .....I stopped after about dozen pages.

The reason this record never surfaced, during the west coast police interviews and background checks, is because it all happened when he was a teenager, and his file had been sealed. You look wiped Wes.... You ok?"

Wes smiled. The last thing he wanted to do was to read a long psychiatrist's report about a sick teenager. Charlie fired one last question.

"Which room is Manuel's?"

CHAPTER 43: CHARLIE'S LOG: A WATCHER

Earlier this morning Sam called and woke me with a warning.

He felt the necessity to remind me of Emma's appointment as the supervisor for the remaining S3 Interrogations at Fort Green. His analysis: Emma, as a scientist, has always depended on logic; she will ensure all scans are completed by the book, no guilty to escape, no innocent to be executed. Dear Emma will be thorough, not prone to allow minor deviations to become part of her work. Anyway, that's his analysis, and you can guess what his advice was.

After a short, boring drive I'm now in the prison parking lot, and I'm trying to be casual, but it's not working. The milieu at Fort Green Prison rattles me; in the car park a traffic jam of ambulances line up to accept bodies. I was warned officials don't know how many are going to be executed each day, so they always order a surplus of ambulances.

The local firms can't deal with all the work. Some of the bodies will be delivered to crematoriums a couple of hours away from the city. I walk the gantlet of ambulances; it's a hot sunny afternoon, and all the drivers are out, leaning or sitting on vehicles. They're smoking or just filling in the time with the usual gossip.

There must be something going on because the guards are in a full battle dress. I don't see any prisoners in the exercise yard, but it sounds like the prison symphony is playing, plates and cups rattling against the bars. When I ask the guard at the first gate about the mini-riot, he shakes his head and gives me a small smile.

"Last night we received the latest Prison Reform amendment; this pissed off many our guests, and things are escalating. I see you haven't heard ….let me summarize.

First, all releases are on hold, even if the original sentence has been served. They're going after repeat offenders. Fucking good news, if you ask me.

Second, all prisoners will have to go through an S1 interrogation. But the part which appears to have the boys most worked up is the definition of an 'injury' has been adjusted: the impact on the victim will be the primary focus. The example is given: a con artist who has repeatedly wiped out the life savings of people could be viewed in the same manner as a serial killer. Shit, I can't believe it.

Our guests are upset…an interrogation revealing three or four serious fraud cases could lead to an S3 brain scan….shit …we will be locked down all weekend."

I begin to understand. Jesus, I hope I'm swifter when get to the Watchers' station. I get the directions and start a slow walk. It's a long walk, through many gates before I get to the assigned room. The good news is they are expecting me and are ready.

I start with the debriefing material, including a live recording of an actual S3 interrogation. The package is impressive. It's well organized and thorough. I understand what is about to happen. Son of a bitch. I have to keep it together for just a few more hours. Ron Bowen will be the last Fort Green prisoner to be interrogated. This gives me time to think about what I'm about to do, that damn Monk.

A Historian will be the only other Watcher, and it's John Wojecki. I'm not sure this is good news or not. John certainly helped us with the Five Star Couple, but these Historians are not known to be the type who will bond with other staff. John will use his expertise to move the scanner as soon as his interpretation of the scene tells him the probe is in the wrong time window.

He does not overly concern himself with the details of the crime. His preparation is to review dress fashions, car models, news events which were current in the relevant time periods. I think he knows I've arrived and am in the room, but I don't get much of an acknowledgment. Good news?

Each Watcher has his viewing screen, supplemented by a huge screen mounted on the back wall. I'm in the main room and see a set of large buttons next to my station. Each button is covered by a bright, bold label. One label reads 'AHEAD'. The other reads 'BACK'. Also, a small red switch is positioned near a microphone: this is to allow a 'sign-off' signal. Of course, the sign-off means: we've seen the relevant images, and the scan can be terminated.

The massive display almost fills the entire far wall which I'm facing; my control panel and individual monitor sit at my station. I'm allowed to decide which monitor I wish to use. I remember all the warnings about keeping focused on the event and not the technology. Christ, enough. I know it's not a movie, and I have to make quick decisions.

Anytime I recognize a scene, I have to decide: before or after the shootings? Once the decision is made I press the proper button to signal the scanning team to move in the appropriate direction, go back in time or jump ahead.

The Historian will be doing the same thing. In case of a disagreement, the scene will play out until resolved. If the scanning team becomes concerned about the time issues, they will go with the Historian's judgment.

Because of Amendment 33-2, if it looks like a crime scene, they will play it, regardless of the time frame being displayed. I'm told switching from one scene to another will not be instantaneous, and there may be a blank screen for 30 seconds, possibly up to five minutes, as they correctly reposition the probing head.

I've been drinking coffee all morning and didn't stop when I got to the prison. Thank God it wasn't beer or I would be gone. Wouldn't that make a great scenario; a hammered Watcher, who doesn't give a damn and can't properly focus on the screen.

A buzzer sounds and the show begins. Jesus, here we go. The outer segments tend to be a bit fuzzy. And, as the scene plays out, it's not a smooth transition from one frame to the next; it jerks along. You still can put it together, but it's not seamless like a TV program.

The first scene is obviously one from early in Ronald's life as a toddler. I see a small pair of hands gripping the horizontal railings of a crib. I don't see him, just his hands and arms. And I see an older woman, must be his grandmother, trying to sooth him with soft words. "Ronnie, my baby, hush my boy….".

Jesus Christ, convict Ron as a child. I'm floored; no matter how many times I heard the warnings about keeping the focus off the technology it's impossible not to be overwhelmed. I'm seeing a read out of a guy's memory cell. Christ, it's fascinating; and I hear the voices as a young Ron cries, and his grandmother tries to comfort him. I have to focus and get in the game: before I can move, a buzzer sounds indicating the Historian has pushed the forward button. I just concur with my 'AHEAD' button.

I get some recovery time; the screen remains blank for a few minutes, and then another stream of images play on the screen. The earlier scans used an automated voice over to give Watchers assurances about blank screens and delays. The computer voice proved more of an irritant than a help and had been dropped.

The AHEAD command drove us too far into the future, and memory displays Ron's trial. My old partner, who took over the case, is on the stand with a judge almost leading his testimony. Poor Ron, he drew Judge Wilber Lewis, who was delighted with his nickname: Hang'em High Lewis. The man never had to buy a drink anytime he decided to do the rounds of cop bars.

I'm watching this as a TV program I can't go on like this; I have to get over this feeling. It isn't the technology; I seem to be thrown because we are invading someone's memories and peeking into his private life. My hesitations and slow response could kill Ron. The Historian beats me to the 'BACK" button.

We do a couple more jumps, and I'm still a few seconds behind the Historian, but we have not had any disagreements, and I'm improving. I'm surprised I'm able to recognize some of the time frames, even though they are not relevant to any crime. I can't relax and wish we would get to the event. Is this taking too long?

The images in combination with the massive video display are almost like reliving the scene, and I understand why Watchers are often overwhelmed by the process. God, I wouldn't want someone looking at what I have stored in my memory. The memory streams are realistic and detailed. It's the voices I find the most disconcerting; they have a ghostly quality, as if they are surfacing from some distance source and being modulated through a long tunnel. This isn't a good description, but it's the best I can do.

We arrive. The wall fills with an image of my cousin's police cruiser. I focus. I see Ronald's image reflected in the windshield of the cruiser. Jesus, I can see myself peering out from the passenger window, a buzz cut for a hair style, a smooth-faced 17-year-old; I stare at my image. Was I ever that young?

I see my cousin get out of the cruiser and walk toward Ronald. Voices flood the room; my cousin is firm and it's obvious Ronald is struggling with his speech. Ronald says he's walking home which is a few blocks down the road; they continue talking; I see my cousin pointing and he says, "Go home….right now.".

I've been slow, but I hit the 'AHEAD' button. The Historian allows it play for a few more seconds; the noise from down the road explodes across the screen. My cousin jumps into the cruise, and we are off down the road with Ron standing in our wake, apparently not part of the unfolding action. At this point, the Historian hits the 'AHEAD' button. I'm not sweating, but damn it, my hand is shaking. Did too much get displayed in the scanning room?

Just because we signal AHEAD, it's no guarantee that we will end up at some future event. This all depends on the skill of the scanner, and I think luck. Not all brain schema behave or present the same, some are very complex and not a simple chronological street address pattern. Dr. Kate used to say she can't explain the scanning process, but she says it's important the scanner not be interrupted. She says it's not logical, but a good scanner will get a feeling for the patterns

I hope the next jump doesn't land us a few hours before the cruiser scene; if we go back a couple of hours in time, Ronald is finished. No way the Historian, or the scanner, will move away from that image, a body, and three drunk teenage boys.

Next image up is a prison setting; good, we have jumped ahead; may the scanner has the pattern; I hope we can keep this rhythm. Both of us hit the 'BACK' button. Again there is a delay before a new set of images develop.

This is it. A perfect scene for our purposes, two men in a substantial discussion. Ronald is arguing with a small unpleasant man; this guy I know, the robber at the liquor store; he was shot during the robbery and died at the hospital a few days later. Before he died, he provided a death bed confession and declaration .... *find my old partner, Ronald......the bastard fled the scene....my old partner shot the clerk........Ronald was the one who panicked.*

He said it was Ron's premature fleeing which pissed him off and lead to his being shot and captured. The monitor displays a small club with a long bar which runs from the front door to the back of the premise. Tall bar stools run in parallel to the bar, and on the wall facing the patrons is a large mirror, the full length of the club. It's in this mirror we see Ron and his buddy.

Reflected in the mirror both faces are clear, even with the many bottles of booze blocking the bottom segments of their bodies. The heavy discussion has escalated into a violent argument. The guy is close to a frenzy. This job is an easy score, and he is already counting the money.

He needs Ron, and the refusal angers him. He begs, but this is not working. Next, he tries physical threats, but this is rather pathetic, given the size discrepancy. Ronald continues to refuse the guy, and after some heavy screaming and cursing, the man walks away. With a few fist shakes, he leaves the bar.

A tall woman with an extreme hair style slides on to the vacant stool next to Ron; they're instant friends, and the drinks arrive for both. This is the woman no one could find and who was his alibi for the time of the robbery and murder.

I still remember the bar and the decor which I considered over the top, many ersatz pieces. This old fashion club proves to be Ron's salvation. One of the gaudy pieces is a huge pulsating wall clock which reflects time and date; the clock hangs slightly above eye level on the mirror, easy to read. I let it play to ensure we get the confirmation to prove he was in the bar at the critical time. I give the 'sign off' signal, the Historian follows.

This killer who died in the hospital was an angry, mean son of a bitch, and his final act of revenge was a false declaration. I leave the room with the Historian. John is teasing me. I never knew the bastard had a sense of humor. He sees my shaking hands and thinks this is funny, a homicide detective stressed with a crime scene. The Historian says his goodbye; he's in a hurry; their team is going to celebrate. The Fort Green project is completed. I'm surprised to hear him say he will join a team celebration.

I'm feeling damn good, and I know the Monk will be dancing when he hears. I won't tell Sam; I'll make him call me for the news. Time to get the hell out of here.

CHAPTER 44: CHARLIE'S LOG: THE PARKING LOT

I think about visiting Ron's cell but reject the idea.

It's a long walk to the parking lot. Jesus, why do they have these long halls and frigging security gates every 20 feet? I want to get out of here. I'm almost through the last gate when I hear my name being called. Oh Christ! It's Red. I knew she was in control of the scanning today, alone because of the staff shortages. What the hell does she want?

"Charlie, I was the Medical Tech for Ronald today and thought I should make you aware of a few things about the process. Even when I have a probing position established, I have to work with various screens and a range of memory pockets. An exciting and confusing array bounce around before I allow an image up to a Watcher's monitor. Often these pockets jump around the main event; some streams are ahead of the event and others after the event. But they all are on my screen for five to ten seconds and then flick to another set of transient images.

These temporary screens are all correct images derived from his memory and assist with the process which we use to establish a focal point and a stable output stream. We don't allow all these images up to the Watcher because it would be confusing. The Watcher would see overlapping pictures with rapidly shifting time frames, a mixed kaleidoscope of future and past all around the event. Hence, we keep that to ourselves. We observe and wait until we have an established firm picture we can feed up to the Watchers. "

She wants a reaction. Well, screw her. I have had enough of her. I don't know where this is going, but it doesn't sound good. It appears she saw too goddamn much. I try not to fidget, try to look calm, which has been my goal all day and ask her. "Alright Miss Scanner, is there a point to this lesson?"

I can't read her; she continues. "Yes. When the Watcher signals AHEAD or BACK, his screen goes blank, but our transmission of images keeps rolling. It's like slamming on the brakes in your car; it takes time to stop the stream from flowing; and, our screens will jump around both forward and backward around the time point. We get to see a great deal more than the Watchers.

Sometimes these images are very clear, and we see a full history of the primary image the Watchers were monitoring, other times more chaos at these transient points.

The reason it took a long time to get the cruiser scene up to your monitor is the first control point landed ahead of the cruise scene. On the early history of that night, I couldn't get a firm setting; the pictures kept jumping, and I could barely follow the story. Finally, the scene stabilized, and the cruiser images arrived at your monitor.

I think the first memory is very emotional for Ronald; that's probably the reason it proved so difficult for me to stabilize the stream and stop the violent jumping of the various images. What do you think?"

I know I'm in real trouble, down the sewer with Ronald. I'm trying to think of a way out, and nothing is coming. Screw it, try and bluff. "OK, you get to see the full show and more. I'm still waiting."

She is smiling and knows she has me. "You're rather fast to move away from the cruise scene. And the guy in the passenger seat looked familiar and rather young to be helping a patrolman."

"Is there a question here, because I am in a hurry?"

"Relax Charlie, I saw and assessed the entire show. Normally, there are two of us in the scanner room, but because of the Dr. Kate issue, I worked alone today. I made the decision about which part of the scan to save for the court records. I didn't think there was anything relevant about the cruiser scene and didn't retain any of the transient images occurring prior to the cruiser scene

I just kept the bar scene. Before you ask: legal representatives have their own facilities. I only send them the memory stream which is relevant, and the Historian has sanctioned; they don't get swamped with all the intermediate hits and misses."

I'm usually not lost for words but not one smart ass comment surfaces; at this point, I remember her reputation, empathy for the less fortunate. I mumble. "Thanks Emma, Ronald will appreciate your expertise."

"Charlie, I know Ron's history, an overzealous prosecutor, a sloppy detective, a biased judge and numerous failed appeals. I thought he was unjustly sentenced and feel Ronald has suffered enough and shouldn't have to pay another penalty for one night of a teenage drunk."

With that she starts walking away down the hall; after a few steps, she turns. "Why don't you call me tomorrow? I will be finished here, and we can go for the dinner and the dance you wanted."

After the bombshell, she turns and walks down the hall. Can you believe this? What a great ass. Jesus Christ!

THE END

From the second Charlie Taylor novel: **KILL SOME OF THE PRIVILEGED**

It was a computer generated sound, a weird combination of tones, edgy with distorted harmonics. I know it's impossible, but the voice sounded psychotic.

I was at Manuel's desk, at his request, and impatient to get back to mine. To face me Manuel shifted his entire upper torso; more rehab was required before he would regain normal flexibility and range of motion in his neck and upper body. A few months ago, the Five Star serial killer stabbed him. The stabbing and subsequent recovery drained some of his confidence; he was a more subdued detective who now frequently asked for direction or permission.

I said, "Again."

Manuel smiled and hit play.

"You may call me Robin Hood. I will be taking from the wealthy and famous and distributing to the less fortunate. You will know I have arrived when you start finding the body parts. My final signature will be a painted target on the chest with an arrow right through the bull's eye. If you want to stop me, solve these audio clues; it will not be easy because I am the avatar of a Hindu god.

It is Tuesday, August 24th, 2021; you have a few days. Have a nice day."

The rest of the audio consisted of four sound bites, each about 30 seconds long with five-second gaps between each sample:

Giggling: was a high-pitched sound, like a young man or a boy, a little wild or out of control, scared, or perhaps hysterical.

Snorting: was an emotional man, taking gulps of air between the snorts: ready to attack or under attack?

Cursing: was an older man who was upset or sounding off: a string of unrelated profanity, loud, angry, some words slurred.

Wailing: was a young woman or girl, frustrated, almost a screaming, moments of silence and then another piercing wail. A cry for help? In pain?

The third Charlie Taylor novel: **KILL ALL OF THEM**

The random scattering of clothing on either side of the bed made it apparent no one gave any consideration to the next wearing or the sloppy housekeeping.

On the bed, the large man left little room for the woman resting on her stomach. The giant lay on his back, snoring, arms positioned like a cross, one arm outside the bed, the other over the top of a woman. She did not complain nor did it wake her. Unfortunately, she would never wake up, not this morning or any morning.

When he did wake up, the hangover headache would not help; but Monk would have some decisions to make.

THE END